The Hummingbird's Cage

TAMARA DIETRICH

An Orion paperback

First published in the United States in 2015
by New American Library
This paperback edition published in 2016
by Orion Books,
an imprint of The Orion Publishing Group Ltd,
Carmelite House, 50 Victoria Embankment
London EC4Y 0DZ

An Hachette UK company

1 3 5 7 9 10 8 6 4 2

A CIP catalogue record for this book
is available from the British Library.

ISBN 978 1 4091 6648 1

Printed and bound by CPI Group (UK) Ltd, Croydon, CR0 4YY

www.orionbooks.co.uk

The Hummingbird's Cage

Tamara Dietrich was born in Germany to a US military family and raised in the Appalachian town of Cumberland, Maryland. She has wanted to write ever since she could read. After earning a degree in English and Creative Writing from the University of New Mexico, Albuquerque, she embarked on a career in journalism. Chasing a newspaper career, she has lived in New Mexico, Maine, upstate New York and Arizona. She has won many journalism awards for news reporting, feature writing and opinion columns. She now lives in Smithfield, Virginia in a colonial cottage that predates the Revolution. She has a grown-up son, a dog, three cats and an English cottage garden. She gets her best writing ideas while out jogging with the dog or cycling. *The Hummingbird's Cage* is her first novel.

To every woman with a story of brokenness.

You are stronger than you know.

Contents

Acknowledgments

Writing can be a solitary business, but getting a novel ready to pass into the hands of readers never is. Every manuscript needs gentle readers, hawkeyed nitpickers and wizards of the Big Picture.

First, to Mike Holtzclaw and Veronica Chufo for giving the first draft an early read and forgiving its countless rough edges. Novelist Leah Price, whose keen sense of plot helped add depth and drama, and whose ongoing moral support is invaluable. My fellow Pagan River Writers—Diana McFarland, Hugh Lessig, Sabine Hirschauer, Felicia Mason and Dave Macaulay. You help keep the creative torch burning every month with pizza and wine, page reviews and good humor when it's sorely needed. To jazz diva, writer and sister-from-another-mother M. J. Wilde, who has always believed in magic and miracles and, most important, in friends.

To Trudy Hale at the Porches on the James River and Cathy and Rhet Tignor at Pretty Byrd Cottage on the Eastern Shore. Their retreats were sanctuaries when I needed them—peace and quiet and blissful views from my window.

My literary agent, Barbara Braun, at Barbara Braun Associates, who took on a would-be novelist and steered her toward her lifelong ambition. Editor Jenn Fisher and editorial director Claire Zion at Penguin/NAL, for seeing promise in the manuscript and shepherding it through to publication.

I can't overlook my sixth-grade teacher at Northeast Elementary. Eons ago, Betty Hinzman was the first to believe in an awkward adolescent who said she wanted to write a book one day. She'll never know how much that meant.

And last, but never least, to my mother, Betty Phillips. (See, Mom? This is what you can do with a creative writing degree.)

To all, my warmest thanks and gratitude.

Part I
Asunder

It’s difficult to discern the blessing in the midst of brokenness.

—Charles F. Stanley

January 1

My husband tells me I look washed up. Ill favored, he says, like old bathwater circling the drain. If my clothes weren't there to hold me together, he says, I'd flush all away. He tells me these things and worse as often as he can, till there are times I start to believe him and I can feel my mind start to dissolve into empty air.

There's no challenging him when he gets like this. No logic will do. No defense. I tried in the past, but no more. Back when I was myself—when I was Joanna, and not the creature I've become at Jim's hands—I would have challenged him. Stood up to him. If there were any speck of that Joanna left now, she would at least tell him he had his similes all wrong. That I am not like the water, but the stone it crashes against, worried over and over by the waves till there's nothing left but to yield, worn down to surrendered surfaces. That every time I cry, more of me washes away.

This is all to Jim's purpose—the unmaking of me. He's like a potter at his wheel, pounding the wet clay to a malleable lump, then building it back up to a form he thinks he might like. Except there is no form of me that could please his eye. He's tried so many, you would think that surely one would have won him by now. Soothed the beast.

In the early years, I was pliant enough. I was young and a pure fool. I thought that was love, and one of the compromises of marriage. I didn't understand then that for Jim the objective is not creation. It's not building a thing up from nothing into something pleasing. What pleases him most is the moment when he can pound it back again into something unrecognizable.

I understand what's happening—I do—but it's all abstraction at this point. I am not stupid. Or, I wasn't always. In high school I was smart, and pretty enough. I completed nearly two years of college in Albuquerque before I left to run away with Jim, a deputy sheriff from McGill County who swept me off my feet with his uniform and bad-boy grin.

In the beginning, it was a few insults or busted dinner plates if his temper kicked up after a hard day. He would always make it up to me with a box of candy or flowers from the grocery store. The first time he raised a welt, he drove to the store for a bag of ice chips, packed some in a towel and held it gently against my face. And when he looked at me, I believed I could see tenderness in his eyes. Regret. And things would be wonderful for a while, as if he were setting out to win me all over again. I told myself this was what they meant when they said marriage is hard work. I had no evidence otherwise.

A part of me knew better. Knew about the cycle of batterer

and battered. And she was right there, sitting on my shoulder, screaming in my ear. Because she knew this wasn't a cycle at all but a spiral, gyring down to a point of no return.

But I wasn't listening. Wouldn't listen. All mounting evidence to the contrary, I believed Jim truly loved me. That I loved him. Sometimes people are that foolish.

I bought books on passive aggression and wondered what I could do to make our life together better because I loved him so. The first time he backhanded me, he wept real tears and swore it would never happen again. I believed that, too, and bought books on anger management.

When I was two months' pregnant, one of his friends winked at me when we told him the news. After he left, Jim accused me of flirting. He called me a whore and punched me hard in the stomach. It doubled me over and choked the breath out of me till I threw up. Two days later, I started to bleed. By the time Jim finally took me to the clinic—the next county over, where no one knew us—I was hemorrhaging blood and tissue. The doctor glanced at the purple bruise on my abdomen and diagnosed a spontaneous abortion. He scraped what was left of the fetus from my womb and offered to run tests to see whether it had been a boy or a girl, and whether there was some medical reason for the miscarriage.

I told him no. In my heart I knew the baby had been a boy. I'd already picked a name for him. And the reason he had to be purged out of me was standing at my shoulder as I lay on the exam table, silent and watchful and coiled.

That was years ago, before the spiral constricted to a noose. I have a daughter now. Laurel—six years old and beautiful. Eyes like cool green quartz and honey blond hair. Clever and sweet and quick to love. Jim has never laid a hand on her—

I've prevented that, at least. When his temper starts to kick in, I scoop her up quickly and bundle her off to her room, pop in her earbuds and turn on babbling, happy music. I tell myself as I shut her bedroom door that the panic in her pale face isn't hers, but my own projection. That it will soon be over. That bruises heal and the scars barely show. That it will be all right. It will be all right. It will be all right.

January 7

Jim has started probation—ninety days for disorderly conduct, unsupervised. Before that, ten days in lockup that were supposed to make an impression. That was the idea, at least. But old habits—they do die hard.

He's working second shift now, which is not to his liking. Or mine. It throws us together during the day, when Laurel is at school and there's nothing to distract him. He tells me if the eggs are too runny, the bacon too dry, the coffee too bitter. He watches while I wash the breakfast dishes to make sure they're properly cleaned and towel dried. Sometimes he criticizes the pace, but if I'm slow it's because I'm deliberate. Two years ago a wet plate slipped from my hands and broke on the floor. He called me butterfingers and twisted my pinkie till it snapped. It was a clean break, he said, and would heal on its own. It did, but the knuckle is misshapen and won't bend anymore.

I clean the house exactly the same way every day. I time myself when I vacuum each rug. I clean the dishes in the same order, with glasses and utensils first and heavy pans last. I count every sweep of the sponge mop. I spray polish on the same corners of the kitchen table, in the same order, before I fold a cloth four times and buff the wood to a streakless, lemony shine. It doesn't mean he won't find some fault—the rules are fickle—but it lessens the likelihood.

Around two p.m., after he showers and pulls on his freshly laundered uniform, slings his Sam Browne belt around his shoulder and holsters his Glock 22, I brace as he kisses me good-bye on the cheek. When the door shuts behind him and his Expedition backs out of the drive, my muscles finally begin to unknot. Sometimes they twitch as they do. Sometimes I cry.

It wasn't always like this. In the beginning I was content to be a homemaker, even if I felt like a throwback. And Jim seemed pleased with my efforts, if not always my results. I learned quickly he was a traditionalist—each gender in it's place. At the time I thought it was quaint, not fusty. I called him a Neanderthal once, and he laughed. I would never call him that now. Not to his face.

He had his moods, and with experience I could sense them cooking up. First came the distracted look; then he'd pull into himself. His muscles would grow rigid, like rubber bands stretched too tight, his fists clenching and unclenching like claws. I'd rub his shoulders, his neck, his back, and he'd be grateful. He'd pull through to the other side.

But over time the black moods stretched longer and longer, the respites shorter and shorter. Something was rotting him from the inside out, like an infection. The man I'd married seemed to be corroding right in front of me.

I learned not to touch him unless he initiated it. If I so much as brushed against him, even by accident, he'd hiss and pull away as if my flesh burned.

I met Jim West ten years ago on a grassy field one October morning just as the sun crested the Sandia Mountains east of Albuquerque and shot a bolt of light onto his dark mahogany hair, rimming it with silver. He was tall and powerfully built, with sweeping dark brows, a Roman nose, cheeks ruddy from the cold and the barest stubble. I thought he was beautiful. It was the first day of the annual Balloon Fiesta, and Jim was tugging hard on a half acre of multicolored nylon, laying it out flat on the frosty ground. He was volunteering on a hot-air balloon crew preparing for the Mass Ascension. All around were a hundred other crews, a hundred other bright balloons in various stages of lift, sucking in air, staggering up and up like some great amorphous herd struggling to its feet.

Jim planted himself in the throat of the balloon envelope, spread eagle, arms wide like Da Vinci's Vitruvian man, holding it open so a massive fan could blow air inside. The balloon streaming behind him was bucking as it inhaled, and Jim trembled and frowned with the cold and the effort. His dark eyes swept the crowd—many of us students from the university—and when they lit on me, they stopped. His frown lifted. He shot me the lopsided grin I hadn't yet learned to hate, and shouted something I couldn't make out over the noise of the fans and the gas burners springing to life, belching jets of fire all around us.

I shook my head. "What?"

Jim shouted something else unintelligible. I shook my head once more and pointed to my ears. I shrugged in an exaggerated *Oh, well,* and Jim nodded. Then he mouthed slowly and distinctly, *Don't . . . go . . . away.*

I turned to my friend Terri, who leaned into me with a giggle. "Oh, my God," she murmured. "He's gorgeous."

"Oh, my God," I groaned back.

A thrill shot from my curling toes to my blushing face, and suddenly I knew how the balloons felt—galvanized by oxygen and fire, bucking skyward despite themselves. It was a mystery to me why such a man would single me out—pretty enough, I guess, but hardly the type to stop a guy in his tracks. Of the two of us, it was Terri, the saucy, leggy blonde with the air of confidence, the guys would go for.

For a half hour or so, Jim toiled away, helping tie down the parachute vent, spotting the man at the propane burner as it spat flames inside the envelope, heating the air till ever so slowly the balloon swelled and ascended, pulling hard at the wicker basket still roped to the earth.

When the basket was unloosed and it lifted off at last, all eyes followed it as it climbed the atmosphere. Or so I thought. I glanced over at Jim and his eyes were fastened on me, strangely solemn. He strode over. "Let's go," he said, and held out his hand.

Gorgeous or not, he was a stranger. In an instant, the voice of my mother—jaded by divorce and decades of bad choices—flooded my head. Warnings about the wickedness of men . . . how they love you and leave you bitter and broken. But daughters seldom use their own mothers as object lessons, do they? This man who took my breath away was holding out his hand to me. Without a word, I took it.

I believed in love at first sight then.

I believed in fate.

February 15

Yesterday, Laurel asked about Tinkerbell again. Jim was there, and looked over at me curiously. I turned toward the stove to hide my face. I clenched my teeth to keep them from chattering. I pulled in a ragged breath and said as lightly as I could:

"Tinkerbell ran away, sweetie. You know that."

Tinkerbell was a little mixed-breed dog that showed up at our door last Valentine's Day—rheumy eyed, scrawny, riddled with fleas. Laurel went ahead and gave her a name before I had a chance to warn her we could never keep a sick stray. Jim would sooner shoot it, put it out of its misery, but I didn't tell her that, either. I had picked up the phone to call county animal control when I watched Laurel pull the dog onto her lap and stroke its head. "Don't worry, Tinkerbell," she said softly. "We'll love you now."

If the dog didn't understand the words, it understood the kindness behind them. It sank its head into the crook of Laurel's arm and didn't just sigh—it moaned.

I put the phone down.

We hid Tinkerbell in the woodshed and fed her till she looked less raggedy. Filled out, rested, bathed and brushed, she was a beautiful dog, with a caramel coat and a white ruff, a tail like a fox, her soft almond eyes lined with dark, trailing streaks like Cleopatra. When she was healthy enough, we presented her to Jim. I suggested she'd make a fine gift for Laurel's upcoming birthday, less than a month away.

Jim was in a good mood that day. He paused and studied Tinkerbell, who stood quietly, almost expectantly, as if she knew what was at stake. Laurel stood at my side, just as still, just as expectant, pressing her face hard against my hand.

The risk here, it occurred to me, was in appearing to want something too much. This gives denial irresistible power.

So I shrugged. "We can always give her away, if you want."

Jim's lips twitched, his eyes narrowed, and my heart sank. Manipulation didn't work with him.

"You want her, Laurel?" he asked at last, breaking out that awful grin. "Well, okay, then. Happy birthday, baby."

Laurel wriggled with pleasure and beamed up at me. She went to Jim and kissed his cheek. "Thank you, Daddy."

I was confused, but only for a moment.

Then I understood.

Jim had one more thing now—one more thing that mattered—to snatch away from me anytime he chose, quick as a heartbeat.

Two weeks before Christmas, just before Jim was jailed to serve ten days for disorderly conduct, he did.

Laurel sits on the porch sometimes, waiting for Tinkerbell to come home again. Sometimes she calls her name over and over.

"Do you think she misses us?" she asked yesterday.

Jim ruffled her hair playfully. "I bet she'd rather be here with you, baby, than where she is right now."

Every Valentine's Day, Jim gives me a heart-shaped box of fine chocolates that, if I ate them, would turn to ash on my tongue. When he touches me, my blood runs so cold I marvel it doesn't freeze to ice in my veins.

February 29

Snow fell last night, dusting the junipers in the yard, the pickets on the fence, the thorny bougainvillea bushes under the front windows, the woodshed's red tin roof. Jim was working his shift, so I bundled Laurel in her parka and mud boots and we danced in the field next to the house, twirling till we were tipsy, catching snowflakes on our tongues, our hair, our cheeks. The sky was black as a peppercorn.

This morning, Jim noticed I took longer at the dishes than I should have, from staring out the kitchen window at the red sandstone mesas still layered with unbroken snow, like icing on red velvet cake.

By noon the sun came out and melted it all away.

March 2

This evening after I put Laurel to bed, I opened the small storage space under the stairs and removed the boxes of Christmas decorations and summer clothing, the beautiful linen shade from the antique lamp that Jim had smashed against a wall, files of legal paperwork for our mortgage and vehicle loan, tax documents. Where the boxes had been stacked, I took a screwdriver and pried up a loose floor plank. In the cubby space beneath is an old tea tin where I keep my Life Before Jim.

Jim doesn't like to be reminded that I had a Life Before. Or, rather, he doesn't like me to remember a time when I had behaviors and ideas uncensored by him. A time when I wrote poetry, and even published a few poems in small regional literary magazines. When I had friends, family. A part-time job writing at the university's public information office. Ambitions. Expectations. Thoughts.

He thinks he's hacked it all away—good wood lopped off a living tree—and he has.

All but one.

My German grandmother, my Oma, who lost her father to the Nazi purge of intellectuals, used to recite a line from an old protest song:

Die Gedanken sind frei.

Thoughts are free.

No man can know them, the song goes. *No hunter can shoot them. The darkest dungeon is futile, for my thoughts tear all gates and walls asunder.*

In my tea tin I keep my first-place certificate from a high school poetry contest, the clinic receipt from the baby I lost nine years ago, a letter my mother wrote before she passed from cancer, and a note scrawled on a slip of paper: *Run, girl, run.*

It's not much of an insurrection, I know. But it's my only evidence of a Life Before, and I cling to it.

By the time Jim moved me to Wheeler, I had already banished Terri from my life. Just after I met Jim, as he began insinuating himself into every waking hour—the classes I took, the books I read, the people I hung with—Terri's enthusiasm for him waned.

"Girl, are you sure about him?" she'd ask.

I was troubled that she doubted his intentions. Or my judgment.

"Why wouldn't I be?" I asked.

"Jo, he's calling you all day. He wants to know where you are, who you're with. He's *tracking* you."

But I'd never had a serious boyfriend before Jim. My role models for romance were Byron, the Brownings, Yeats and a manic-depressive mother who cycled through the wrong men all her life. What I saw in Jim was passion and commitment. He took me on picnics in the Sandias. We rode the tram to the peak, and he proposed on the observation deck. We spent our first weekend together in a bed-and-breakfast in the Sangre de Cristo Mountains outside Santa Fe, watching the sunrise from our bedroom window. I felt caught up in a whirlwind, breathless, but happy to let it have its way with me.

Still, when he urged me to drop a study group for semester finals so we could spend even more time together, I balked. It was our first argument. There wouldn't be many more. He told me he cared for me, wanted to be with me, thought I felt the same. Disappointment infused every syllable.

I felt cornered. I blurted, "Terri thinks we spend too much time together already."

Jim's face went blank. For several seconds he didn't speak. Then, "She said that?"

I didn't answer.

"Well," Jim said quietly, "I didn't want to tell you this, but there's more to Terri than you realize. Remember when we met? Terri called me a few days later. She said she thought we should get together sometime. I told her I was interested in you, and that was the end of it."

He was studying me as he spoke.

"I chalked it up to a misunderstanding on her part. She's never called since. I didn't want you to think less of her."

My heart began to thud against my rib cage. Blood pulsed in my ears. Terri, the sleek golden girl who excelled at everything she ever tried her hand at, who could have any man she wanted—did she want mine? Was she looking out for me, or just sowing seeds of doubt to clear a path for herself?

"I thought you trusted me. Trusted *us*." Jim shook his head sadly. "I don't want to break up with you over this."

There must be a moment when every animal caught in a leg trap runs through the minutes, the seconds, before the coil springs. Before the swing and snap of hard metal on bone. The reversible moment—the one it would take back if only it could.

Winter break was coming up, and Terri was heading home to Boston. We had been best friends since the first day of college, but suddenly she seemed like a stranger to me. By the time she returned, Jim and I were engaged and I had dropped out of school. I wouldn't take her calls anymore or return her messages. After a while, the calls stopped.

Just before the wedding, I returned home to my apartment to find a message on a slip of paper wedged in the doorjamb:

Run, girl, run.

But the reversible moment was gone.

March 6

We live just outside Wheeler, a city of twenty thousand bordering the Navajo reservation. The town is roughly equal parts Caucasian, Hispanic and Indian—not just Navajo, but Zuni and Hopi, too. It's been described as a down-and-dirty sort of place. Billboards crowd the two interstates that run into town and out again. Signs are always advertising half-off sales on Indian jewelry—mostly questionable grades of turquoise and silver crafted into belts, earrings and squash blossom necklaces, but also smatterings of other things, like tiger's eye cabochons set in thick rings and looping strands of red branch coral. The town is notorious for its saturation of bars, liquor stores and plasma donation centers. Unless you live there, or need gas or a night's sleep, or you're in the market for souvenirs of Indian Country, it's more of a drive-through than a destination.

The McGill County sheriff's office is headquartered in

Wheeler, but its jurisdiction actually lies outside the city limits—about five thousand square miles of high desert. The rugged sandstone mesas that make up the northern horizon begin about twenty miles east, and they are something to behold, rising up out of the earth in a sloping, unbroken line, bloodred and striated.

In any given year, the county might see two murders and a half dozen rapes. I know, because Jim likes to tell me, studying my face as he recounts the details, which are far more lurid than what makes it into a deputy's report. A dozen arsons, two dozen stolen cars. Four hundred people will drive drunk. Thirty will go missing, and some will never be seen again. Three hundred will be assaulted—at least, those are the ones that make their way into a report. These usually consist of brawls between men who've had a few too many, or jealous fights over a girl, or squabbles between neighbors. Less often, young men will jump a stranger for his wallet or whatever contents of his car they can easily pawn. And some are what are commonly known as domestic disputes.

If you wonder why I never became a statistic with the sheriff's office, it wasn't for lack of trying, and not just on Jim's part. If you've never been in my shoes, you likely could never understand. Ten years ago, I couldn't have. The closest metaphor I know is the one about the boiling frog: Put a frog in a pot of boiling water, and he will jump out at once. But put him in a pot of cold water and turn up the heat by degrees, and he'll cook to death before he realizes it.

After the slap comes the fist. After the black eye, the split lip. The punch that caused me to miscarry was a bad one. After that, came the fear: That I did not know this man. That I didn't know myself. That he could seriously hurt me. That he might even kill me. That there was no one to turn to, so thoroughly had he separated me from familiar people and places. He had moved me into his world where he was an authority, an officer of the law, and I was the outsider, an unknown quantity.

Then there was the shame. That somehow I had caused this. That somehow I deserved this. That this was, as he so often told me, my fault. If only I were smarter or prettier, took better care of the house, were more cheerful. If only I had salted the beans right, or hadn't left the toothpaste tube face-down instead of faceup.

In point of fact, when I finally felt the water start to boil, I did try to get help. But Jim was ready. It happened the first time he cracked one of my ribs, and I dialed 911. He didn't stop me. This was an object lesson, only I didn't know it. The deputy who knocked on the door was a longtime fishing buddy who still had one of Jim's favorite trout spinners in his own tackle box at home. By the time the deputy left the house, he and Jim had plans that Sunday for Clearwater Lake.

Jim waved the man out of the driveway, came inside and closed the door. I was leaning against the china cabinet, holding my side. Laurel was a toddler then, and wailing in her crib. It hurt so bad to bend that I couldn't pick her up. Jim came at me so fast I thought he intended to ram right through me. I shuffled back against the wall. He braced one broad hand against the doorjamb, and with the other shoved hard against the china cabinet. It toppled over and crashed to the floor, shattering our wedding set to bits, scattering eggshell porcelain shards from one end of the room to the other.

Jim was red with rage, snorting like a bull. "You stupid bitch," he said, panting hard. "Clean this up."

He stepped toward me again, this time more slowly. His

hand came up and I winced in anticipation, but he only cupped my cheek in his palm, stroking my skin. When he spoke again, the pitch of his voice was changed utterly—low and gentle, like a caress.

"And if you ever call them again, I swear to Christ I will cut your fucking fingers off before they even get here."

After that, you feel the heat, but not the burn. After that, you get on your knees and pick up the pieces, grateful you can still do that much. And after that, you lean over your daughter's crib no matter how much it hurts and pick her up and hold her so tight you think you'll smother both of you.

March 10

Laurel turned seven yesterday, and it was a good day. Jim was off and had picked up presents—a dress with ruffles and matching shoes, a DVD of *Sleeping Beauty* and a stuffed rabbit with a pink bow around its neck holding a heart-shaped pillow that read, *Daddy's Girl.* He'd suggested a coconut cake, even though Laurel's favorite is chocolate. I made chocolate, but covered it with coconut icing.

Laurel doesn't like ruffles, either, or matching sets of clothing. Left to herself, she'll pair pink stripes with purple polka dots and top it with a yellow sunhat freckled with red daisies. It will look like she's pulled on whatever has risen to the top of the laundry basket, but in fact she will spend a half hour in careful consideration of this piece with that before making her final decision. Jim jokes that she must be color-blind. He calls it "clownwear," and if he's home to see it, he makes her change. But I let her mix and match as she pleases, because she says she is a rainbow and doesn't want any color to feel left out.

March 13

Jim's probation has ended. Three months of good behavior, ten days served, an official reprimand and a misdemeanor conviction that a career man can overcome with enough time and a little effort. That was the sheriff's encouraging speech when he met with Jim and me this morning to, as he says, close the book on an unfortunate incident.

As far as he knew, we had merely argued. And I, being foolish, had taken the stairs too fast and slipped. And if it was anything more serious than this, well, he was a big believer in the healing power of time.

"I've known you two for—how long? I never met a nicer couple," he said. "You're young; you can get beyond this. You've got a daughter—Laura? Think of her. Go home. Get your family back. Forget it ever happened." He wagged his finger at Jim and laughed. "But don't ever let it happen again, Corporal."

Jim grinned. "No, sir. It won't."

As jail time goes, Jim had it easy. He was kept in a separate cell to protect him from other prisoners, some of whom he might have arrested. His buddies brought him men's magazines to pass the time, and burgers and burritos instead of jailhouse food. They shot the breeze with him and played cards to ease the boredom, the cell door open for their visits. It might as well have been an extended sleepover. Jim joked with them, lost good-naturedly at poker, winked when they delivered the magazines.

When he was finally released . . .

No, not yet. Not yet. Not yet. I can't tell it yet.

What I can say is that it wasn't my fault Jim went to jail—it was the doctor in the clinic across the Arizona state line that Jim took me to in case it was something serious. Wheeler is only a few miles from the border.

I can't remember what set him off this time—some trouble at work, most likely, that carried over. And it was mid-November, and Jim never does well during the holidays. But this time I was vomiting blood, and feverish. I was afraid I was bleeding inside, and convinced him to take me to a doctor. I swore I wouldn't say anything.

To all appearances, Jim was the concerned and loving husband, holding me up as he walked me through the doors of the clinic. He was near tears as he explained he'd come home to find me half conscious at the base of the stairs, our little daughter frantic, trying to rouse her mother. The nurses seemed as concerned for his welfare as for mine.

But the clinic doctor was young, fresh off a hospital residency in Phoenix and clearly not stupid. He could tell a bad beating from a fall. He called the local police department, which referred it back to McGill County for investigation as suspected domestic assault.

The doctor had me admitted to the small regional hospital, where I stayed for two days. During that time, he visited me to check on my progress, and to press for details.

I could tell he meant well. He asked what happened to my bent pinkie. How I came by the scar that bisects my left eyebrow. The scalding burn on my back. He said he would send someone from the local domestic violence center to speak with me, if I wished.

I didn't wish anything of the sort. He was young and earnest. To men like him, illness and injury are the enemy, and they are soldiers in some noble cause. I felt like he was flaying me alive.

"You're safe here," the doctor said.

I stared at him. He was a fool.

"Where's my daughter?" It was not a question.

Jim didn't visit me—he wasn't allowed to visit while the report was under investigation. He was put on paid leave from the sheriff's office, so he stayed in our house outside Wheeler, putting Laurel on the school bus every morning, waiting for her when she got home again every afternoon.

When I was released from the hospital, I returned home and Jim moved in with a buddy and his family. They commiserated over what was clearly a misunderstanding. A bad patch in a good marriage.

An assistant county attorney met with me once. She came to the door in heels and a tailored skirt suit that showed lots of shapely leg. Her hair was pulled back in a sleek ponytail. She wore dark-rimmed glasses, but only for effect. They made her look like a college student. I'd never met her, but knew of her—

police officers and officers of the court are members of the same team. And cops gossip like schoolgirls.

Her name was Alicia and she was full of swagger, lugging an expensive briefcase, a cell phone clipped to her belt. She couldn't have looked more out of place in Wheeler than if she'd parachuted in from the moon. If I'd had the smallest sliver of hope for rescue, which I didn't, Alicia dashed it just by showing up.

We sat at the kitchen table, the better for her to take notes. I poured her a cup of coffee that she didn't drink and set out a plate of oatmeal cookies that she didn't touch. I fed her the story Jim had made up, and she saw right through it. Just like the doctor in Arizona, Alicia pressed for "the truth," as if it were something tangible you could serve up on demand, like those cookies.

"According to the medical report, your injuries are consistent with a beating," Alicia snapped, impatient, glaring at me over her dark rims. "We can't do anything unless you help us. He'll get away with it. Is that what you want?"

I was calmer than I thought I'd be. I shook my head. "He already has."

Alicia's penetrating stare bordered on disgust. She slapped her folder closed and stood up. I was surprised—she had a reputation as a terrier, and I thought she'd put up more of a fight.

"Women like you—" she muttered under her breath, shoving her folder in her briefcase.

Something snapped inside. I stood up, too, heat rushing to my face.

"And women like *you*, Alicia," I said through clenched teeth.

She froze for a second, studying me. "What are you talking about?"

"You really should be more careful. When your boyfriend,

Bobby, knocks you around, don't call Escobar at the station house to cry on his shoulder. The man can't keep a secret. And, my God, you should know it's a recorded line."

Her pretty face turned scarlet. Later, I would regret being so blunt, so mean. But caught up in the moment, I couldn't stop myself. Laying into her felt electrifying, like busting loose from a straitjacket, and for the barest second I wondered if this was how Jim felt when he lit into me.

She slammed the front door behind her and we never spoke again. I did see her in court at the hearing for the plea agreement. Without the cooperation of the victim—that would be me—the case was weak. Jim's defense attorney and Alicia worked out a deal: if he pleaded guilty to misdemeanor disorderly conduct, the felony assault charge would be dropped and he'd serve minimal time. A felony conviction was too great a risk for Jim—it would mean the end of his police career, not to mention a lengthy jail sentence.

The judge agreed. It took all of two minutes.

To this day, if anyone should ask—and no one ever does—I would tell them the same thing I told everyone else: I got upset that day, slipped and tumbled down the stairs. I would swear it on any Bible put in front of me.

I would swear it because Jim wants it that way.

What they don't know is what happened the same afternoon that Alicia stalked out of our house.

After she left, I opened the back door to call Tinkerbell in from the yard. It was chilly, and after a run she liked to curl up on her blanket by the kitchen stove. Usually she was ready and waiting, but not that day. I called again and again, listening for her yippy bark, expecting to see her fox tail fly around the corner. But there was only uneasy silence.

I stepped outside, and that was when I saw Jim's Expedition parked to the side of the road a short way from the house. The windows were tinted, so I couldn't make out if there was anyone sitting inside. I scanned the yard again, panic rising.

That was when I saw Jim.

He was standing next to the shed, watching me. It was a bloodless stare, and it stopped me cold. I stood there transfixed, unable to speak or move. Or turn and run.

He took a slow step toward me, then another. All the while his eyes fixed on me, pinning me like an insect to a mounting board. Then he stopped. I noticed then he was carrying something in his arms. His hand moved over it, like a caress. It whimpered. It was Tinkerbell.

I opened my dry mouth, but it took several tries before I could manage words.

"Jim, you're not supposed to be here."

He smiled—but that, too, was bloodless.

"Now, that's not very nice, is it, girl?" he baby-talked playfully in the dog's ear. "Not a 'Hello,' not a 'How are you?'" He looked at me and sighed. "Just trying to get rid of me as fast as she can."

"How . . . how are you, Jim?" I stuttered, struggling to sound wifely and concerned. "Are you eating well?"

He laughed softly.

"Come here."

"We're not supposed to talk."

"Come here."

"Laurel will be home from school soon."

"We'll be done by then. Come here."

His voice was pitched so pleasant, so light, he might have been talking about the weather. I started to shake.

I moved toward him. When I was close enough, he told me to stop. He turned to the shed, opened the door and gently dropped the dog inside. Then he closed the door again.

I could have bolted then, but to what purpose? Jim was faster, stronger, cleverer. And at that moment, I didn't trust my legs to hold me up, much less handle a footrace.

Before he returned, he grabbed something that was leaning against the shed. I hadn't noticed it until then. It was a shovel—the one with the spear-headed steel blade he'd bought last summer when he needed to cut through the roots of a dead cottonwood tree. It still had the brand sticker on it: *When a regular shovel won't do the job.*

When he came back, he offered it to me. I shrank from him and shook my head.

"It's okay," he said softly. "Go on. Take it."

The shovel was heavier than I'd expected, or maybe I wasn't as strong. It weighted my arm and I had to grasp it with both hands.

"Follow me," he said.

He led me behind the shed, just short of the six-foot wooden fence that lined the rear and sides of the property. He searched the ground for a moment, considering, as if he were picking out a likely spot to plant rosebushes. Then he pointed.

"There," he said.

"Jim . . . I don't understand."

"What's to understand, idiot? You got a shovel. Use it."

His voice was mild, his mouth quirked in what might have passed for a smile. But his stare was like a knife. Like a spear-headed steel blade that would have gladly cut me in two if only it could.

I didn't dare disobey. I took a deep breath and stabbed the

shovel in the dirt. I set my foot on the shoulder of the blade and kicked. I began to dig.

The tool was built for plowing through rough ground with the least resistance. Spear it in, kick the blade deep, carve out wedge after wedge of red earth. It was easier work than I would have thought, except for one thing: I wasn't sure what I was digging.

But I had an idea.

A ragged hole was getting carved out, the pile of fresh dirt along the edge growing bigger, when Jim dragged his foot along the ground, drawing invisible lines.

"Here to here," he said.

I straightened and wiped the sweat from my face with my forearm. I leaned on the shovel handle, panting, and considered the perimeter he'd just marked off.

A rectangle. Just big enough to hold a grown woman, maybe, if her arms and legs were tucked tight.

A grave.

One wedge of earth at a time.

Jim had pulled a bare stem from the bougainvillea bush near the fence and was twirling it aimlessly in his fingers.

"You aren't done yet," he said.

I could hear scratching coming from inside the shed. Tinkerbell was pawing at the door, anxious to escape. I turned in desperation toward the wood fence that was boxing me in. With Jim. With no way out. I knew how the dog felt.

"That goddamn hole won't dig itself," Jim said mildly. "Ticktock. You want Laurel to see?"

Instinctively, I glanced at my wrist, but I wasn't wearing my watch. My mind reeled. I could try to stall until the school bus came. A busload of children, a driver—I could dash out and scream for help. Jim wouldn't dare do anything then, would he? Not in front of witnesses?

No, of course he wouldn't.

But what he would do was take no chances. The second we heard the rumble of the bus engine, he'd do exactly what he'd come here to do, before I had a chance to run away or make a peep. Before the bus ever got close.

And after the bus had dropped Laurel off, after it had rumbled away again, Jim would still be here, with blood on his hands. And what would happen to her then?

I picked up the shovel and stabbed it back in the dirt. I had a hole to dig, and now there was a deadline.

By the time I'd finished to Jim's specifications, I was queasy from the effort. I stepped back, leaning against the fence to catch my breath, still grasping the shovel. Jim walked to the edge of the hole and peered in, cocking his head and pursing his lips. It wasn't awfully deep, but apparently deep enough.

He walked over and wrested the shovel from my grip. I cringed.

"Stay put," he said.

Then he turned and headed to the front of the shed.

I heard the shed door unlatch, heard it open, heard him mutter to Tinkerbell to stay put, just as he'd ordered me. I heard the door close.

It wasn't but a few seconds until I heard the whine again . . .

Then nothing.

I pushed myself off the fence and stood frozen in place, still trying to catch my breath. Straining hard to listen.

I heard the shed door again, this time opening. Then Jim rounded the corner, the shovel in one hand, Tinkerbell in the other, toted by the scruff of her neck.

The dog was limp, her head lolling. As I stared at her broken body, an incongruent thought raced through my mind: *When a regular shovel won't do the job.*

It wasn't my grave I'd been digging, but hers.

Jim halted in front of me, the corners of his mouth working like a tic, his eyes bright. "Take it," he said, holding the body out.

Numbly I gathered the dog in my arms; she was still warm, still soft. I could feel her firm ribs, so familiar. But there was no trace of the familiar thrum of a beating heart.

I looked at Jim, awaiting orders.

"Go on, stupid," he said. "Dump it in."

At once I turned and knelt at the hole. I leaned forward and slid her body into it. I arranged the legs, the head, to approximate something natural. I smoothed her white ruff, my hand lingering, but only for a moment. Then I stood up again.

Jim leaned the shovel back against the shed and wiped his hands on his trousers. "Don't forget to clean this. Use the hose. And oil the blade so it won't rust."

He nodded at the dog.

"Now cover that up."

There was no malice in his voice. No exultation. He sounded like any sane man might.

My legs buckled. I was on my hands and knees when he drove off.

May 18

On Jim's last day off, he took Laurel and me grocery shopping. He drove us into Wheeler to the Food Land market, and as a family we walked the aisles, Jim holding Laurel by the hand and I pushing the cart. He has lived in this town for thirteen years, since moving here from some town or other in Utah—the exact location keeps changing when he talks about it—and one way or another he knows everybody. They greet him warmly in the produce section or at the meat counter or by the bakery, and he shakes their hands and asks after the family, the kids, chatting about work, the weather, what's biting right now.

I can tell by their easy banter that they like him. They like us. They don't like me necessarily, because I am so reserved with them, and so very quiet, so deficient in small talk that I give them nothing of substance to form any real opinion. If pressed, they would probably say there's nothing about me to actively *dislike.* But they do like us as a unit.

As often as not, Jim will take us shopping like this. If he knows he'll be working, and a grocery trip is required, he will make out a list ahead of time and go over the particulars with me so I understand to buy the multigrain bread he likes, for instance, and not the whole wheat. Or the rump roast rather than the round. He will estimate the total cost, including tax, and give me enough cash to cover it. Afterward, he will check the receipt against the change, which he pockets.

Besides the Expedition, we also have a car, an old Toyota compact, which I may use with permission, for approved trips. Before and after his shifts, he writes down the mileage in a small notebook. He alone gases it up, and I know from the fuel gauge that he never puts in more than a quarter tank. He changes the oil himself. Rotates the tires. If it needs servicing, which it rarely does, he has a mechanic friend who does the work on his time off for spare cash.

From outside our fishbowl, Jim is a solicitous husband who takes care of his family. He is a hard worker with a responsible job. Good company with his friends. To women, still a striking man in his uniform.

He's invited out often for a beer after work, a weekend barbecue, but usually begs off. Family time, he'll say. For us as a couple, the invitations come less often and are nearly always refused. Some invitations aren't so easy to turn down—when a colleague retires, for instance, usually a ranking officer—and the occasion must be observed.

Two nights ago, for instance, the sheriff's wife threw a retirement party for a captain with twenty-seven years under his belt. She held it in their lovely home on a southside hill overlooking Wheeler. The weather was warm and the night was so soft, the party spilled over into their garden—it was well irrigated, green with new sod, landscaped with huge bougainvillea bushes that were heavy with scarlet bracts. I sat in a corner under a trellis of flowering vines, smelling their sweetness, listening to the Tejano music in the background, the bursts of laughter. Lanterns hung over the brick walkway; the boughs of an acacia tree glittered with strings of lights. If you closed your eyes, you could be almost anywhere.

The evening was going so well that a band of Jim's buddies didn't want it to end. After the speeches, the toasts, the cake decorated like a fishing boat, after the sheriff's wife began thanking everyone for coming, they urged Jim to join them as they moved the festivities to the Javelina Saloon, and Jim had had just enough rum and Cokes to break with habit and accept this time.

The Javelina isn't as rough as it once was. I understand that years ago it was a dive frequented by the sort of drunks who pried hubcaps from the cars parked in the business lot next door so they could bankroll their next binge—usually on a cheap, fortified wine called Garden Delight. Then it was turned into a biker bar, with loud Harleys in and out at all hours, straddled by rough-looking riders who wore dark T-shirts with slogans like *Bikers Eat Their Dead.* The bikers scared off the hard-core winos, many of whom turned in desperation to infusing Aqua Net hair spray into big gallon jugs of water. It made a cheap and wretched home brew they called "ocean."

One winter night, a brushfire ignited behind the saloon and ripped through an adjacent field where a half dozen hardcores were camped out with their wine bottles and jugs of ocean. Most managed to stagger off, but one woman couldn't get out in time. She burned alive. They never determined the exact cause of the blaze. It might have been a campfire that the wind had whipped out of control. Or it might have been a lit cigarette deliberately tossed into a patch of dry grass by someone who wasn't about to have his Harley stripped for parts.

Life is cheap in such places, but that brushfire convinced the city council to demand a crackdown on liquor establishments that cater to rough trade. The Javelina closed down. It reopened again weeks later under new management, the Harley decor still in place, because it was too costly to change out. Some bikers still drop in when they pass through town on the interstates. But now its main clientele is mostly working class—not least of all local police officers and deputies looking to kick back or decompress.

I had never been inside the Javelina before, but I'd often seen its big billboard from the east-west highway—the giant wild boar, tusked and razor-backed, charging at some unknown target in the distance.

You could hear classic country music from the parking lot and smell the Marlboro smoke and beer. I could swear I caught a whiff of gunpowder, too. Inside, the music thumped and a small disco ball revolved above couples slow dancing or boot-scooting on a dance floor thick with sawdust and stained with tobacco juice. But the color scheme was still orange and black, and a vintage Harley Davidson, stripped of its engine, hung from the ceiling above the bar.

I felt conspicuous from the start in a dress that was two sizes too big and shapeless from neck to knees. Jim's choice. The other wives seemed to glisten in their tight, pretty, shiny fabrics. In their high-heeled sandals and sling-backs. Hair curled and tucked just so, or flat-ironed till it streamed like water. Their lips were painted red, mauve and pink, and more often than not parted wide in laughter. They leaned into their men, slapping their shoulders playfully, pulling them to the dance floor. I watched them and my heart began to race, my palms to sweat. I struggled to catch my breath.

"You all right, honey?"

I looked up at a waitress with short champagne hair and gray roots, ruby lips and a look of concern in her eyes.

"Could I have some water, please?" I asked.

"You sure can," she said. "And what can I get for the rest of you?"

"Hey, Edie, when you gonna throw out that crap?" said an officer named Munoz, gesturing at the Harley suspended from the ceiling.

"Well, hell, I like that crap," Edie said. "Reminds me of the good ol' days when we had a classier clientele."

The officers hooted.

"You miss those biker freaks?" snorted an officer named Sandoval.

"I miss their *tips*." Edie rubbed her thumb and forefingers together. "You SOBs are tight as a frog's ass."

The others broke into more gales of laughter, but not Jim. He didn't like profanity in women. I thought he was choosing to ignore Edie, but after she left with the drink orders, he grinned and said:

"Well, there goes her tip."

The others thought he was joking.

The banter went on and on. I watched them as if I were outside looking in. As if I were pressing my face against a cold windowpane, marveling that people inside the bright room could be so easy with one another, so quick to laugh. I marveled the way I would if I were to parachute into some tribal village in the Amazon or Africa. It had all become something foreign to me. An alien culture. I had understood it once—once, I'd even enjoyed it—but not anymore.

I had lost all facility with people. All interest. All connection.

Worse, I began to look around the table, suspicious, searching their faces for telltale signs. For cracks in those happy, deceitful masks they presented to the world. Wondering what awful things they, too, were hiding.

The waitress returned to hand out the drinks. Sandoval's wife—CeCe, I think—called out: "Edie, when you gonna get a mechanical bull in here?"

Her husband grimaced. "Now, what in the hell would you want with a thing like that?"

"You never know—I might like to do a little bull ridin'."

He swept his arm around her and grinned. "Well, sweetheart, it's your lucky night."

In the midst of the guffaws, two big hands came down on Jim's shoulders from behind and a voice boomed, "You son of a bitch!"

Jim recognized it at once; so did I. It was the same deputy who had come knocking on our door one day to help Jim deliver an object lesson. The buddy who had turned a 911 call into a fishing date. His name was Frank.

Jim and Frank shook hands in greeting and slapped each other's shoulders and inquired after each other's wives, as if I weren't there to answer for myself. Then Frank leaned in close and muttered something in Jim's ear. Whatever the news was, it wasn't good. The grin froze on Jim's face. He stared back at

Frank and said something I couldn't hear; then they both moved away to the bar. Jim didn't return for a long time.

Close to midnight, most of the couples at our table had left. I was spent, nursing a single Dos Equis all evening, but Jim was downing Coors after Coors and growing more garrulous. When Edie came around next, he gave a *What the hell* shrug and ordered a double tequila with lime. This was not a good sign.

Munoz shook his head at him. "How in hell you expect to get home, man?"

Jim leaned back in his chair, bloodshot eyes glistening. "The way I always do when I tie one on—lights up, siren wailing."

Munoz chuckled, but his eyes were wary. He gestured at me and my Dos Equis and smiled. "Joanna here will drive you guys home. She's been a good girl."

"Fuck that," Jim snorted. "We'd just end up in a ditch somewhere."

Crack.

Munoz exchanged a surprised look with his wife, both clearly uncomfortable now.

Edie brought Jim his double shot. He slammed it and ordered another. "Easy," Munoz murmured. "Easy."

When the second one came, Jim smirked and toasted him with it.

Before Munoz could respond—if he had even planned to—he glanced past Jim to something at the other side of the saloon, and his jaw dropped a bit. "Ho-ly," he murmured. Jim turned to look. So did I.

A woman had walked into the Javelina.

That's the truest way I can describe it, except to amend it

this way: a woman didn't just walk into the Javelina—she commandeered it.

She was tall and lithe and sturdy. As tall as Jim—taller, if you counted the two-inch heels on her biker boots. Her hair was so black it shone blue, and all of it cascaded down her back like a waterfall. She looked to be in her early thirties, and wore jeans and a studded black leather jacket. She stripped off her leather riding gloves as she strode to the bar like she owned the place. The crowd parted to make room.

At her side, leaving no less of a wake, was a big man with salt-and-pepper hair and a mustache. He was also dressed in leather, and gave every impression that he could, should circumstances call for it, eat the dead.

"Is that Bernadette?" Munoz murmured.

And suddenly I understood everything—Frank's muttered message, Jim's abrupt mood shift and his hard drinking, which was so uncharacteristic for him. I had never met Bernadette, but for years Jim had made certain I knew *of* her, usually in explicit detail. She was his girlfriend from long ago, and the woman he most enjoyed comparing me to. Never, of course, in my favor.

I knew she was a mix of Navajo, Hispanic and Irish and grew up on a sheep ranch on the northern end of the reservation, near Cuba. She had left Wheeler—and Jim—before I'd ever come here. As far as I knew, this was her first time back.

Seeing the woman in the flesh, I understood why in Jim's estimation I had always come up short, and always would.

Jim was staring intently at her, glowering, working his jaw. He was breaking into a sweat, his fist squeezing the empty shot glass. Bernadette was speaking with the bartender, who nodded in our direction. She turned to look. If she was put off by

Jim's presence, she didn't show it in the least; she didn't take in my presence at all. She turned her back and resumed her conversation with the man she'd come in with.

Jim stood, and for a moment I thought he intended to leave. I stood, too, and picked up my handbag and jacket. But he took no note of me and headed for the bar. Uncertain, I trailed behind.

He stood staring at her back for some time without speaking. He stared so hard I thought he would bore tiny, smoking holes in her leather jacket. If she knew he was there, she didn't show it.

Finally he said, "I see you're still drinking tequila."

She took her time turning around. When she did, she surprised me. She barely glanced at Jim at all when she raised her shot glass and answered with a dismissive, "I still have a lot of regrets."

Mostly, she turned her attention past Jim and on me, appraising me in a puzzled way that became almost sad. Then pitying. I hugged my jacket for protection against that look, suddenly and profoundly mortified.

When she finished with me, she turned to Jim. "I hear you're still on the force. Congratulations—never thought you'd last." She smiled over her shoulder at her burly friend. "Where are my manners? Allow me to make introductions. Jim, this is my *hombre*, Sam. And, Sam, this is the reason I got my *Jim Is a Prick* tattoo."

Sam chuckled.

Bernadette leaned back against Sam and stroked his stubble lovingly. "He laughs because it's true." She turned to Jim. "Want to know where I put it?"

Now others at the bar were beginning to laugh, too. Jim's face was turning white; I could feel him vibrate with rage.

With an effort he spat out between clenched teeth: "And how does Sam here like worn-out pussy?"

Sam shifted forward menacingly, but Bernadette raised a finger that stopped him in his tracks. She was appraising Jim now with the dead calm of a stone Madonna. When she smiled, it was beatific.

"Once he gets past the worn-out part," she purred, "he likes it just fine."

The bar burst into roars of laughter. Still smiling, Bernadette leaned back against Sam, who clasped her in a bear hug and spun her on her heels back to their bottle of tequila.

When Jim became aware of me at last, he wrenched my arm so hard I thought his fingers would tear muscle. Before he pulled me toward the exit, I threw a last glance at Bernadette, who caught it as she turned toward us from the bar.

The look on my face wiped the laughter from hers.

May 20

Around two thirty in the afternoon came the growling racket of a motorcycle muffler in the drive. Then a knock on the front door. I didn't answer. I didn't intend to, but the knock came again. Then again. And, finally, a voice:

"I know you're in there."

With a jolt, I recognized the voice: it was Bernadette's.

She was the last person I expected on my doorstep, and a small part of me was intrigued. The rest of me, though, was shot through with panic. And curiosity alone couldn't tamp that down, nor stir me from my blanket on the couch. I held myself as still as I could. I didn't dare breathe.

Knock knock knock knock.

"I can keep this up all afternoon," she called out, but it sounded more like determination than threat, so I called back, my voice croaking from disuse: "Jim's not here."

"I'm not here to see that bastard," she said quietly. "I'm here to see you."

My first instinct was to batten down the hatches. To look around for something heavy to defend myself. To make up some story to shoo her off my porch and back on her bike, heading west toward Wheeler. But both would have taken more strength than I had in me.

It took a while to push myself off the couch and shuffle to the door, clutching at my bathrobe. I slipped the chain from the lock and pulled the door wide. I let her look at me.

She didn't speak for a long while. Then she muttered, "Holy shit."

I couldn't look her in the eye. I waited for her to have her fill, to assess me one more time, then leave me alone. Instead she said:

"Let's have some tea, Joanna."

She stepped inside and gently took my elbow as I shuffled painfully back to the couch. She eased me back onto the blanket. She pulled off her leather jacket and pushed up her shirtsleeves, heading to the kitchen. She put the kettle on to boil and rummaged in the cabinets for cups and tea bags and sugar. She fixed a tray with china cups in their matching saucers, napkins, some saltine crackers, a box of tissues and a bottle of ibuprofen. She was efficient, with an eye for detail. She sat opposite me in the overstuffed chair, and we sipped Earl Grey in a weirdly companionable silence. Then she smiled.

"You ever have a tea party with a biker chick before?"

I laughed despite myself, but I felt out of practice, and it came out more of a hiccup, which hurt my sore ribs. I hiccupped again, and then again. It became a sob. My hand flew to my mouth, where the bottom lip was split and stinging.

Tears sprang to my puffy eyes, one still swelled nearly closed, spilling down my bruised cheeks. Swiftly, Bernadette was beside me on the couch, handing me tissues, letting me cry it out, in no particular hurry.

When I was done, she didn't ask what had happened. Instead, she said, "Let me show you something."

She cocked her head and pushed her long black hair to the side, holding it back so I could see the spot she was pointing to just above her left ear. I could clearly make out a gnarled white scar running five inches along her scalp.

"Bottle of Jose Cuervo," she said. "Five staples to close. Concussion."

"Did you go to the police?"

"Now, now, Jo. You're smarter than that. Even back then, he *was* the police. And he had a police buddy who said he'd swear I was whoring on Bernalillo Road, resisted arrest, assaulted an officer, got what I had coming."

I gasped. "Frank."

"I see you've met. Anyway, a split scalp—I got off easy, all things considered. I left town and never looked back."

"You were afraid he'd kill you."

She snorted. "Honey, I was afraid I'd kill *him.* I grew up on the rez. I've butchered enough game and livestock to know where the knife goes. So I guess you could say he got off easy, too. He just doesn't know it."

The prospect made my heart leap. If only she'd stayed in Wheeler, if only she hadn't left, had put her hunting knife to good use . . . "I wish you *had* killed him."

She shrugged. "That's the bruises talking."

Her indifference stung—clearly she had no idea.

Finally I asked, "Did you meet him here, or in Utah?"

"Utah? Did he tell you he was from Utah? Honey, he's from Tucumcari. The way I hear it, they ran the whole family out of town. He's never been very clear about parents, siblings, that sort of thing. I think he's pure self-invention by now." She shrugged. "Nothing wrong with that, necessarily. We're all entitled to second chances, right? But I always did wonder what he did with his first one. We were only together a few months, but that was enough. I've always been a sucker for a handsome devil—only, between us girls, I prefer them more handsome than devil. Jim was a helluva wild man then. Not so much family oriented. Did he tell you about the time he shot up a motel room?"

"Why on earth?"

"Why on earth not? That's just the way he was. Half the men in uniform back then should have been behind bars at one time or another." She gave me a sidelong glance. "I hear Jim finally made it inside a jail cell a few months ago. I only regret I wasn't here to take a picture. I would have framed it."

"A picture?" I spat the words out.

Her laughter stopped short. "Sorry. I shouldn't take pleasure in that bastard's misery, when I know damn well he takes plenty of company with him. Honey, the stories I could tell you . . ."

Her voice trailed off bitterly; her dark eyes grew darker.

I didn't know what she expected when she came knocking on my door—checking up on a batterer's wife, an hour of tea and sympathy. Penitence for poking a rattlesnake that was sleeping in someone else's lap. And I wasn't sure what I could expect of her.

But, for the first time ever, there was someone sitting right in front of me who knew Jim—the real Jim, not the affable doppelgänger he presented to everyone else. She knew him—if not to all his dark depths, then at least to his capacity for them. She had loved him, too. Once. And he'd made her bleed. Even her.

"The stories—" I stuttered. "The stories I could tell . . ."

And the next thing I knew, I was telling her—the dark things, the forbidden things, the things I'd never told anyone, could never tell anyone, especially when they pressed and prodded and tried to wring it out of me for my own good. The bruises, the bones, the burns, the scars—these are just the tangibles they can check off on any medical report. How do you quantify the words that cut as deep? The bottomless, wretched fear of more of the same?

The dam cracked; the truth gushed out. I told her about my tea tin, the groceries, the gas. The fishbowl isolation. The suffocating prison of this tin-roofed house.

The steady erosion of my own sanity. The no way out. The gut-churning horror of being forced to live every day with a monster.

I took a deep breath and braced and told her about Tinkerbell. About the grave he made me dig, the limp body, the spear-headed shovel.

About Laurel, and how hard it is to pretend to your clever child that everything's all right, that Daddy loves her, that Daddy's a good man, that Daddy would never, ever turn on her one day.

Bernadette was staring at me, expressionless. I searched her face for traces of disgust, for judgment, for compassion, for absolution. I couldn't stop myself.

I took another shuddering breath and told her what I hadn't even allowed myself to think too much about, for fear of making it real. Making it true. About the night Jim returned home from his jail stint, just after New Year's. The welcoming meal I'd prepared—pot roast, potatoes, coconut cake. Laurel had dressed pretty for her daddy in a crimson velvet dress with bows. We'd sat down as a family, and Jim seemed happy to be home, kissing Laurel good night, even tucking her in. When she was finally asleep, as I was washing the dinner dishes, Jim called for me from outside. He was in the backyard near the woodshed. He was wearing gloves, and I thought he was restacking the cordwood, but it wasn't that. As I got close, I could see his face in the lantern light, and it was twisted with the old familiar rage. My stomach heaved. He grabbed my hair and pulled me inside, yanking out hunks till I gasped. He dragged me across the shed, pulled me upright, and with his other hand grabbed an object hanging on the wall. He held it close to my face so I could make it out. It was a machete.

People disappear all the time, he'd said. He's a cop; he should know. No one would miss you, he said. Hell, no one would even notice. And if they did, he'd just tell them I'd left him and gone back to my family in another state. No one would check. No one would care.

This is my future, he told me. This is my end, if I ever, ever, ever humiliate him like that again.

Bernadette was still staring at me, her eyes still blank. I waited for her to say something. To say anything. To tell me what a pathetic wreck I was. What a terrible mother. To hop on her motorcycle and leave a trail of diesel fumes all the way to the Javelina so she could sit with Sam and tell him all about the nutcase outside town.

Instead, she said, "Show me."

She helped me up again, and slowly I led her through the

kitchen, through the back door, through the yard. When I got to the shed, I hesitated. I hadn't been inside since that night. Bernadette paused, too, for a second, then moved past to unlatch the rough plank door. She opened it and stepped in. I forced myself to follow. It was musty and close and smelled of motor oil. "This is bad," she muttered, glancing around. "Bad energy." The afternoon sun cut through the dusty window like a blade; the light was weak, but it was enough for her to scan the walls, taking in the rakes, the spades, all the garden hand tools. Then her gaze rested on one item in particular. It was a machete, hanging just where Jim had left it.

She shook her head, backing away.

She didn't speak again until we returned to the house. Then she paced the living room, her steel-toed boots clicking up and down the wood floor. I waited expectantly, not knowing for what.

"Where's your daughter?" she asked.

I told her Laurel was staying with a school friend for a few days. Bernadette nodded.

"Now, think hard. Give me a name and a number. Someone you can trust. Someone who will take you and your daughter at a moment's notice."

I shook my head, desperate. "No one. There's no one. They're all Jim's friends here. My family's gone. It's been ten years—"

"It doesn't have to be someone you know well, or even recently," Bernadette said. "You'd be surprised how many people are willing to help, if they're only asked. But make it someone as far away from here as possible."

A name sprang to mind.

"I used to know someone in Boston."

Bernadette seemed pleased. "Very good. Write it down."

There was a notepad and pen on the end table beside the telephone. She grabbed it and handed it to me.

"In two days, when Jim has left for his shift," she continued, "I'm coming back here and giving you cash and two plane tickets out of Albuquerque for Boston. Do you know where the Albuquerque airport is? Never mind—I'll give you a map anyway. You'll leave as soon as I get here, gas up your car and drive hell-bent for leather. Take nothing with you. Nothing—do you understand? By the time Jim gets home, you'll be in coach, eating peanuts somewhere over Chicago."

Suddenly the enormity of what she was plotting overwhelmed me. The insurrection was too massive, too fast. The blood was draining to my feet. I began to shake, murmuring protests.

"I can't. Wait. Please. Two days is too soon. I can barely walk. Laurel has to finish school. Laurel has to finish school. Please, she has to."

Bernadette stared at me again, but not unkindly. I was ashamed at my weakness. Oma used to tell me stories of how she and her husband and their young daughter—my mother—had fled East Germany and the communist occupation. Left their lovely home one night without warning or preparation, their dinner half eaten on the table, racing on foot toward the western border with nothing but the clothes on their backs, the barking of search dogs in the distance. I was just a child at the time, and shivered at the story, but Oma would hug me and kiss my cheek. *Mut,* she'd say. *Courage.* And here I was, frantic over pulling my seven-year-old from school early.

But of course my panic was more than that—when you're released suddenly from a dungeon, sunlight is a painful thing.

Prisoners need time to adjust. Bernadette must have understood.

She nodded. "When's the school year over?"

I did the calculation as fast as my feverish brain could manage. "Fourteen days. June fourth."

"Does Jim work that day?"

Another calculation. "Yes."

"Good. June fourth. Until then, pretend everything is okay. Nothing has changed—understand?"

"I can do that."

"No doubt. We're staying at the Palomino Motel, just up the road." She took the notepad and pen from my hand and began writing. "This is the number. Put it somewhere Jim won't find it. But don't call, understand me? Don't call unless it's life or death."

She stopped herself and chuckled. "I mean, *imminent*."

It struck me that, whatever I was risking, this virtual stranger was willing to risk just as much. And for no good reason that I could see. I was confused, light-headed, struggling for words, trying to stammer out gratitude.

"I don't know how to repay you . . . I don't know why you're doing this."

"Don't you?" She cocked her head and smiled down at me as if I were a child who'd just said something precocious.

"Because you asked."

May 29

Something jarred me awake—not a noise or movement, but instinct. The digital clock on the dresser read 2:31 a.m., and Jim wasn't in bed beside me. The sheets where he lay were cold to the touch.

I sprang from bed, adrenaline surging, and made my way to the hallway. There, I could hear a tinny melody drifting from Laurel's room. Cautiously I followed the sound. I recognized it—a song about wishing upon a star, coming from a Cinderella music box Laurel had gotten from Santa last Christmas.

There was a night-light close enough to Laurel's little canopy bed that I could make out Jim bending over her sleeping form. My breath caught in my throat. I froze in place, staring.

Whenever Laurel had nightmares, I was the one to sit at her bedside till she fell back to sleep. She must have had a bad dream, and Jim must have heard. Watching him with her then—so gentle, so warm—was like stumbling on a stranger. At a Jim that *might* have been, but for whatever reason—because of whatever devil hunched on his shoulder, hissing in his ear—could never quite close the deal.

I watched as his fingers trailed along Laurel's cheek, the way he used to brush mine a million years ago. His expression in the obscure light so tender, it jolted me to the bone.

"Sleep, baby," he shushed.

June 3

The two weeks after Bernadette left the house passed like a forced march through a minefield. For the first time, I was glad of regimentation and rules. They ate up the hours. They helped settle my mind and keep the lies sorted into the right piles.

An odd sensation began to brew in my chest, churning it up. Night after night, I lay in bed taut as a bowstring as Jim slept next to me. I examined this new feeling, turning it over and over in my head like a found foreign object.

Finally, I identified it: *hope.*

I didn't like it. Resignation doesn't ask for anything. Pain can be numbing.

Hope has expectations. Hope can be dashed.

At times, I even found myself bitterly resenting Bernadette for laying this new burden on me—a terrible secret that seemed to press against my lips, straining to burst through as if daring to be caught. But always the resentment lifted the moment Jim left the house, the risk of discovery easing for one more shift at the station. His absences washed over me like a death house reprieve.

It helped not at all that nothing was expected of me, except to be ready when the moment came. I couldn't bear a second's idleness. Chores done, I'd rake the leafless yard, dump clean clothes out of bureau drawers just so I could relaunder them. Scrub the kitchen floor, then change the bucket water and scrub it all over again. Bite my lips till they bled.

Sometimes I'd hear the stuttering roar of a bike engine in the distance and imagine it was Bernadette or Sam. I'd wonder whether she'd ridden the two hours to Albuquerque for the plane tickets yet, or if she'd bought them over the phone and was having them mailed to her at the Palomino. Maybe the tickets were lying on her nightstand even now, just waiting for the jailbreak.

Then another thought would crush me: What if she'd changed her mind altogether? Decided to dump Jim's loser wife like deadweight? Was she even now in Durango or Flagstaff or San Antonio? At those times, it was all I could do not to pick up the phone and call the number she'd left. What stayed my hand was the realization that the only thing I could do if she answered was to pinch out a pathetic, "Are you still coming?"

The easiest thing was keeping it from Laurel. I was so well practiced in that already. And there was so much at stake.

That last night as I lay in bed, my mind could level on only one thing:

Tomorrow.

June 4

Insurrection Day

As scheduled, Laurel had early dismissal from school. The bus dropped her off around twelve thirty. She showed off her certificate for passing first grade and I suggested a fried-chicken lunch on Saturday to celebrate. Jim approved. I fought to hide my nerves, fixing my face into something neutral, waiting for him to hit the shower before work. I laid out his fresh uniform with shaking hands.

By the time he was strapping on his Sam Browne, my face was flushed. When he kissed my cheek, he paused for a second to ask if I had a fever. I don't know if it was concern in his eyes or suspicion. I blamed it on the excitement of Laurel's special day.

At 1:58 his Expedition pulled away.

Laurel changed into her play clothes of many colors and I sent her out to the backyard. I stationed myself in a chair at the front window and stared out at the road, my fingers knit together so tight my knuckles cracked, listening to every tick of the sunburst clock above the couch. I grew light-headed, and realized I was holding my breath. So I decided to time myself to the deliberate beat of the big clock—*tick, breathe in; tock, breathe out.*

At 2:33 came the distant roar of a Harley.

My heart twisted in my chest like a snared rabbit. This time, my breath caught and held till I could see motes of light. I didn't care. I sat as fixed as a tombstone, head bowed, willing with all my might for the roar to come closer.

And it did—a faraway growl from the west, growing louder and louder as it approached the house, closer to the ticking clock, closer to the harp-backed chair that was the only thing, it seemed, keeping me from sinking down to the molten core of the earth.

Closer and closer, until—

Bernadette rode up like an archangel in studded black leather on a steed of steel and chrome, a bandanna capping her head, her long hair flowing behind like a banner.

I exploded through the front door and nearly knocked her down before she had a chance to set the kickstand, hugging her hard, weeping, my eyes and nose running shamelessly.

"I wasn't sure you'd come," I choked out at last. "Thank you, thank you, thank you."

"Hell!" She gasped, laughing, staggering under the impact.

When I let her go at last, wiping at my wet face, stammering out an apology, she stripped off her gloves without a word, reached into a zippered pocket of her jacket and handed me a blank envelope. Inside were the tickets, five hundred dollars in cash, an Albuquerque street map with the airport circled in bold red marker, and a phone number and address on a sheet of lined paper.

"Your friend will be waiting for you at the airport in Boston," she said.

I swayed on my feet. "She remembers me?"

"Of course she does." Bernadette was regarding me with frank amusement. "I told her it was a family emergency and you had to leave town fast. She didn't even ask what it was—I figure you can explain when you see her. She says you and your daughter can crash with her and her husband as long as you need to."

I stared speechless at the bounty in my hands. When I looked up again, Laurel was watching us uncertainly from the side of the house. She'd heard the motorcycle rumble to the edge of the front lawn and had come to see. We'd never had such a visitor before, and she wasn't sure how to take it. Her little hands were knotting anxiously.

"Hello, *niña*!" Bernadette called out, smiling. Then she turned back to me and murmured low: "Remember—the gas station just this edge of town."

I nodded. I knew this. Of course I knew this. The game plan was ridiculously simple, straightforward. But even so, it helped to have her spell it out one more time.

"Then turn right around, and it's a straight shot to Albuquerque. Don't stop—no food, no nothing. McGill is a big county, and there's more prying eyes and gossiping tongues around than you know. Get out fast, and don't look back."

"What about you? It might mean trouble."

She grunted. "Knowing that *pendejo*, there's no 'might'

about it. Which is why—as much as I'd *love* to stay and watch the meltdown—Sam and I decided to pack up tonight and head out. We're thinking Reno—honey, I'm feeling lucky."

She winked and began pulling her gloves back on. "Don't linger, Jo," she murmured again, this time in earnest. "I mean it. Get your ass in gear."

I nodded, clutching the envelope to my chest. It struck me that this would likely be the last time I would ever see Bernadette—a stranger who was sticking her neck out, at no inconsiderable risk, to help a woman she'd just met. And why? Was the goodness of her heart that profound? Or was her desire for revenge against Jim that deep?

Maybe it was a mix of both, and if so, that was fine by me.

"Wait—how do I get in touch with you? How do I thank you?"

Bernadette didn't answer. She swung onto the bike and kicked it to life. She punched the throttle twice and the big engine growled back in response. Laurel covered her ears as Bernadette laughed. Then she nodded in my direction. *"Adiós, hermana!"*

She accelerated hard, her rear tire raking the edge of the lawn, spraying grass and dirt behind. The front of her bike was airborne for a second; then it squealed on the pavement as she raised a hand in salute, barreling back toward Wheeler.

"She's *loud*," Laurel said in wonder. I laughed as I dried my face on my sleeve.

"Yes, sweetie, she is that. How do you feel about going for a drive?"

For us, it was an outrageous idea. I might as well have asked if she wanted to sprout handlebars and spoked tires and go bicycling on the roof. Her eyes widened, but she didn't ask questions. I fetched the car keys from the hook inside the front door.

The air was warm; the sun was shining. The engine started right up. I felt giddy, and so weightless I could have floated up like a hot-air balloon. Laurel was studying my face so earnestly that I laughed. She smiled back, but her eyes were still so anxious I felt a pang of guilt.

No matter. I was doing this for her. For both of us.

It was four miles to that first gas station on the outskirts of town. I gave the attendant a twenty from Bernadette's envelope and began to tank up, the meter clicking away.

It was clicking for a minute or so before I noticed the choking odor of gasoline getting stronger by the second. It was then that I saw liquid running out from underneath the car, streaming toward the road.

I froze—fairly sure what it was, but not daring to believe it.

I forced myself to pull the pump handle from the filler neck of the car and set it back in its cradle. Then I dropped to my hands and knees and peered under the chassis. I saw the gas tank and understood: a hole had been punched in the side of it, near the middle. Gasoline had chugged out onto the pavement.

No wonder Jim never kept more than a few gallons in the thing. No wonder he never took it in for service, but maintained it himself or had a friend tend to what he couldn't.

A starving gas tank meant a short leash on me. And this was his insurance policy.

I pushed myself back to my feet, rocking on legs ready to buckle. I could never make it to Albuquerque on just a few gallons. There were gas stations along the way, sure, but not many. And in between were long stretches of nothing. I couldn't begin to guess if I could make it from one filling station to the next, or if I'd end up stranded on the interstate waiting for Jim to track us down—which he surely would, and most efficiently. Then there'd be nothing left but to get hauled back to the house, and what was waiting for us in the shed.

Jesus, I'd even handed him the perfect story to tell anyone who asked—his miserable, mental wife had taken their child and run off to distant parts, never to be seen around here again. He'd play the abandoned husband as skillfully as he'd played the doting one.

I groped for options. First was giving up—abandoning hope like the fickle cheat it was and driving back to the house. Chasing this last hour, these last two weeks, out of my memory. Burning the envelope and its contents, swearing Laurel to secrecy. But Jim would be checking the car's mileage after his shift, and how would I explain the extra miles? An emergency trip to the grocer's?

"Joanna?"

I turned toward a familiar voice, guts twisting. There stood Deputy Munoz in civilian clothes, tanking up an SUV with two kids inside. There was genuine concern on his face.

"You okay? You're shaking like a leaf. Is that gas coming from your car? Let me take a look."

"No!" I barked as he flinched. I caught myself, pitched my voice to something less full-on crazy. "We're all right. We're fine. We're . . . going home now."

I was backing away as I spoke, till I collided with the Toyota. Then I turned and snatched at the door handle. I fell into the driver's seat and cranked the ignition, Laurel watching, her eyes as big as hen's eggs. Munoz was heading toward the car, leaning over to peer inside. I pulled out so fast the tires squealed.

My one thought was the Palomino. Bernadette would know what to do. Maybe we could hide out there. Sleep on the floor if we had to.

It was a stupid idea, and I knew it. Selfish, too, because it would put her in more danger than she already was. But in the end it didn't matter—at the motel there was no sign of a motorcycle anywhere.

Bernadette and Sam might be back any second, or they could have checked out already and left for good. There was no time to wait and find out. And no way I'd ask at the motel office and implicate Bernadette even further.

One thing I was absolutely sure about: Munoz would be calling Jim up by now. Munoz was a good guy. He'd figure Jim would want to know his wife was having car trouble and needed help. That she looked really upset. Maybe she was sick. Maybe someone could call the motor club. Maybe Jim could swing by in his unit and help her out himself. Wives appreciate that sort of thing.

I sat idling in the motel parking lot, gripping the wheel, weighing terrible options. But the one image that crowded out every other was that of the shed behind the house and what was buried behind. The machete on the wall.

Laurel was staring at me. Willing me to do the right thing. More than ever, I felt the weight of her little life in my hands.

As I looked back into those frightened eyes, it was clear what I had to do. For her sake, if not for mine. She'd lived long enough in the shadow of a psycho.

I shoved the car in gear and pulled from the lot, beelining for the highway.

For Albuquerque, for freedom, one way or another.

The insurrection was still on.

The gas got us to the big truck stop near Continental Divide, about halfway to Grants. Grants is a good-sized town, and there'd be more stations once we got there. By now I was beginning to believe we might.

I bought three plastic gas cans, gallon size, and filled them. I loaded them in the trunk, then started to tank up.

It's a popular truck stop along Interstate 40. A family-style restaurant inside, and a bank of showers for truckers and long-distance travelers. The pumps were busy. I glanced around uneasily, trying not to stand out. Laurel's face was fixed on me through the rear window.

There was an undersized, tinny-looking car at the next pump. The driver gassing up was a young man who looked sixteen trying to pass for thirty. He wore a torn T-shirt with the sleeves rolled up and black skinny jeans. His red hair was cropped close, except where it spiked into a cowlick at the crown like a rooster, or some ironic Dennis the Menace. He was wearing earbuds, listening to music on a player that was bulging in his back pocket. His leg jiggled to a beat only he could hear. The lobes of his ears looked freakishly large, till I realized they were stretched out by plugs the size of wine corks.

Red Dennis pulled his music maker from his pocket and was glancing down at it when something on the ground caught his eye. He looked over at me and pointed under my car.

"Whoa, lady!" he said. "You're leaking!"

He said it loud enough to hear himself over his own music. Loud enough for half the people at the pumps to hear. Some of them turned to stare.

I yanked the nozzle from my car and shoved it hard back on the pump cradle. Red Dennis was heading toward me, tugging out his earbuds. His T-shirt had a Rolling Rock beer logo and a big picture of a baby in a diaper lying on its back sucking on a beer bottle. *No harm here,* the shirt read. *The kid's already shittin' green.*

Before he could get anywhere close, I was in the car slamming the door and locking it, cranking the ignition and aiming for the highway.

A quarter tank and three gallons extra would get us to Grants. Yes, yes, I was sure of it.

I checked the speedometer, determined to stick to the limit and under. I noted the mileage. I gripped the wheel with sweating palms, holding it steady, smack in the center of the right lane. I wouldn't give a patrolman any excuse to pull me over.

Two miles out, I glanced in the rearview mirror.

And there in the distance I saw it: flashing lights, red and blue. Far off, but coming up fast as a bullet train.

And I heard it: the scree and whoop of a siren.

It was eating up the distance between us with a vengeance. And I knew exactly who was behind the wheel.

Laurel heard it, too. She twisted in her seat to peer through the rear window and started to whimper.

I could barely draw a breath.

"Oh, my God," I whispered. "Help."

Part II

Borne Away

No rack can torture me,
My soul's at liberty
Behind this mortal bone
There knits a bolder one.

You cannot prick with saw,
Nor rend with scymitar.
Two bodies therefore be;
Bind one, and one will flee.

—Emily Dickinson

The First Day

There was an open window with white eyelet curtains. There was a breeze through it. There was a brass footrail with porcelain finials. A rocking chair. The smell of baking bread. Laurel's voice outside, the call of birds.

The Second Day

An old woman came with a bowl. Chicken broth. A napkin. She tucked it under my chin and fed me with a spoon. She had a severe face, thin, but her eyes were kind. Her hair was gunmetal gray, pinned back in a bun. She wiped my chin when I spilled. I tried to thank her, but my voice wouldn't come. "You sleep now," she told me, turning out the lamp, so I did.

Morning

"Mommy?"

Laurel's voice pulled me from a jagged sleep. A dream where I was running knee-deep in red sand and rattlesnakes. I could taste blood, like sucking on a copper penny. Someone was screaming.

I opened my eyes and Laurel was standing by the bed with a tray. It was laid with a bowl of oatmeal, a plate of apple slices, orange juice, a slice of toast.

"Let me take that, child." The old woman was there, too, lifting the tray from Laurel's hands, setting it on the nightstand. I pulled myself up, arms shaking with the effort. The woman adjusted the pillow so I could sit, then settled the tray in my lap.

"I feel better," I told her, my voice strange, croaking out of a throat nearly too parched for sound.

"Now, that's a blessing," said the woman. "You eat now."

As I did, she sat down in the rocking chair, its rails clicking against the pine floor. Laurel climbed onto the bed with me, handing me a spoon as if I were younger than she was. Then the napkin, the oatmeal bowl.

"My name's Jessie," the woman said. "Jessica Farnsworth—but you call me Jessie. This here is our farm. My husband's out sneakin' a smoke, as if I don't know. You remember how you got here?"

I shook my head.

"Simon found you out in the scrub wandering around with your little girl here. You couldn't tell us much—you were in a bad way. Laurel says you had some trouble with her daddy out there on the road."

The oatmeal caught in my throat. I took a sip of juice. When I could speak again, I said, "My name is Joanna . . . Benneman." I threw a warning glance at Laurel. "Simon's your husband?"

Her severe face broke into a delighted cackle. "Lord, no! My husband's Olin, the old fool. Simon Greenwood—he's a local man. Works in our café. Short-order cook."

I licked my lips with a tongue as dry as ashes.

I didn't remember anything about being found. Nothing about how we got here, or even where *here* was. I remembered leaving the Palomino, making for Albuquerque. Had the car run out of gas? Broken down? Did I ditch it somewhere and try to hike with Laurel through the desert? To Grants or Thoreau or some other town?

I shoved feebly at the tray with arms like bricks, the food half eaten.

"Let me take that." Jessie pushed herself up from the rocking chair. "You'll have a real appetite before long."

She smiled down, her gray eyes steady. Her skin was thin and clear and remarkably unlined. It seemed to radiate like rice paper backlit by a candle.

"You rest."

She bustled off with the tray.

When she was gone, Laurel nestled next to me on the pillow. "Mommy," she whispered. "Our name's not Benneman."

"I know, sweetie. But that was my Oma's name when she was a little girl like you. So I think it's okay if we use it for a little while. Can you do that?"

She nodded solemnly, her pointer finger tracing a big X across her heart. "Our secret."

Rain

I slept so much, I felt hungover with it. I didn't ache or hurt; I was just tired—down to my last particle. Eating wore me out. I slept through so many meals, I couldn't tell you. I'd hear kitchen noises downstairs—the rattle of pots, the clatter of dishes, the murmur of voices. Laughter. Then I'd sleep again for hours. Or years, for all I could tell.

Sometimes images of Jim flared up, but they didn't linger. He seemed to come on like a bloodhound fixed on a scent he couldn't quite make out.

I thought of Terri, too. Waiting in vain at the airport, glancing at her watch. Wondering who to call to find out why I wasn't on that plane when it landed.

But I didn't have the strength or the will to hold on to such thoughts for long.

The room kept me quilted up and safe. I drifted in and out

of sleep. When I woke, I'd watch sunbeams slant their way across the wood floor. Or listen to raindrops pinging against the roof and the windowpane in a broken staccato, like Morse code.

Laurel would visit to tell me stories of her day. Chattering on about helping Miz Jessie with the baking, the sweeping. How she went with Mr. Olin to feed the chickens and hunt for eggs. She felt bad for the hens, she said, when they discovered their eggs were gone.

Sunshine

One morning, Jessie came to help me out of bed. She laid out a white blouse with pearl buttons, a simple skirt. They fit well. She brushed my hair till it gleamed and snapped in a barrette as if I were Laurel's age.

"Now," she said. "Aren't you the prettiest thing?"

I wasn't at all sure I was ready or able to leave my little cocoon, but she led me by the hand out the bedroom door and down the stairs. My legs weren't as wobbly as I'd expected after lying in bed for so long.

Through a big kitchen, then a rear screen door to a long trestle table under a giant oak tree. Half the table was laid with embroidered white linen and floral china. Laurel was there on a wooden bench, her slim legs kicking back and forth. She jumped up and ran to me.

"Mommy!" She wrapped her arms tight around my waist. "Come sit beside me."

Someone had managed to clothe her in nearly every color found in a crayon box. A feather boa of pink and white was looped around her neck. She took my hand from Jessie and brought me to the table.

The sights and smells were overwhelming. Smoked ham, bacon, sausage. Sliced tomatoes, home fries, biscuits, pots of jam. A pitcher of orange juice and a pot of coffee. My mouth watered painfully.

"How'd you like your eggs?" Jessie asked.

Such plenty—I thought she was joking.

A man with a rough shag of white hair and a handlebar mustache was rounding the corner of the house. He was compact, dressed in a worn work shirt and a straw hat, wiping sawdust from his dungarees.

Jessie wagged her head at him. "Sneakin' another smoke, I see," she scolded. "Breakfast is on. Pour out the coffee." She headed back to the kitchen.

The man set his hat next to his plate and took a seat. He ran his hand through hair that lifted from his scalp in thick, cottony tufts that looked fit to blow off like dandelion seeds. His face was leathery and lined.

When he reached to shake my hand, his grip was firm but gentle, his calloused fingers as coarse as pumice stones. He took me in with eyes that shone a vivid blue.

"We ain't been properly introduced, ma'am. I'm Olin."

"Joanna," I said.

"Pleased to make your acquaintance. And pleased you're feelin' better."

I tried to smile. He poured out the coffee and juice while I looked around at their farm. Their house nestled in a narrow green valley that ran east to west in a long arcing curve;

it was bordered on the north by a crooked line of midrange hills.

I turned in my seat toward the south and couldn't help but gasp.

At my back was a toothy break of foothills . . . and they fed into the biggest mountain I'd ever laid eyes on. I had to crane my neck to take it all in.

Its face was deeply scored, with jagged outcroppings thrusting through thick green forests that covered all but the snowbound crest. The crest jutted into a rocky, bladelike ridge that looked sharp enough to cut steel.

The mountain dominated the valley, swallowing up a quarter of the sky. It seemed out of all time and place, like a transplanted Alp.

And it seemed almost . . . *animate.*

Aware.

And staring back at me.

I started to shiver, the ground shifting under my feet. I felt a force pulling at me. Summoning me. I gripped the edge of the bench seat to anchor myself in place.

It was as though the mountain had its own force of gravity. As if it were pivoting slowly on its axis, reaching down to collect me in its orbit. I was sure I was about to take a tumble—but just as sure I'd be rolling *up* the mountainside, not down, and plunging off—

"A sight, ain't it?"

It took what strength I had to drag my eyes away and turn back to Olin. When I did, he was cradling his coffee cup, watching me calmly. I tried to answer, but words wouldn't come, so I nodded.

"Folks give it all sorts of names," he continued. "Hereabouts, we just call it the Mountain."

I pressed my napkin to my lips. I felt flushed—a mild fever was muddling me, that was all. I'd overdone it coming down to breakfast.

"You have a pretty place," I managed finally.

Their farmhouse was stately—two stories of smooth gray stones, facing west, with wide windows and a deep porch wrapping around.

"Built it myself," Olin said. "We had ourselves a little low-slung place snug to the road at first, but I kept plowin' up fieldstones every year, and the missus, she hankered for a stone house like she seen in some magazine. So I put fieldstones by till I had enough to make it for her. Sure took a while."

A red barn and a slope-roofed coop for the chickens stood behind the house. Next to the barn was an empty corral, and farther down the valley were thick groves of nut trees and fruit trees, shade trees and varieties of pine. There were many others I couldn't identify. Beyond that stood half-grown fields of wheat and corn.

I could hear water running nearby that Olin said was Willow Creek, cutting down from the Mountain. A hundred yards or so out was a little arching footbridge. And on the far side of the bridge was a boxlike building of yellow stucco with turquoise trim. It sat along a hardpan road that bisected the valley north to south, with a neon sign on the roof facing away. I couldn't make out what it said.

"Yonder's our place—the Crow's Nest Café," said Olin.

A pickup truck, mustard yellow, sat in the shade of the building. I could only guess it belonged to the short-order cook who worked there—the one Jessie said had found us and brought us to their door.

"You can't get much business out here," I said. "Remote as it is."

There looked to be miles of empty in every direction, and I was grateful for it. A moat of wilderness to keep the world out.

"We get enough," said Olin. "Not brisk—regulars, mostly. And every now and then strangers blow through."

I checked out both ends of the road. If Jim were to find us, that was how he'd come.

Olin nodded south.

"Up the road there, round the bend, is our little town—Morro. Used to be mines all through here till one day the copper played out. Most folks up and left, but some of us stayed on."

He looked about, taking in the landscape in a way that was almost loving. As if all he surveyed in every direction was as much a work in progress as his house and his fields.

Jessie was back with the eggs. "Here, honey," she said, sliding two of them onto my plate and two onto Laurel's. "Eat up."

"It's our little corner," said Olin. "Summers are hot, but they don't burn you. Winters are cold, but they don't bite. A few of us, we was born hereabouts. Others was movin' through and decided to stay on. But nobody makes it here that don't make for good company."

His blue eyes locked with mine as if he were scouting for something. I couldn't look away if I wanted to.

Finally he nodded.

"And every now and again," he said, "we get us a short-timer. I figure you for one of them."

For some reason, it stung me to hear it.

"Why do you say that?" I asked.

He smiled encouragingly.

"I figure you for a gal with a thing or two to accomplish yet," he said. He chucked Laurel under the chin. "This li'l gal, too."

Jessie turned to Laurel. "My, my! You ate every last bit on your plate," she said. "You want seconds?"

"No, ma'am. I'm full," said Laurel.

"Run along, then, and take your plate to the kitchen. Then I know for a fact there's a new swing under that tree yonder, made for a little girl just your size."

Laurel ran to the kitchen with her plate and fork, then over to a big chestnut tree near the barn. She slid into a wooden swing seat that looked freshly hewn and sanded, and kicked off. Her slim legs pumped hard. Her hair and feather boa flew.

"Mommy, watch!" she called.

"I see you, sweetie! Hold tight!"

"She'll be fine," Olin said. "She's a strong little thing."

Higher and higher she swung till she was almost parallel to the sky. She looked tiny and fragile next to the craggy old chestnut. If she lost her seat and flew off, if the rope broke, she could break a bone, or worse. But she wasn't thinking about disaster. She had a sure reservoir of courage.

"She doesn't get that from me," I murmured.

Olin and his wife traded a long look, and suddenly I could see myself through their eyes. They had to be wondering what kind of refugees had landed in their laps.

"I don't know how to thank you," I said. "I've been so confused the past few . . . days?"

Just how long had I been in that room upstairs? They weren't volunteering a timeline.

Jessie patted my arm. "You stay just as long as you need to. Laurel hasn't said much. But from what she has, well, when a woman takes it on herself to grab her child and run off from her own husband, like as not there's a reason behind it."

I stared at my coffee cup. Such people couldn't begin to understand what Laurel and I were running from. What could be hard on our heels even now.

Jessie had said Laurel told them her father had given us trouble on the road. Had he? I had no memory of it.

And just where was Jim? If only I could pinpoint him on a map . . .

"How far are we from Wheeler?" I asked.

"Head about three miles to the highway, just over the hills," said Olin, indicating the breaks to the north. "Then cut west a good thirty miles and you'll hit Wheeler right enough."

"So close," I murmured.

From the looks of this lush valley, I would've thought we were much farther from town than that. Where were the red mesas? The high desert? This place looked more like Colorado than western New Mexico.

And thirty miles out meant we were likely still in McGill County and the sheriff's jurisdiction. It would be only a matter of time before Jim tracked us here.

"Has anyone been around?" I asked. "Looking for me?"

"Not a one," Olin replied promptly, as if waiting for the question.

I hesitated, not sure what I could expect from these people.

What was it Bernadette had said? People are ready to help, if only they're asked. Even so, these two people were strangers to me. And I to them. How can you know who to trust?

I couldn't take a leap of faith like that.

But I might manage a small step.

"What Laurel said is true," I ventured. "We can't go back. We *can't.* If anyone should come asking around—even someone official—they can't know we're here. Please."

"I wouldn't fret. We ain't seen no one official in . . . how long?" Olin glanced at his wife, who shrugged. "We ain't county, you see, nor reservation. Hardly on any maps anymore."

I knew there were pockets of land leased from the federal government by homesteaders and entrepreneurs. One family east of Wheeler had leased a large tract and put up a store, a post office and an apartment compound for teachers at the nearby Indian boarding school. Decades later, they still had the land under contract.

Still, I doubted such land could be outside any sort of law enforcement.

"Morro must have police officers," I said.

"Oh, honey," said Jessie, "we haven't had need of a lawman in a long, long while."

"Ain't nothin' here we can't handle," Olin said.

Not yet, anyway. They couldn't possibly handle Jim, or see through the snake-oil charm of a sociopath when nearly everyone in Wheeler had failed for so long.

I was torn. If I tried to find out how we got here, that would lead Jim straight to us. Even reaching out to Terri was a risk—when Laurel and I didn't arrive on that plane, she would have tried to find out why. That would mean calling Bernadette, if Terri had a number for her, which was unlikely.

No, most likely it would have meant contacting Jim.

The only thing I wanted at that moment was to hide out. To lay low until I got my strength back, and my bearings. Figure out the next move for Laurel and me. Something that wouldn't land us back in that tin-roofed house, or worse.

"Listen, if anyone should come 'round . . ." I hesitated. My voice sounded thin and childlike to my own ears.

Olin leaned in again, and this time his eyes were piercing, with no hint of humor. He laid his rough hand over mine, and his touch was warm. The warmth spread up my arm like an infusion.

"Joanna." His voice was deep and soothing, the way I talk to Laurel when she wakes up in tears from a bad dream. "If such a situation should arise, I'll know how to handle it."

Olin had to be eighty, at least. Not a big man. But at that moment I understood that his frame, however slight it might seem, was forged of iron. He wasn't giving me easy assurances—he was giving me his word.

"Thank you," I choked out.

"You got any people, honey?" Jessie asked. "Family?"

I shook my head.

"Well, then." She rose briskly to gather the breakfast dishes. "About time I had some female company around here. We were never blessed with children of our own, and after a while we stopped praying for them. It's like having a family laid right in our lap, ready-made. I figure to enjoy it while it lasts."

Vantage Point

It was a struggle to settle my mind on coherent thought. It wanted to wander. It wanted to kick off like Laurel in that swing under the chestnut tree, shoot for the sky and keep going.

Staying occupied, going through familiar motions, helped to ground me. I didn't keep to my bed anymore, but helped Jessie with the chores—weeded the vegetable garden, kneaded dough, swept the heart pine floors and beat the rag rugs, hanging them over the fieldstone fence.

Jessie had to show me how to launder clothes in her big-bellied hand-crank machine—the old-fashioned kind I'd seen only in pictures. It had to be decades old, but they'd kept it in fine condition, and she insisted it still served her well. I'd hang the clothes on the line out back, fetching them in again when they were dry and smelling as sweet as buckbrush. Sometimes I'd bury my face in them and just *breathe.*

Always that terrible mountain was at my shoulder, reigning over the valley, hanging on my every move. I resisted looking at it the way you avoid looking directly at the sun, for fear it could blind you. But as with any forbidden thing, there was a strong temptation, too. To give in. To turn and steal a peek. To see what might happen if I did. But when I'd do so, the ground wanted to slide out from under me all over again, and I was reeling on the edge of a cliff.

The Mountain didn't seem to bother Laurel—she played for hours under its shadow, oblivious. I didn't dare tell the old couple how it disturbed me, or they might wonder if their houseguest was losing her mind. For all I know, they'd be right.

We landed at this place like true refugees—with just the clothes on our backs, and not so much as a toothbrush. Jessie bought clothes for Laurel at a general store in Morro—dungarees and shirts, a jacket, sneakers and socks. For me she bought yards of fabric and sewing patterns. From the styles of the dresses and skirts, some of those patterns must have been lying in store bins for years. Still, they were pretty in a vintage sort of way.

Jessie had an old Singer machine—black and gleaming, smelling faintly of machine oil—stored in a walnut housing cabinet. She'd mail-ordered it ages ago, she said, from a catalog. After supper, Olin and Laurel would play dominoes or checkers, while Jessie and I would sit in the corner, the machine whirring away.

Nearly every day, Jessie and her husband assured me they'd heard of no police search for a woman and child, but I failed to see how they'd know—they owned no television and took no newspaper. From what I could tell, their only link to the outside world was a radio—a boxy antique that picked up a single station that broadcast oldies music and radio shows.

It was as if the old couple had decided one day—decades ago—that a rustic life suited them, and they would keep just as they were for as long as they could. As if they had extricated themselves from the evolving world, and not just from its modern conveniences. Sometimes when I looked at them, I got the unsettled feeling that I was watching them through a rearview mirror, slowly receding from me.

Despite their reassurances, Jim never strayed far from my mind. I couldn't seem to shake him, however hard I threw myself into routine. I couldn't peer out a front window without expecting to see a deputy's unit speed up the dirt road or beeline for the house. In fitful dreams, police lights strobed outside, but were never there when I woke.

Back in Wheeler, whenever Jim would drive us to town, I'd stare out the car window and note all the places to hide. Every house with busted windows and an overgrown yard. Every shed with no padlocked door. Every boarded-up business. Every playhouse, doghouse, culvert.

In my mind, there was no hole so tiny that Laurel and I couldn't squeeze inside and disappear. I never imagined past that. Never imagined coming out again.

Most days, this farm felt like a good hiding place. Most days it felt safe. It was less easy to feel that way at night. After the supper dishes were washed and everyone settled in, I'd sit in a wicker chair on the porch and leave the light off. It was a good vantage point. Now and then headlights traveled up the road or down, but they never stopped.

I sat and wondered about Bernadette—by now long gone with Sam to Reno or whatever town had appeal for a woman with spirit. And about Terri, who was a true wild card. The Terri I used to know would be ballsy enough to catch a flight from Boston to Albuquerque to find out why her friend hadn't arrived. Especially if she hadn't bought whatever story Jim had fed her. *That* Terri was no fool.

But that Terri was fixed more than—what, ten years in the past? I didn't know her anymore and she didn't know me. Terri today might decide I'd flaked out on her one more time, and adios.

And that thought gave me comfort. I didn't want to be tracked down—not by anybody.

I wanted to crawl into a hole and disappear, once and for all.

A few nights ago, I asked Olin if he kept guns in the house. He told me he had a vintage carbine, two long-range Winchester rifles for hunting—one lightweight and one heavy—and a 12-gauge double-barrel shotgun. He showed me the cabinet where he kept the cartridges. He didn't ask questions.

Simon

If it seemed Jessie and her husband had removed themselves from the world, it wasn't entirely so. After some weeks, they said there'd be company for Saturday supper—Simon Greenwood, the short-order cook who'd found Laurel and me wandering in the desert. He used to come every week before they took us in, they said. And after that, they thought it best to wait till I was up to it. Apparently they thought that time had come.

I knew this just meant another plate at the table. I should be able to manage that for an hour or so—if Jim had taught me anything, it was how to shut down and fake it on many levels.

But when Saturday came, I could barely function. Back home, for those rare evenings with Jim's friends, everything was decided for me—what to wear, what to say, how to behave. I was groomed to be insignificant. To ask no questions, but to answer them like a Good Wife. To lie if need be.

That evening, I couldn't so much as decide what to wear. I simply couldn't *make a choice.* Any choice. I felt like I couldn't bear to make the wrong one.

I gathered the clothes Jessie and I had sewn together and laid them out. Laurel came in, stroking each piece. She had no trouble dressing herself—a green skirt with white daisies, a blue-and-black blouse, red socks.

"Let me pick for you, Mommy," she said.

At least I knew better than that. I chose something close at hand and buttoned myself into it—a subdued sleeveless column dress of soft cotton. But as I turned to head downstairs, I caught myself in the standing mirror in the corner of the bedroom. I don't have much to do with mirrors anymore, but this time I straightened and drew close for a better look.

What my reflection told me was that Jessie was a fine seamstress and knew how to cut and sew fabric to fit. I was still too pale, my eyes too guarded. But I wasn't as bony as I remembered. And the dress, though simple, skimmed my figure in an elegant line. Its bronze hue tempered my complexion from sallow to cream and brought out the color of my eyes, which are the same quartz green as Laurel's.

I ran a finger along the scar bisecting my left eyebrow. I looked at myself so rarely anymore, it startled me to see it.

My hair was still a lank, neutral brown, without the body or auburn hues it once had. There was a time when women would stop me on the street to ask what brand of color I used. They wouldn't believe me when I told them it didn't come from a bottle.

Those days were gone.

I pulled it back from my face, twisting it behind in a swift, practiced movement, fastened it with clips and headed downstairs.

Laurel sat in a wicker chair on the porch, keeping an eye out for the dinner guest. It was the same chair I used every evening to keep a lookout for her father.

The table was laid with bone china, old polished silver and fresh linen. There were tall beeswax candles in silver candlesticks. Olin made a last sweep of the kitchen, dipping his finger in the pear glaze for the chicken before Jessie smacked his hand away. I filled the water pitcher and set it on the table.

Finally Laurel called out from the porch: "Here he comes!"

I peered through the screen door at a man heading toward the arching footbridge, a big tan dog at his heels.

He was taller than most, slim, his hair springing up in short, woolly waves—light brown, with streaks of sun-bleached blond. He was wearing a butcher-style apron, carrying a bottle of wine in one hand and a fistful of flowers in the other. I could hear him talking to the dog as they neared.

He noticed Laurel, now chafing at the porch railing, and smiled and waved to her.

"Laurel," I murmured. "Come inside."

"But, Mommy, I want to say hi."

"Now."

She grumbled, but obeyed. I pulled her close.

Olin stepped outside to greet Simon like an old friend. "Go on in," Olin told him. "The ol' woman's waitin'."

I retreated with Laurel to the far side of the room.

The man stepped through the door, where Jessie was waiting to plant a kiss on his cheek.

"'Bout time," she said, and there was rare affection in her voice. "That your apple wine?"

He handed her the bottle. "Yours now."

With a word he sent his big dog to lie on a hook rug by the fireplace. Then he looked up. Something flickered in his eyes when he saw me—recognition? I certainly didn't recognize him.

But he did surprise me. He was younger than I'd expected—mid-thirties, maybe. I imagined he'd be closer in age to Olin and Jessie.

His face was tanned, his eyes a gray-blue, heavily hooded in a sleepy sort of way, with creases that deepened when he smiled.

Laurel twisted her hand from mine and rushed to him.

"I'm Laurel," she said.

He crouched to one knee. "Simon. Pleased to make your acquaintance."

"Those flowers are pretty," she said. "Are they for Miz Jessie?"

"Matter of fact, they're for you. Picked them in a meadow behind my cabin this morning. You look like a field of wildflowers yourself, so I figure they'll feel right at home."

"Come on, honey," Jessie said as Laurel took the bouquet. "Let's go put those in a vase. Won't they look nice on the table?"

Simon straightened and turned to me.

"This here's Joanna," said Olin. "But I reckon you two already met, after a fashion."

"How're you feeling?" Simon asked.

He sounded too earnest to be making small talk, and it unsettled me. "Good," I said. "I'm good. And you?"

He smiled. "Just fine, thanks." He looked quizzically at Olin. "Mind?"

"Go on up," Olin said.

Simon nodded as he passed, heading for the stairway. I turned in confusion to Olin.

"He needs to wash up before supper, workin' a grill all day," Olin explained. "This way, he don't have to drive out to his place, turn around and drive all the way back."

I could hear the shower start upstairs.

Laurel and Jessie returned with the flower vase and set it between the candlesticks. Then Laurel ran to the dog, still lying on the rug. As she stroked his neck, his tale thumped the floor. "What's his name?"

"Pal," said Olin, settling into a chair beside her. "Golden retriever mostly, but collie and shepherd in there, too."

"We had a dog once," Laurel said thoughtfully, running her fingers through the fur. "She ran away."

"Now, that's a pity," Olin said. "Pal here—he must've strayed from his people, too. Simon gives him a good home, though. No dog could have a better."

Jessie returned with the wine bottle, uncorked now, and two glasses. She handed me one and poured. "Just taste," she said.

"Simon makes this?" I asked.

"With apples from his own orchard," Jessie said. "Doesn't lay in many bottles every year, but that just makes them worth the wait."

"How long have you known him?"

"Why, I met that boy when he first entered this world, bare beamed and buck nekkid."

Laurel whooped.

"Helped deliver him," Jessie said with a smile. "Women did, in those days. Doctors were scarce."

Upstairs, the shower shut off.

"Has he worked for you long?" I asked.

Jessie pursed her lips in thought.

"After the war, he drifted a bit," she said. "Had to find his way again. Happens sometimes to men who see too much. When he came back, he built that little cabin of his and took a job at the café. Been there ever since."

I wasn't sure which war she meant—the Gulf War? Iraq? Afghanistan?

Before I could sort it out, Simon came bounding down the stairs, dressed now in jeans and a blue plaid shirt open at the collar. His hair was damp, the waves combed back from his face. He was freshly shaven, trailing a light scent of something warm and spicy.

"You smell nice," Laurel told him.

"Not me," he said with a smile. "That's bay rum."

Olin stood and stretched, his joints cracking. "Let's dig in!"

Laurel claimed the seat beside Simon, stealing sidelong glances. He took the chair across from me. Soon he, Olin and Jessie began rattling on about who was traveling where, building what, spending time with so-and-so.

If I'd been uneasy before, it was all the worse now. Family dinners back home were strained, even on good days. Small talk only irritated Jim, and for me it carried risk. I never knew from one day to the next which word or comment, however innocent, might set him off. Silence became my sanctuary.

Suddenly I was picturing that table again—wondering if Jim was sitting there, a single plate in front of him, a single glass, a knife, a fork, a spoon. Did he even bother with such things anymore? Or did he just root through the fridge, then stand at the counter eating over the sink like a bachelor? Was he thinking of us, wondering where we might be, biding his time, stoking his rage?

I glanced furtively around Jessie and Olin's table, only vaguely aware that Olin was regaling them with a story about a horse he'd had as a young boy—a big, feisty Appaloosa that first taught him to swear. The others were laughing—even Laurel, her eyes bright. I took the cue and forced a smile.

A faint ringing started in my ears, growing louder.

More words then, more banter, but coming as if from a distance—disconnected, like static buzzing on that old radio in the front room, the needle casting back and forth for a clear signal to lock onto.

I wiped cold sweat from my upper lip and sipped at my water, willing my hand not to shake, fighting the rising panic.

I'd dreaded—even resented—the thought of company tonight, as if it were an intrusion on me. But now it was clear that I was the intruder. I was the outsider, a stranger in every sense, not this man sitting so easy, so appreciated, at their table.

I took up my knife and fork and began to saw pieces of chicken—sweet with the pear glaze but tasteless on my tongue. I cut the bits smaller and smaller and smaller . . .

Finally I stopped and stared at my plate, now sliding out of focus. My chest was tightening, squeezing the air from my lungs. I could feel myself surrendering to the growing static, drifting with it, the voices fusing together, receding to a rushing noise not unlike that creek outside . . .

"How about you, Joanna?"

The sound of my own name cut through the panic—through the rattle and noise filling my head to bursting. It seemed to come from a far place, but it was coming only from across the table, where Simon was watching me, holding the wine bottle, waiting. I blinked at him stupidly.

"Sorry?"

"More wine?" he asked.

I drew a steadying breath. "Yes, please. A little."

He poured a small glass. "I understand you like to write. You must like books, then."

"Yes."

He waited, apparently expecting I had more to say on the subject. I struggled to oblige him.

"I don't read much anymore," I said. "Not since . . . not for a long time."

"What did you like to read, when you did?"

His expression was open, friendly. He was only trying to engage me.

"Poetry," I said at last.

"Anyone in particular?"

At least that question was easy. "I always liked Yeats."

Simon paused, then began to recite: " 'Where the wandering water gushes from the hills above Glen-Car . . .' "

I gave him a thin smile. This poem I knew—as familiar as Laurel's favorite bedtime books, read and reread a thousand times.

I finished the line for him: " 'In pools among the rushes that scarce could bathe a star.' That's from 'The Stolen Child.' "

Laurel looked startled. "Somebody stole a child?"

"It's a poem, sweetie," I said. "About a fairy that tries to tempt a mortal child away from the troubles of the world."

"Did she go?"

"Well, yes. The last stanza goes like this:

'He'll hear no more the lowing
Of the calves on the warm hillside
Or the kettle on the hob
Sing peace into his breast,
Or see the brown mice bob
Round and round the oatmeal chest.' "

I surprised myself, recalling those lines. I hadn't thought of that poem in years. And the book was long gone.

"That's sad," said Laurel. "Not seeing the mice anymore. Or the calves."

"That would be sad," I said. "But think of the wonderful life with the fairies. And no reason to be unhappy again, ever. That's a good thing, don't you think?"

"Maybe. But if you didn't come, too, I wouldn't go."

"That's right, honey," Jessie said, patting her hand. "You stick with your mama. And if those fairies come round, you tell 'em to scat."

Later, as Jessie passed around the dessert plates, I felt Simon's eyes on me. I forced myself to glance up. His gaze was steady, speculative.

Olin cleared his throat, then spoke: "Simon, how you holdin' up down at the café? We sure did leave you shorthanded of late."

"I understand—you've been busy."

Jessie was shaking her head. "Still, a shame you don't have some help. Even for a day or so a week."

I took their meaning then. It wasn't that I was unwilling to help out in their café, but I'd never done restaurant work before. Or held any real job. After we were married, Jim wouldn't allow it.

But it wasn't only lack of experience that unnerved me. It was imagining Jim pulling up at that café one day—stepping out of his unit with his spit-shined shoes, his Sam Browne and .40-caliber pistol, unsnapping his holster. Working there, I'd be sticking my head out of my hiding place.

On the other hand, I realized he could just as easily pull up at Olin and Jessie's door.

So what I really had to decide was when I would stop letting Jim make my decisions for me—control me, even in absentia. Again I was staring at my plate, this time wrestling down my own survival instinct. I took a deep breath.

"If you like," I said at last, "I could help. But I've never waitressed before—I might be lousy at it."

"Oh, honey," said Jessie, "the way you do around here, you can handle yourself. I'll teach you all you need. Then I'll leave you in Simon's hands."

I glanced at Simon, who was still watching me steadily. And for some unearthly reason, I blushed.

The Café

It took a few days to muster the nerve to cross the footbridge, but one morning I woke before dawn feeling something like resolve, pulled on a skirt and blouse and left a note for Jessie.

I paused on the front porch. The yellow pickup was already parked next to the building and the neon sign and windows were lit up.

To the left of me, the Mountain was a massive silhouette under its snowcapped peak. I stepped off the porch, averting my gaze even as I sensed *it* still watching *me*.

I started toward the café, my eyes fastened on the path. There was little ambient light, but enough to navigate. My movement must have startled something in the brush—I could hear a rustle and scurry of some small animal, receding fast. Something was throwing shadows of piñon and juniper all around me, and I glanced up ahead to see a full moon on the wane, low and fat in the sky and visible just above the flat roof of the café.

And there it was again—that inescapable force of gravity, latching on to me. It wanted me to turn. Wanted me to look. The prospect was terrifying—and yet thrilling at the same time.

I'm not sure it was my decision to stop.

Or to turn.

The sun hadn't breached yet, but light was spreading out from the east. There was an anemic layer of stratus clouds hanging low in the sky, and as the dawn grew their underbellies bled out from scarlet to salmon to pink.

The face of the Mountain was changing, too—from flat silhouette to deep shadows, cut with shards of light. It seemed to be shifting, rearranging, from the rising sun or some other catalyst.

And there at the summit I saw it, shining from the crags.

A fixed, flawless white light.

I'd never noticed this before—in fact, I'd never seen the top of the Mountain except in daylight. The light seemed set at such an altitude, and so inaccessible, I couldn't imagine what it might be. Or how someone had managed to put it there. Or why.

It didn't move or blink or strobe. A beacon of some kind? A warning?

A cool breeze swept in from the east and I pulled my sweater close.

The sun was cresting now, inching higher with each passing second. As it rose, the light on the Mountain faded in kind, shrinking to a pinpoint, then to extinction, even as the Mountain itself seemed to rouse to life.

It took an effort to disengage and turn back to the path. The air held a new snap and static, as if a thunderstorm had just passed through.

Across the footbridge, I rounded the café to the front. Through the windows I could see the place was compact and retro, with little red tables and a curving Formica counter. In a corner was a large, silent jukebox with art deco chrome and blinking colored lights.

I opened the door and a bell jangled overhead; I could hear soft music coming from the back. There was movement near the jukebox, where Pal was rising stiffly from a rag rug. He pushed his nose into my hand till I scratched his ears.

"It's me!" I called out. "Joanna!"

Simon's head appeared above the half wall that separated the dining area from the kitchen. He broke into a smile.

"You've come to rescue me."

"I'm hardly the cavalry," I said.

"Can you tell time?"

"I . . . Of course."

"Then in ten minutes, open this oven and pull out the biscuits." He handed me a pair of oven mitts. "I got a feeling we'll be busy today. Relatively. Jessie on the way?"

"I left a note," I said. "But this morning I wanted to . . ."

"Fly solo?"

"I guess. Can I help with anything while I wait on the biscuits?"

The next half hour flew. I wiped down tables and counters, wrapped sets of silverware in paper napkins, refilled napkin holders, straw dispensers and condiment bottles.

When Jessie arrived, she walked me through the menu,

showed me how to take orders and leave the slips for Simon. To serve and clear and work the cash register. She was direct and encouraging.

Soon customers began filing through the door. My heart skipped with every jangle of the bell, but every face was that of a stranger. The first time I screwed up an order, I froze and braced for the fallout. But the customer waved off my apologies, insisting the blueberry pancakes I brought him were better than the buttermilk he'd ordered.

A dozen people must have come through that morning—farmers, ranchers, store owners, laborers. None of them asked prying questions. At lunchtime came a second round.

"To get a look at the new waitress," said Jessie.

"They didn't know there'd be a new waitress," I said. "Even I didn't know till I woke up this morning."

Jessie smiled but didn't answer. By two o'clock, she untied her apron and left for the day. Only four customers remained. I refilled their coffee mugs as Simon beckoned me to the counter.

"How about lunch?" he asked.

I'd been so busy, I hadn't thought to break for a meal.

"How does it work?" I asked.

He shrugged. "Just tell me what you'd like."

I hesitated. It had been a long time since I'd ordered in a restaurant.

"Well," I said, "I haven't had a cheeseburger and shake in ages."

I took a seat by a window on the western end of the valley. The sun through the glass was warm on my face and arms. Only two trucks remained in the parking lot, belonging to the last customers.

Simon set two plates on the table—one in front of me with a cheeseburger and fries, and an identical plate on the other side. He left and returned with a chocolate shake for me, a vanilla one for himself. He sat down and thumped a ketchup bottle over his fries.

"So tell me," he said. "How was your day?"

I shook my head. "I'm surprised I survived."

"You did great."

"How would you know? You were back at the grill."

"I see and hear plenty back there," he said. "And careful—you have a limited quota of discouraging words before you violate the menu."

I blinked at him. "What?"

He flipped over a menu and ran his finger along a line at the bottom: *Seldom is heard a discouraging word.*

"Olin's idea," he said. "To keep folks civil. And if they aren't . . ."

"You kick them out?"

He paused, considering me carefully. "For you, a new rule," he said. "You'll have to drop a coin in the jukebox over there and play any song I choose."

"I don't know," I said. "You might have rotten taste in music."

"I happen to have swell taste in music. And every record is crackerjack."

"Are those real vinyls? Forty-fives?"

"Not just forty-fives," he said. "Some are seventy-eights—all of them requests from customers. Jessie orders them special. Sometimes people would just like to hear a song that means something."

"What's your favorite?"

He smiled at me over his burger. "One of these days, I might tell you."

I pegged him for country-western. A ballad, though, not a rowdy bar song. Nothing about cheating—Simon didn't seem the type. And not a patriotic anthem, either. Not after what Jessie had told me about his war experience.

Jim had a particular taste for country-western. I'd listened to song after song about whiskey and beer and pickup trucks, true lovers and cheaters. After a while, it all ran together like manic-depressive white noise.

A few years ago, though, Jim took a break from music. All of it. That was after a country band came out with a song about a wife who'd had enough of her abusive husband and decided to get rid of the problem—rat poison in the grits and rolling out the tarp . . .

One day Jim came home from work and caught me listening to it. I hadn't planned to—it just came over the radio as I was cooking. But as it began, as I listened, it stopped me in my tracks. Jim caught me standing there, so focused, so fascinated. Maybe he thought I was taking notes. Maybe I was.

He yanked the power cord from the wall, then slammed the radio against my head.

It was cheap plastic and splintered easily, so it didn't do as much damage as you'd think. Jim must have thought so, too, because for good measure he took the pot of stew cooling on the stove, stood over me where I lay stunned on the linoleum and poured it on my back. I was five months' pregnant with Laurel then.

"Is something wrong?" Simon asked.

I couldn't look at him.

"If I ask you something," I said, "will you answer it?"

"I don't see why not."

I swallowed hard.

"That day . . . that day you found us. I don't remember it. Any of it. And I need to know what happened."

"It's no mystery, Joanna. I was driving down the road here, heading toward the highway. Once you're over that hill, it's all steep curves toward the interstate, and soon enough you hit desert again. I saw buzzards circling half a mile or so from the road. And on the ground right under them, I thought I saw something move."

His tone was mild. Matter-of-fact. Almost indifferent. When he said the word "buzzards," I looked up to lock eyes with him.

I didn't see indifference there, but sympathy. It stung me.

"I was able to off-road the pickup halfway in," he continued. "By then, I could tell it was someone staggering along, barely able to keep to their feet. I got out and sprinted the rest of the way. You were stumbling, but still standing. You were holding Laurel, and she was passed out—it was all I could do to pry your arms off her. You didn't want to let her go—in fact, you fought me quite a bit.

"You must have been out there awhile. You were dehydrated, sick from the heat. Your clothes were ripped up, legs swelled from cactus spines. I slung Laurel over my shoulder, propped you up as best I could and half carried you back to my truck. Olin and Jessie were the closest. I knew they'd take good care of you."

I couldn't bear to look at him anymore, and turned to stare out the window. But this time I wasn't seeing the green valley, but the awful scene Simon had just described.

"Did you find our car?" I asked finally. "A little Toyota. Silver."

"No car. I even drove back along the road once you were safe at the house, and back and forth along the interstate looking for one. In case there was an accident and someone else might be hurt."

"Did I . . . Was there blood . . . on my clothes?"

Simon might have been picturing an accident, but I wasn't. I was picturing rat poison and just deserts with a sick fascination.

"Some," he said. "From scrapes and cuts. Not much, though. You heal up fast."

"I have lots of practice with that," I said bitterly.

We both went quiet.

It was nearly three o'clock—closing time—and the last customers were leaving, calling their good-byes to Simon, dropping cash on their tables. The bell on the door jangled as they left. Their trucks pulled out and headed south toward the foothills.

Then all was silent again.

"Guess you'll have to kick me out after all," I said.

Simon didn't answer. He pushed his chair back and headed to the jukebox. He studied the selections, then slid a coin in the slot and punched some buttons. The machine whirred and clacked; a record slid into place.

It was soft rock from the sixties, a hit from before I was born. But it was timeless, and I knew it well. This was the more recent remake, the same version Terri and I would play in our dorm room at Hokona Hall whenever we pulled an all-nighter or just wanted to cut loose.

Don't worry, baby—everything will turn out all right. Don't worry, baby . . .

I smiled, and Simon looked pleased. We listened to it together without speaking, and when it was over he sent me back out the door.

Good Night Air

I tugged Laurel's nightgown over her head. Her hair was damp from her evening bath, the ends rolling like tiny sausages. She could use a trim.

Before she slipped under the covers, she pulled a thin book from the nightstand and handed it to me. Jessie had borrowed it from the library in town. Laurel was too old for it, really, but she loved it. So did I. It was comfort reading, the book equivalent of tomato soup and grilled cheese sandwiches.

After the book ended, after all the familiar "good nights" were said, Laurel was still wide-awake, watching me solemnly from her pillow.

"Mommy, are we living here now?"

I set the book on my lap.

"For a while, sweetie. Do you like it here?"

She nodded, rubbing one eye with her knuckles.

"But are we staying? Is this forever?"

"Well, forever's a long time," I said.

Laurel's hand dropped to the covers and she leveled a look at me even more solemn than before. It was a piercing, knowing look, and I'd never seen it come from such a young face before. Especially hers. It gave me the distinct impression she knew something I didn't. And *knew* she knew, and was only waiting for me to catch up.

I set the book back on the nightstand.

"Laurel, honey," I said. "Do you remember the day we got here?"

She squinted at me, puzzled.

"I woke up," she said. "And I was here."

"Here?"

She jiggled her feet under the covers and smiled.

"Here. In bed. Miz Jessie brought me strawberries."

I brushed stray hair from her temple.

"And what about before that?" I tried to keep my voice light. "Do you remember Mr. Simon bringing us here?"

She thought for a moment, then shook her head.

"And before that?" I asked even more lightly than before. "Do you remember Daddy? Out on the road?"

This time her eyes were fixed on me intently.

"Do *you*?" she asked finally.

I couldn't tell if she was being curious or trying to prod my memory. Either way, it was disconcerting.

"No," I said. "Maybe you can help me remember."

She shook her head once more.

"I can't."

Can't? I thought. *Or won't?*

How old does your child have to be before she starts keeping big secrets? I felt a pang of guilt. Maybe that was something she'd learned from me.

Laurel yawned and stretched, settling deeper under the covers. "Mommy?" she asked.

"Yes, sweetie?"

"I heard Tinkerbell today."

My breath caught in my throat. "Wh-what?"

"She was barking. Up on the Mountain. I think she's trying to find us."

In a flash I was back in our yard in Wheeler, Tinkerbell scratching at the shed door, Jim heading inside with the shovel . . .

"That . . . that's just not possible, Laurel. If you heard a dog, it could have been any dog. They sound alike from far off."

"No, Mommy. It was Tinkerbell. And we gotta go get her."

I stood up from the bed, rattled to the core. I wasn't going up on that mountain. And certainly not to hunt for a dog I knew full well I'd never find.

"Time to go to sleep now," I said.

"But, Mommy . . ."

I stooped for a quick kiss to her cheek, then switched off the table lamp.

"Good night."

Bee in a Thunderstorm

Not long after Laurel told me about Tinkerbell, Jessie said a few ladies from town would arrive the next morning—they were holding a bee to finish up a wedding quilt for the local schoolteacher. She invited me to join them, and pressed till I felt no choice but to accept. She looked pleased when I did.

"It'll be fine weather for it," she said. "These old bones know."

Olin was behind her at the dining room table playing dominoes with Laurel. He looked up at me and winked.

Early the next morning came a menacing rumble. I glanced out my bedroom window to see heavy clouds crowding in from the east. A gust of wind lashed the bedroom curtains. You could smell the storm brewing.

Wooden deck chairs already sat under the oak tree, arranged in a tight circle that Olin had set up the night before at Jessie's instruction. But it seemed the ladies were about to get rained out.

Then I noticed Jessie in the vegetable garden below, standing between rows of tomato plants. Her hands were on her hips and she was glaring. She raised the skirt of her apron and waved it, the way she does to chase off a stray hen.

"Shoo, now! Shoo!"

But there was no hen in sight, and Jessie wasn't looking down, but up—up at the storm clouds.

Another rumble, a louder volley than before. She shook her head and retreated back inside.

We didn't eat breakfast at the outside trestle table, but at the little oak one in the kitchen—all but Olin, who said he had business in the fields.

He'd been outside all morning, but had been vague about where or why. Earlier, I'd spotted him off in the distance—as still and straight as a soldier at inspection, far outside his fieldstone fence. He had faced east, too, just like Jessie.

I almost called out to him then, but something stopped me. Somehow it felt like an intrusion. Now here he was again, running off.

Another battery of thunder; the storm was drawing nigh.

"A pity about your bee," I told Jessie. "You could always bring it inside."

She looked at me thoughtfully. "We always have it outside. Never you mind."

The ladies arrived soon after breakfast. Liz LaGow was dark and sturdy—not tall, but vigorous. She was carrying a thick bundle wrapped in cloth and trussed with twine. Her dark, probing eyes took me in from ponytail to sandals. I knew she and her husband owned the general store. She arrived with her sister, Molly Knox, who was taller than Liz, and slimmer, with finer features. She had a coil of brunette braid at the crown of her head and eyes that were less penetrating than her sister's. Molly owned the hotel in town.

Like Jessie, the sisters wore simple belted dresses hemmed a prim distance below the knee. I couldn't get a handle on how old they might be—they seemed ageless, but had the same bold energy as Jessie. For some reason, I could clearly picture the three of them marching hundreds of miles alongside Conestoga wagons, raising children on hardscrabble farms on the frontier.

The teacher, though, was altogether different. Bree Wythe was younger than I—petite and lively in jeans and a sleeveless blouse of coral silk. She wore a string of small turquoise nuggets around her neck. Her hair was ash blond, styled to her shoulders. Her smile was warm as she took my hand.

"I'm so happy to meet you," she said in a voice with slight Southern notes. She linked her arm through mine as we followed the others through the house toward the back door. "Thanks for helping on the quilt—I don't know about you, but I've never finished a stitch in my life."

We stopped just inside the kitchen, where Jessie and the sisters stood at the open doorway to the backyard, staring at a bank of black clouds that now nearly eclipsed the sky. Wind whipped the branches of the old oak. Lightning crackled; thunder growled.

The three women exchanged grim looks, then without a word forged ahead into the yard. The wind smacked their long skirts about their legs and tore at their hair, pulling it loose from buns and braids.

I paused in the doorway with Bree and stared after them. I expected Bree to be as rattled as I was, but she only smiled and tugged on me until we were heading for the oak, too.

Liz was loosening the twine around her bundle, drawing out a large quilt. The others opened small sewing bags to withdraw scissors, needles, thimbles and spools of thread. Deftly they stretched the quilt into a four-legged frame, then settled back in their chairs. Bree and I took our seats, and the five of us tucked into the quilt as if the wind weren't howling or the clouds about to split open.

The scene was so outrageous, so surreal, I couldn't speak.

Molly handed me a needle, spool and thimble, and Jessie did the same for Bree. Numbly I snipped off a length and bent to thread the needle, but of course it was impossible with the wind whipping the thread, and though it was only midmorning, it had grown as dark as dusk. I was about to give up when Molly passed me the needle she'd just threaded, apparently with little trouble.

Conversation would only have been drowned out, so the women bent to their own work, needles darting.

Thunder exploded directly over our heads in a long, furious roar that rattled the windows of the house. I could taste the electrical charge.

"We should go inside!" I shouted.

The women paused long enough to stare at me, then shook their heads. Molly leaned in close. "This is nothing, Joanna. Just wait."

Thunder again, followed hard by lightning. I stared about, my heart in my throat.

Then, just as I was about to bolt for the house, everything abruptly changed.

The banshee noise broke off as suddenly as flipping a switch. The thrashing branches of the oak eased till they were rocking like cradles. A rift began to open in the clouds directly overhead, wider by the second, splitting apart to expose a strip of cobalt blue sky. Shafts of yellow sunlight cut through the rift and hit the oak tree.

"There, now," Jessie muttered with a sigh. "Much better."

She and the sisters laid down their needles and calmly began to tuck their hair back in place. I watched them, stunned. I could only guess we were in the eye of the storm, although I'd never heard of thunderstorms having eyes. But they must, for this storm was clearly far from over.

On every side of us it still raged, hammering down the grass all along the bowl of the valley, whipsawing the trees. Fields of corn and wheat rolled like great waves. Clouds boiled, black and green and sickly yellow. In the distance, rain fell in flat unbroken sheets. Lightning flashed—not in single jagged bolts but in branching spectacles that lit up the sky. Thunder bellowed, but it wasn't rattling the windows anymore.

There was chaos all around while we sat undisturbed in an acre of oasis.

Liz began to rub her shoulder as if she'd strained it. "About time," she muttered. "Couldn't hear myself think with that racket."

"I . . . I don't understand," I said. "What's happening?"

Liz frowned at me dismissively, then turned to Bree. "Honey," she said, "tell us about the wedding. At the hotel, is it?"

Bree looked relieved to lay down her needle. "Middle of

December. Reuben says it's a slow time at the ranch. Joanna, you're more than welcome."

I stared at her, still confused. December was a long way off—I couldn't imagine still being in Morro by then. Bree was just being polite.

"Thank you," I managed finally. "If I'm still here."

Jessie dropped her hands to her lap and stared toward the barn just as Olin emerged with a deck chair under each arm, Laurel trailing behind. "Speak of the devil," she muttered. "What's that old fool up to now?"

He stopped in a patch of grass well within our sight and set the chairs side by side facing the western end of the valley, which was now bearing the brunt of the storm. Then the two of them took their seats to watch as calmly as if they were in a movie theater.

Liz was bristling, clearly feeling provoked. Molly was stifling a smile.

"Pay him no mind," Jessie said airily. "Don't give him the satisfaction."

Olin pulled the caps off two pop bottles and handed one to Laurel. It was then I noticed Bree studying me curiously.

"Joanna, summer's about over," she said. "School's starting soon. Will you be enrolling your daughter?"

The question caught me off guard. The last time Laurel had left school, she'd brought home her first-grade certificate, launching our escape.

I shrugged, feigning indifference. "I haven't made any plans."

I was sure Jim had alerted Laurel's school by now, and they'd let him know about any request to transfer her records. Enrolling her anywhere else would be firing off a flare.

"If it's a matter of documents, I wouldn't worry," said Bree. "I'd never turn a child away because of paperwork."

"And don't forget," said Jessie. "We're not county. We do things our own way out here."

"But there must be a school board," I protested. "Officials to account to."

"Honey"—Jessie gestured around the circle—"most of the school board is sitting right here." She looked meaningfully at Liz and Molly, who nodded in return. "All right, then. It's settled."

Apparently the discussion was over. And Laurel was enrolled in school.

"You been to town yet?" Liz asked. "No sense putting it off," she said when I shook my head. "We don't bite. Come on up and visit the store. We got everything you need, and most everything you'd want."

"Check out the hotel, too," Bree urged. "A lovely old Victorian. High tea on weekends. Very authentic."

"Yes, indeed." Liz smirked. *"Authentic."*

Molly's cheeks reddened. "And why not?" she said. "George has been very helpful."

Liz and Jessie said nothing.

"Who's George?" I asked finally.

"Oh," said Jessie. "He's Molly's gentleman caller."

"George is from Bristol," Molly said stiffly. "England."

I didn't ask how they'd managed to meet, but couldn't imagine it was through any online dating site. In fact, I couldn't picture Molly—or her sister or Jessie—on a computer at all. Jessie didn't keep so much as a microwave in her house.

What I could picture—quite suddenly and with utter

clarity—was one or the other placing a lonely-hearts newspaper ad. I could see photos exchanged—formal poses in sepia tones—then letters back and forth over many months, many years. The progression of their courtship washed over me with surprising surety.

Jessie laid down her needle and gazed about. "Storm broke."

It had broken long ago over our heads, of course, but now it was breaking in earnest over the rest of the valley. Lightning streaked soundlessly far off to the west, where thunderheads were in galloping retreat.

I paused, too, taking in the aftermath. The valley appeared to be standing still, catching its breath, set loose from time and space. It felt as if every clock in the world had wound down and suddenly stopped.

Even the air was motionless, leaving the valley as composed and vivid as a diorama. As wild and reckless as the storm had been, so profound now was the calm that followed it. The lull was contagious—it washed over me and through me in a wave of warmth. I'd never felt so at peace. I didn't want it to end.

None of us spoke. None of us moved. We sat together in stillness and silence under the oak tree, caught up in a consecrated moment.

A second passed. Then another. And with the next, the clocks began to tick again. Rain began to drip from the leaves and the rooflines. Birds stirred in the branches, and in the distance Willow Creek rushed noisily from the downpour.

The valley felt purged. Revived.

"Well, ladies." Jessie sighed. "Gather up."

Sewing bags opened up again, and back went needles, thread and thimbles. Liz and Molly unframed the quilt, folded it and slid it back into its fabric bag.

Olin still sat with Laurel at the far corner of the barn. He turned toward me and raised his pop bottle in salute.

And I knew what he was telling me: *You're welcome.*

A Still, Small Space

After the storm, after the sisters had left with Bree, I packed the last of the deck chairs back in the barn and stood alone in the open doorway. Dusk was falling, and lights were switching on in the farmhouse. Scraps of voices drifted outside, rising and falling in conversation. The radio broke into a twangy two-step, something about "Too Old to Cut the Mustard."

I stared about me at every homely and familiar object, every bit of landscape, as if they had suddenly become alien to me. As if at any moment they could transform into something else altogether, or vanish outright. Plow, tiller, scythe. Fence, tree, house. Even as I turned from one to the next, they seemed to pulsate, their lines blurring. I blinked, and they were back.

It was then I realized that the question I'd been asking—*How did we get here?*—was painfully inadequate. Suddenly it was almost irrelevant that I couldn't remember what happened that last day in Wheeler, between the frantic sprint toward Albuquerque, the flashing lights in the rearview and waking up in that bed upstairs.

This wasn't just a matter of recall.

It was a matter of *here itself.*

My stomach heaved and my knees buckled. I slid down the doorjamb, pushing off to land on a ladder that was lying along the barn wall. I closed my eyes and sucked in deep breaths, willing every particle to be very, very still.

"Gettin' a handle on the moment?"

I blinked up at Olin, standing over me in the doorway, his head quirked. His fingers worked a leaf of rolling paper packed with a line of loose tobacco, deftly snugging it into a cigarette. He licked the seal closed, stuck one end in his mouth and pulled a matchbook from his shirt pocket. When the cigarette was lit, he puffed twice as he slid the matches back into place. Then he offered me his hand.

"Join me outside," he said.

He eased me up and led me from the barn to the trestle table. As we sat, I barely noticed or cared that its benches were still soaked from the rain. Olin watched me for a long moment over his cigarette. He seemed expectant.

"Stew for supper," he said finally. "If you can eat."

I shook my head. I started to say something, then stopped. Words had become meaningless.

"Or," Olin continued, "we could just sit here and talk about the weather."

I stared at him and he gazed back, placid as ever. His lines never wavered, never shifted out of focus. It gave me encouragement.

"I thought it was me," I said. "With the Mountain. The way it pulls at me. Almost . . . talks to me. But it isn't me, is it?"

Olin took a drag on his cigarette, the tip flaring cherry red in the gathering dusk, mirroring pinpoints of light in his eyes. The smoke when he exhaled smelled sweet. He waited for me to continue.

"And you and Jessie—you're not just old-fashioned, are you? I can't explain it, but you're . . . somehow you're out of time and place."

If I expected Olin to be offended, he wasn't. Nor did he protest. Instead, he smiled indulgently.

I glanced at the western sky as the first stars sparked into place, much like the lights in the farmhouse. There was no trace of storm clouds left.

"And that thunderstorm. Deny it if you want, but . . ." I hesitated. The evening air wasn't cool, but I was starting to shiver.

"Go on," Olin urged.

"I think . . . I think you made it. Called it down. Whatever. And Jessie and the sisters—" I shook my head again as if to clear it. "Somehow they busted it up right over us, didn't they? Stopped it smack in its tracks. So they could have their bee. Jessie said they always have their bee outside."

"They surely do."

"Rain or shine, right? Only it never rains. At least not where they are. Olin, what is this place? You have to tell me. And tell me like I'm four years old, because that's about all I can handle right now."

He bent his head and flicked ash off the tip of his cigarette. He scraped his thumbnail thoughtfully along his chin, as if considering how best to approach the subject. I watched him in fascination and fear, hardly daring to breathe.

"A while ago," Olin began slowly, "we had a fella come through, said he was a rabbi. From Brooklyn, he said. And him and me, we got to talkin'. He told me about this place by the name of *Olam HaEmet.* A 'Place of Truth,' he called it. He said there comes a time when you go to this Place of Truth, and you stay put till you figure things out. Reflect on all the things you did in your life. Or maybe on all the things you should've done but didn't. He said that's where he was headed."

I started to laugh, but it snagged in my throat. A rabbi? Olin in a tête-à-tête with a rabbi—a tallit slung over his shoulders and tefillin boxes strapped to his head? But overriding the sense of the surreal was the gist of Olin's words. And even more, the meaning between them. I wanted him to fill in those gaps for me unbidden. At the same time, I wanted to scream at the top of my lungs for him to stop. I tried to lick my lips, but my tongue was as dry as dust.

"And this place, where do you find it?" I asked.

"Not so much *where*," Olin said gently, "as *how*."

I was shivering so hard now my teeth began to clatter. I tried to rub the gooseflesh from my bare arms, but my fingers were icicles. The fact was, I remembered reading something about Olam HaEmet, a long time ago. Except the writer had called it the "World of Truth." It's a place observant Jews believe waits on the Other Side. A place for reflection.

A place for departed souls.

"No," I whispered.

"You never know about expectations," Olin said mildly. "Everybody's got his own, I guess. When they first cross over."

Cross over? What the hell . . . ?

A faint ringing started in my ears and my body felt as weightless as balsa wood.

"You're crazy," I said. "Or I am. This isn't happening."

"Give me your hands, Joanna."

I glared back at him as if this—all this—were somehow his fault. Some cruel prank.

He said it again, this time more firmly: "Give me your hands."

His tone was still soothing, but there was a note of command in it, too. I found myself reaching for him, my hands now shaking so violently they looked palsied. I shuddered as he took them. The infusion of warmth I felt the first time he ever touched me—that first morning at breakfast, at this very same table—was nothing compared to the jolt of heat that coursed through me now, driving out the bone-chill. The shivering began to ease.

"This can't be." Tears were sliding down my cheeks. "*I* can't be."

"Go ahead; cry it out if you want. Won't make it any less so."

"But how? I don't know how . . ." An accident on the road? Had I hit another car or careened off the highway to escape that speeding cruiser? Another realization struck, and I pulled my hands from Olin's to stare in horror at the house. "Oh, dear God . . . Laurel . . ."

"Now, now. It's all right. Don't she look all right to you?"

All right? Since we'd come here, Laurel had never looked healthier. Or seemed happier. Suddenly I thought about that night in her room when she'd asked if we were here forever. If *this* were our forever . . .

"Does she know?" I asked.

Olin considered for a moment. "Not exactly. She's workin' it out—children, they catch on when they're ready. But she ain't quite there yet."

Five minutes ago, I would've said I wasn't quite there yet, either. Not ready to catch on. Not ready at all. But I had been suspicious, asking questions and grasping for answers, and Olin had only been obliging me.

Now he was regarding me with sympathy, as if another shoe were about to drop.

"Joanna, when we first met, you recall what I said? That you had the look of a gal who wouldn't be stayin' long."

"A short-timer. I remember."

He nodded. "Now, that's the thing. Near all the folks who come through, they go on eventually. But there's some, a few—they up and turn back."

"I don't understand."

"It ain't their time. They ain't fixed in one place yet, nor the other. So they got a choice to make. To stay or go back."

"Are you— Olin, what are you saying?"

"Near as I can tell," he continued, "you're here for a reason. You were in a bad way, and for a long time. Back in Wheeler."

I ducked my head, unsure how much Olin knew, even without my telling.

"This here—" Olin glanced up and down the valley, nearly eclipsed now by the gathering dusk. "Think of this as a place to rest. To get strong and straight inside. Think of it like your own Place of Truth. To consider where you come from, and what you might do different if you go back."

Jim's face flashed in front of me, and I shuddered involuntarily.

"That man of yours," Olin said knowingly. "Seems to me he was bleedin' the life out of you for a long time before you ever made it here."

"And he sure as hell won't stop if he gets the chance to do it again."

"No, he won't. It ain't in him to stop."

"So why would I *ever* want to go back?"

"That ain't for me to say."

I leaned on the table, burying my face in my hands, anxious for the moment to be over. More than anything I wanted to look up again and find no trace of Olin or the farm or that Mountain. I wasn't ruling out insanity, either—his or mine. I'd sidled up to it often enough over these last few years. But when you've finally lost it—lost it good and proper—do you even realize it? Do you know if you've given up, crawled inside your own head and pulled the ladder up after you? *Die Gedanken sind frei*, my Oma used to sing. *Thoughts are free . . . The darkest dungeon is futile, for my thoughts tear all gates and walls asunder . . .* For all I knew, I was still out there staggering in the desert, just as Simon had said, my broken brain cooking up this mirage . . .

And yet . . .

And yet I did know—knew marrow-deep—this was no delusion. No mirage. I knew because, with all my heart and soul, I wanted it to be. But no such luck. Not for me.

Finally I raised my head. "I don't— Olin, I have so many questions . . ."

"You hold on to them," he said. "Now ain't the time for questions, and I sure ain't the one for answers. What's important—well, it's best we all figure out the important things on our own. In our own way."

Suddenly I felt wrung out, weak as an infant. "What should I do?" I asked. "I don't know what to do."

"First off, you go on inside and get yourself some supper. You get yourself a good night's sleep. You wake up tomorrow and praise the day. You be mindful. And the next day, and the day after that, you get up and do it all over again. *You live.*"

Was that all? Eat, sleep, wake, work—in the afterlife, the same rules applied? I had no idea of the proprieties here. The physics. Were there other short-timers? Was everyone who crossed paths here a departed spirit? If not, would I know the difference? Would *they*? Olin and Jessie spoke of Wheeler as if they'd been there many times. As if they went there still . . .

"Olin," I whispered, as if Jim could be within earshot. "Can my husband find us here?"

Olin looked past me for so long I thought he didn't intend to answer. Then he did.

"That ain't for me to say, neither."

Little Yellow Boots

I woke on the porch, curled up like a fetus on the wicker settee. It was early morning and a dank chill hung in the air. I pushed myself up and a blanket slid off—someone must have laid it over me while I slept. I felt sluggish, as if my brain had been working overtime through the night. I rubbed at eyes that were dry and sore, trying to recall how I ended up sleeping outside.

And in a flash it came back . . . The sisters and the bee. The thunderstorm. Olin. The Place of Truth.

I swung my legs to the floor and nearly toppled an empty wine bottle sitting at my feet. It was one of Simon's—the apple wine he supplied at Saturday suppers. I'd sneaked it from Jessie's cupboard after they'd all gone off to bed. Then I'd slipped outside to get as snockered as circumstances would allow. I considered it a necessity. A palliative. Even an experiment. And what I discovered was that circumstances allowed snockered, sure enough. But apparently not sloppy. Or maybe for sloppy you needed two bottles.

The noises of a waking household were coming from inside. Jessie would be back in the kitchen, setting her cast-iron skillet on the stove, grinding coffee beans, sending Olin to the henhouse for eggs. I pulled the blanket back over my shoulders and stood. The planks of the porch felt cool and sure against my bare feet. I padded to the front railing, keen for any signs of the supernatural. I wasn't sure what that might be—a melting landscape like something out of Dalí, maybe. A second sun flaring overhead. A herd of bush elephants trumpeting across the valley floor, white tusks flashing . . .

How had Olin called it? *Getting a handle on the moment.* But how do you get a handle on a moment like this? Take it one day at a time, like a recovery program?

Then again, maybe this was meant to be an easy, familiar passage. Like leaving one room to enter another. Otherwise, how could you bear it?

The rattle of an engine came from the hills to the north where the road reared up and disappeared. An old Ford pickup appeared, its black paint faded to dull, piebald grays, coughing blue smoke from its tailpipe. It puttered past the diner on its way south, a ladder poking from its bed, a red rag knotted around the last rung, whipping in the wind like the wings of a scarlet bird.

For some reason, the sheer banality of it heartened me. This, I could handle.

I picked up the empty wine bottle and slipped it under the blanket, out of sight. When no one was looking, I'd drop it in a waste can. Apart from sparing myself some embarrassment,

I intended to use it as another experiment—to see if I was entitled to secrets here.

Breakfast proceeded the same as every other morning. Olin gave no hint that anything was amiss. As if he hadn't lobbed a virtual grenade in my lap hours before.

Hours. Were there still hours? I wasn't sure anymore.

But there was continuity. Familiarity. You sugar your coffee. Spoon the jam. Sop gravy off your plate with hunks of biscuit. You talk about the day ahead, ticking off what needs doing. By the end of breakfast, I was reacquainted with the rhythm, nearly myself again. If I wasn't ready to praise the day, at least I was ready to participate.

Dishes washed and dried, I stepped back outside to find the chill had gone, the sun blazing overhead. It was what Laurel calls a shiny day—so bright and clear your eyes ache with it. She'd gone with Olin to the coop earlier, and her sneakers were caked with mud from the storm the day before. I took a bucket to the yard and was scrubbing her sneakers when Jessie suggested we walk to town to get Laurel a pair of rain boots. I wiped a stray bit of hair from my face and stared at Jessie, searching for a sign on hers—anything to indicate she was aware of what Olin had told me last evening. A hint of complicity. Of *knowing*. Maybe even of sympathy.

But it was Jessie as Jessie had always been—her gray hair coiled to a tight bun, her sturdy frame as straight as a fence post, brooking no argument.

She tied on a straw sunbonnet and handed me another. It was wide brimmed, and from long habit I slung it low to hide my face. I brushed Laurel's hair into a ponytail and the three of us set out.

This was the first time I'd ventured off the farm, and even

now—even now—I couldn't imagine heading along this road without running into a deputy's cruiser, slanted off to the side, engine idling, windows dark. And Jim hunched like a vulture behind the wheel. But I knew that if I hid out on this farm much longer, I'd only be making myself a prisoner on purpose.

We struck out for town—toward the Mountain—an easy walk not only for its length, a mere two miles or so, but also because it felt as if the road sloped down a tick, although to my eyes it seemed level enough. The effect was of some force drawing me on, compelling me to *come.*

As we walked, Jessie pointed out wildflowers on either side of the road. So many, and such variety. She began to name them: fiddlehead and soap tree yucca, thistle and red pussytoes, lupine and Indian paintbrush, chicory and biscuit-root, sagebrush and mountain dandelion, heartleaf and pearly everlasting.

The only sound aside from Jessie's voice was the faint basal hum of cicadas. Their drowsy noise always reminded me of high-voltage transmission wires, and a thought struck. I looked about, and there were no transmission towers in sight. No power lines anywhere, in fact. No telephone lines or utility cables. No poles to string them on. No cell towers, no radio towers. Behind us, no poles or lines running electricity to the farmhouse. Yet the house *had* electricity. Something was powering the lamps, the radio, the sewing machine, the oven, the clocks . . .

I glanced at Jessie, at my daughter walking so easily with her, the two of them holding hands like great friends.

Jessie glanced back at me, her expression obscure, still reciting the names of flowers in a singsong voice as soothing as a lullaby.

. . .

By the time we rounded that first foothill, I had few expectations of Morro. Olin had said it was long forgotten, and I'd seen bypassed towns before: the bitter decay of empty storefronts and boarded-up windows, littered streets and broken sidewalks.

But Morro was nothing like that.

It wasn't big, consisting of but a single street. But that street was more like a broad boulevard that ran for blocks, and smoothly paved. At the town line a sign read:

WELCOME TO MORRO

Beyond the sign, sidewalks with rows of shade trees that branched thirty feet and higher lined each side of the boulevard. On the outskirts of town stood handsome family homes with deep lawns, while at the center well-kept commercial buildings bustled with people. And right in the middle of the boulevard stood a large domed gazebo.

Jessie stepped briskly to the sidewalk, making for the business center of town. Laurel and I followed. There were few cars, and no traffic signals. We passed a sidewalk café and an Italian bakery selling gelato from a walk-up window. An antiques store, an art gallery, a butcher shop, a green grocer's. Across the street was a lending library and a redbrick building with a sign that read, *Town Hall.* Beyond that were more shops, then more homes lining the far end of town.

But the anchors of this place were clearly the general store—a three-story building that took up the better part of a block—and across from it a grand Victorian hotel called the Wild Rose, painted in flamboyant shades of red.

I walked slowly, the better to take it all in.

There wasn't a single crack in the sidewalk, no hole in the asphalt. No chipping paint. Not a stray bit of litter skittering down the street.

Morro was idyllic—a town Norman Rockwell might have dreamed up.

Or me.

Jessie led us past the hotel, where a couple emerged—very elegant, in their thirties, with dark hair and skin. The man wore a tan sport coat and open-collared shirt; the woman, a beautiful sari of apricot silk. I tried not to stare—they seemed so cosmopolitan, and in their way as anachronistic as Olin and Jessie.

At the general store, its massive front windows were papered with flyers for club meetings, recitals, the weekly farmers' market, a school play. And inside, the building seemed cavernous, with row after row of well-stocked aisles.

Jessie led us to the shoe section, where we searched the shelves for rain boots in Laurel's size. But we found few children's boots at all, and none small enough for her.

Jessie called out for assistance, and a big man sorting boxes nearby left his pallet and joined us. I recognized him from the café—Faro LaGow was the customer I'd brought blueberry pancakes by mistake but who graciously took them anyway.

He was muscular and ruddy, with a short graying beard and close-cropped ginger hair. He put me in mind of an old ring fighter.

He grinned at Jessie. "What can I do you for today?"

"We'll take a pair of rubber boots. For this child here. Something sturdy."

Faro considered Laurel for a moment. "You're seven if you're a day."

Laurel nodded.

"Not sure we got anything on the floor to fit," Faro said. "But a shipment's just come in. First, young lady, why don't you tell me what sort of boots you had in mind."

Laurel's eyes widened. I could tell she was delighted to be consulted, but with an imagination like hers the possibilities were endless. So I answered for her: "Just rain boots. Anything her size."

Laurel yanked her hand from mine and tossed her head at me. *"No!"* she said.

Faro leaned low till he was level with her. "I take it you got your own ideas."

I didn't like where this was going. Of course Laurel would have ideas, but they would likely be wildly unrealistic. Faro seemed to be needlessly stoking her hopes, inviting disappointment. Just the sort of game Jim liked to play.

Laurel took a moment to consider the options, biting her lip thoughtfully.

"Yellow boots," she said finally. "With polka dots."

"What color polka dots?"

This time she didn't hesitate: "All colors."

Faro straightened, rubbing his chin with a hand the size of a boy's baseball mitt. His knuckles were stitched with faint scars. "Well, now, let me go poke through my stock."

By now I was sure the man was toying with her. Whether he meant it unkindly or not didn't matter.

"No," I insisted. "Don't bother."

"Worth a look," he said, and winked. Then he turned on his

heel and headed toward the back, disappearing behind an unmarked door.

"Laurel, honey, he's gone to check," I said. "That doesn't mean he has them."

"If he doesn't," she said, "I don't want any."

Her young face was pure petulance now, and I only hoped she wouldn't pitch a fit right there in the aisle when Faro LaGow showed up empty-handed.

While we waited, Jessie wandered off for boxes of salt crackers and roasted coffee beans. She collected a can of boiled linseed oil and a horsehair brush for Olin to refinish his gunstocks.

At last Laurel hissed with excitement. "Here he comes!"

Faro was approaching, his hands hidden behind him. "Well, now, young lady. Will these fit the bill?"

And from behind his back he drew a pair of rain boots: bright yellow, covered in polka dots of every color.

Laurel squealed, snatched the boots up and ran to me. I turned them over, checking for signs of fraud, however well intentioned. But there was no drying paint, no stickers. And they were just the right size: seven.

I stared at Faro in disbelief, and he grinned back.

"These are . . . perfect," I managed. Then to Laurel, "What do you say, honey?"

"Thank you, Mr. Faro. Can I put 'em on now?"

He looked at me and I nodded. Laurel pulled on the boots and paraded back and forth for us to admire them properly.

I struggled with how to feel about this. The man had either dug up Laurel's dream boots back in that stockroom through sheer serendipity or had somehow managed to conjure them out of thin air, made-to-order. I lacked the nerve to ask the obvious question: Where on earth had these come from?

Jessie linked her arm through mine. She was gazing at Laurel indulgently, the ghost of a smile on her lips.

We checked out and left with our parcels, returning the same way we'd come, Laurel bounding ahead.

Let There Be Light

That evening, Laurel kept her boots on all through supper. She kept them on as she and Olin played checkers at the table, Jessie reading nearby, half-moon glasses tipped low on her nose. The radio was playing a set by the Artie Shaw orchestra.

I sat for a good hour alone on the dark porch, watching the road, recapping the day, struggling yet again to ground myself. Now and then my attention strayed to the foothills, and to Morro beyond—the pitch-perfect town where whims can come true.

When I came back inside, I paused at the table lamp by Olin's empty chair near the fireplace. The base was a ceramic Remington cowboy astride a cattle pony.

I turned the switch and the lamp sprang to life—the round bulb glowing under the linen shade. I studied the base again, checking all around the pony's four hooves where they attached to the heavy metal stand. I could find no power cord to run to an electrical outlet. On the nearest wall, there was no outlet.

I turned the lamp off again.

Then on.

Anatomy Lesson

I slept fitfully. Every time I woke, I'd lie very still and listen to the silence. An old wind-up alarm clock had sat on the night-stand, but I went and buried it in a laundry basket inside the closet where I couldn't hear its *tick-tick-tick*—like a heartbeat, but mechanical and mocking. In the dark, too, I listened to my own heart. I could feel the steady pulse at my neck, my wrist. And when I pressed my palm against my chest, there it was.

Tick-tick-tick.

The upshot was to make me doubt Olin, or want to. But I couldn't tell if my resistance sprang from strength or weakness. I kept shifting back and forth. One minute, Olin was an old soul doing me a kindness. The next, an old coot feeding me a line. In the dark, anything and everything seemed possible.

My brain wouldn't shut off.

I rubbed my temples, feeling the soft skin stretch across

the hard cradle of skull. Anatomy itself was a mystery now. In the Place of Truth, in Morro, in whatever or wherever this was, how much was illusion and how much was real?

And what was the purpose? Or even the power source? What keeps a lamp going here? Or a heart?

One night when I was a little girl my mother drove us down some desert highway in our old Rambler wagon. I lay in the backseat staring at a black sky bristling with stars. My brain wouldn't shut off then, either. For the first time, I was struck by the vastness of the universe, pure and perfect, and my own place in it. As I stared, the stars began to shift, inching across the sky like a pinwheel. And I knew it was revealing itself to me, and only me. And a voice that was no voice at all began to fill my head with thoughts so big, so frightening, they set it to spinning, too . . . and soon enough my whole body seemed to spiral like those stars, toppling headfirst toward the sky.

The shock, the enormity, had made me pull back. I closed my eyes and shut my brain down—like pulling a pot off a stove before it boils over. As if whatever I was about to discover threatened to burn me alive. It was all too vast. Too terrible.

After that, the stars were never the same. In time, like anyone else, I learned the names of the major constellations, the North Star, the Evening Star. But I never again trusted myself to get lost in them.

That had been a lesson learned, and I decided to apply it again. There are things too big to take in all at once. And thoughts so deep they might send you pinwheeling off to disappear in the dark.

I couldn't handle Awe when I was four, and still couldn't as a woman of thirty.

I wanted surety and safety and continuity. I wanted to wake in this bed in the morning, wash my face, comb my hair, wake Laurel and get her ready for an unremarkable day. I wanted a long march of unremarkable days just like it.

I wanted it for as long as I was able. Or allowed.

The Lady from Mississippi

Since sleep wouldn't come, I decided to get up early to make my second trip to the café. This time the dog, Pal, wasn't dozing in his corner but sitting just inside the door as if expecting me. Simon came from the kitchen to hand me a mug of hot coffee, already flavored with cream and sweetener.

"How'd you know?" I asked, unable to hide a note of suspicion.

He shrugged. "I've seen how you take your coffee."

"No, I meant how'd you know I'd be here this morning?" It had been well over a week since I'd first helped out.

He nodded toward the back. "There's a window. I could see you heading down the path. Didn't think I was psychic, did you?"

His explanation came as a relief, and I smiled. "Not psychic. Just . . . nosy."

"I prefer 'observant.'"

"Most nosy people would."

He laughed and turned back to his work. He was dressed in a red plaid shirt, the sleeves rolled up past his elbows; his forearms were tanned.

He gestured toward a radio on a stool. "Mind if I turn this on?"

Soon a piano was playing in the background—classical, which surprised me. Chopin, I think. Apparently Simon wasn't such a country-western fan after all.

I took a deep breath and dove in, setting to work as I had the first day, wiping down surfaces, refilling canisters. I slid trays of loaves and biscuits in and out of the oven, setting them on racks to cool. Now and then I glanced at Simon, moving so easily, so confidently, about his work. I would take my cue from him.

There weren't as many customers this morning. One was a plump and pensive woman who said she was the town librarian, although she hardly fit the type.

Jean Toliver wore a skirt to her ankles, a long-sleeved velour blouse cinched at the waist with a silver concho belt. Hanging low on her chest was a magnificent squash blossom necklace of silver and turquoise.

I learned she was from a small town in upstate New York near the Adirondack mountains, but had a lifelong interest in Southwestern Indians, so I imagined she meant it as an homage to dress like many traditional Navajo women. I'd also seen very traditional ones wear their hair twisted at the nape into a sort of stiff, vertical double twist, but Jean wore hers in a simple braid down the back.

Her skin was so milky I suspected she rarely made it beyond the library stacks. Her eyes were the color of nougat behind round-rimmed glasses.

"You're the new one," she said.

I wasn't sure how to answer her.

"You like books—I can tell. Not everyone does," she continued, glancing around the café with disapproval. "A few of us started a monthly book club. You should come."

She opened a canvas tote, drew out a flyer and handed it to me. "Our next meeting." Then she smiled, and two deep dimples gave her a girlish look.

I slid the flyer into my apron pocket. As I turned to leave, Jean tapped my arm.

"We have monthly poetry workshops, too," she murmured. "At the library. You should bring some of your work."

I hadn't told Jean I wrote poetry. Or rather, that I used to, eons ago. In fact, I hadn't told anyone.

"I wouldn't be good enough," I said. "But I might sit in one day, if that's all right."

Jean nodded. "Anytime."

By late morning the breakfast shift had eased up, and it was my first chance for a break. I poured a glass of lemonade and took a seat on a stool. Simon turned off the grill and leaned on the counter, a dish towel slung over his shoulder.

"This is the speed most days," he said, nodding at the tables, most of them empty. "Second gear. Occasional shifts into fourth."

He struck me as a curiosity. A short-order cook who liked Yeats and classical music. Served in the military. Traveled. Had even, as Jessie said, fought in a war.

"Don't you ever get bored here?" I asked.

He paused. "There's a saying: 'May you live in interesting times.' That happens to be a Chinese curse. There's a lot to be said for the simple life."

"That's funny—I said the same thing once to a college friend about a hundred years ago. But interesting times have a way of ambushing you, don't they?"

"They do."

Simon had a frankness about him. An easiness that invited conversation. Even, to an extent, confidences. But just how far did that extend?

I bent over my lemonade, unable to look him in the eye.

"You're from Morro originally, aren't you?" I asked.

"Third generation. My people are from Maryland and Virginia, but my grandparents settled here before the Civil War."

"Then you left."

"Not strictly by choice. Sometimes there's a job to do, and you're called to do it. A lot of men were."

"Jessie said you were in the war. Iraq was it?"

He drew a deep breath and turned away. His strained expression made me regret probing the subject. Roadside bombs, snipers, multiple deployments, post-traumatic stress—not every veteran could reassimilate easily or quickly after trauma like that.

"I'm sorry," I said. "I shouldn't have asked."

"Don't look so distressed, Joanna. I made it home just fine."

"I see."

"Besides, *simple* isn't the same as simplistic. Don't get me wrong—some days all I want to do is drop everything and head out for some far corner of the earth."

"Why don't you, then?"

He grinned. "Who says I don't?"

I looked at him then, full on. There was humor in his eyes, but there was earnestness there, too. Did he really get a wild hair some days and strike out for far-flung places? And if he did, did he book a plane ticket or just click his heels together like Dorothy and let out something like, *There's no place like Nepal?*

All at once Simon broke into a laugh that made me blush. Then he turned to head back to the grill.

I was ringing up a customer when the man muttered, "Oh, my Lord." He was gaping over my shoulder through the front windows, and I turned to look, too.

The *prettiest* car I'd ever seen had just pulled up—a two-tone convertible, powder blue and white, stretching from a chrome hood ornament to what looked like chrome missiles mounted on the rear fender. It had whitewall tires with polished rims. The soft top was down, and the noon sun set the white leather seats to shimmer.

Simon came out front to look, too, and gave a long whistle. *"That,"* he said, "is a 1956 Cadillac Eldorado."

The car door swung open and the driver stepped out—a tiny black woman in a lavender suit and red kid gloves. A red silk scarf was wrapped around her head, its ends dangling down her back like two giant rose petals. She removed oversized white sunglasses to glance at the café sign, then headed inside. She took a seat, stripped off her gloves and untied her scarf to reveal a cap of smooth, marcelled hair.

"Honey, you got sweet tea?" she asked, picking up a menu. Her voice was high-pitched and Deep South.

I brought the tea, and the woman ordered pork chops and fried apples. When I gave Simon the order, I asked if she'd been in before.

"Nope," he said. "I'd remember the car."

Simon brought her plate without waiting for me to retrieve it. Then he stood beside me for a better view of the convertible.

From what I could see, it had no dents, no scratches, no markings of any kind. As pristine as if it were still sitting on a showroom floor.

"Not a speck of dirt," I murmured.

The woman gave me a puzzled look.

"Take a load off, honey," she said, nodding at an empty chair at her table. "I know how it is, on your feet all day. My name's Lula. You had lunch yet?"

Soon Simon was back at the grill, frying up more pork chops and apples while Lula told me about her home in Mississippi.

"Natchez—on a bluff over the river, up from New Orleans," she said. "I was a hotel maid there from fifteen on—and they *worked* you. Big white house, portico two stories high, big ol' columns, acres of lawn."

"Like a plantation," I said.

"Used to be, long time since," said Lula. "Family fell on hard times and sold it for a hotel. One night a car pulled up like what I got now, and out they stepped—him in black tails and her in yellow satin—lookin' like *somebody.* Swore to God one day I'd get me a car like that. See what there was to see in this world. Stay in fine places, too."

Simon arrived with two more plates and joined us.

"What if you break down out there on the road?" I asked.

Lula leveled her eyes at me over her tea glass. "What if I don't?"

And in a flash of certainty I knew that the Eldorado outside would never break down on her. It would take Lula wherever she wanted to go, with never a blown tire or a boiling radiator. It would never run out of gas. And should she ever want to drive to China one day, or whatever destination she might fancy, somehow it would get her there.

"You still have people back in Natchez?" I asked.

"Not for ages," said Lula. "My grandmother, she raised me. We lived in a shotgun shack outside Dunleith till she passed. I took on my two brothers and went to work. Otis, he up and died—wasn't but seven at the time. Been seizin' up all his life, and one day he just grabbed ahold of his head and dropped. My brother Lester, he took to the bottle. Gone a long time. Heart give out."

She shook her head. "I'd say wasn't nothin' of family left in Dunleith but what they planted in the old Baptist cemetery, but even that ain't there no more. A few years ago, they up and moved it."

"Excuse me?" I said. "They moved the cemetery?"

"The church house, anyway—loaded it on flatbeds and drove down the gravel road to Long Switch. Wasn't no congregation no more—folks died off or left. So a big company come and turned the land to crops."

"What'd they do with the people buried there?" I asked.

"Not a blessed thing."

I wasn't sure she understood me. "I mean, before they started plowing—what did they do with the bodies in the cemetery?"

Lula braced her forearms on the table and leaned toward me, her smile indulgent.

"Honey, they left 'em. Said they wasn't no bodies. I know for a fact that cemetery started out back in the slave days. Wasn't much used after that but by a few old families. When I was young, they was a boy sweet on me—he's there. His great-grandmother, too—she had the *sugar.* By the time the company come, grave markers was mostly gone. Onliest thing left was that ol' beat-down church, and land turnin' wild like it was back when the Indians had it."

"You mean . . . they're *farming* the graveyard?"

Lula nodded. "Soybeans mostly. Some cotton."

It was a horrifying image—furrows dug, seeds planted, then roots growing down, down toward bones lying six feet under, smooth as those stones Olin pulls from his fields every spring.

Lula leaned toward me again. "Don't you fret none—they's more to eternal rest than where your bones are planted. It don't make the situation less despisable to me, but ain't a thing to be done but get on with life."

She sat back with a smile and asked if we had chocolate cake for dessert. She had a thick slice and a cup of coffee before wrapping her scarf back around her head and picking up her gloves. She paid her bill and turned to leave, but before she got to the door she stopped to throw her arms around my neck.

"You take care of yourself," she said. "Your little daughter, too."

Her earnestness startled me. But it wasn't until the café had closed for the day, the farmhouse chores were finished, Laurel was tucked in and I was back in my room readying for bed that it struck me:

I hadn't told Lula I had a daughter.

Rain, Rain, Come

I'd been working in the vegetable garden for a good hour when I stood to give my back a stretch. The air was listless and hot. We'd gone nearly two weeks without a good soaking, and the plants weren't the only things feeling it. I fingered the wilting butterhead lettuce in my basket, then looked up, eager for signs of weather. But the clouds were as thick and dry as cotton batting, and stalled out.

I licked at my parched lips as sweat slid down my back. I was about to head inside for a drink of water when a notion struck that stopped me short.

I turned toward the same field where Olin had stood the morning of the quilting bee—so motionless and unyielding he might have been carved from his own fieldstone, looking for all the world like a man with a purpose. And when he was done, a thunderstorm had swept through this valley.

Olin was a man of many skills; was rainmaking one of them?

Tentatively I looked around, but no one was in sight. I closed my eyes.

So . . . what does a rainmaker say? What does a rainmaker *think*?

Does she think *rain* and the clouds come? Can thoughts get caught in an updraft, pulling in water vapor, seeding the atmosphere until they're plumped up and ready to fall as raindrops?

Suddenly the absurdity of the moment—standing in a garden, trying to catalyze a downpour—cut me to the quick. I felt like a grown woman caught playing hopscotch. I opened my eyes.

But there was more to it than mere discomfiture. While a part of me knew, all evidence to the contrary, that conjuring up a storm was a load of hocus-pocus, still another was sure that even if it *were* possible, it wasn't child's play. It couldn't be.

And yet . . .

I turned toward the Mountain. A prickle ran up my spine as I sensed it looking back, as if taking my measure. Curious to see what I could do.

Skepticism? Or a challenge?

I set my basket at my feet and shut my eyes again.

This time I didn't think—not in words, anyway. Instead, I pictured the sky overhead just as it was—a palette of white and blue, the sun a brilliant ball radiating ferocious heat and light. The images clicked into place almost willfully, like pieces of a jigsaw puzzle.

Then I added a rain cloud. Just one.

I concentrated with all I had to shape it, sculpt it. To make it realer than real. I made it darker than the others—gray as

granite, and swelling with moisture. I placed it just at the sh
arête of the Mountain. Heavier and heavier it grew—until it
was so swollen, so heavy, it couldn't keep its altitude anymore. It began to sink . . . skimming lower and lower . . . whipping down the Mountain slope . . . out of control now and picking up speed . . . making for the garden . . . for me . . .

My eyes flew open and I was startled to find I was panting, struggling to catch my breath. Sweat was running down my face, the salt of it stinging my eyes. I used my shirttail to wipe it away.

I glanced up again, and the sky was just as it had been. The Mountain . . . still vigilant.

But what was that hugging the ridge?

It was a cloud like the others—only this one was not quite so white, not quite so high. Its underbelly was a pigeon gray, as if a charcoal pencil had only begun to shade it in.

Even as I watched, the cloud began to shred and dissipate. Fainter and fainter, until finally it dissolved into the same thin air it was made of.

As if it had never been there at all.

Nastas

Olin had built a freestanding fireplace and grill on the patio behind the house, with a pumice stone core and faced with sandstone flags. Jessie said they used it deep into winter, bundling up like Eskimos. There was no need to bundle yet—it was only the end of August, according to Jessie, although I couldn't see how she kept track. The two of them owned no calendar—Olin said there was nothing a calendar could tell him that the elements couldn't.

"Except birthdays," Laurel said.

"That's what the wife's for," said Olin.

Simon suggested a barbecue, and he'd bring the venison steaks. By now Saturday suppers were settling into routine, and no longer a cause for panic. I still left the bulk of the conversation to the others—I'm not garrulous by nature, but can appreciate those who are. Even Laurel has a better talent for it than me.

We were on the patio when Simon arrived. He showered and joined us, his eyes skimming my yellow sundress. I turned my back to finish laying the table, awkwardly smoothing the fabric over my hips.

Simon was a creature of habit, too, and as usual he took a seat facing me while Laurel claimed the chair next to his.

Olin took charge of the grill, forking the steaks onto a platter for Jessie to distribute. She started with Laurel.

"Ever had venison before, honey?" Jessie asked her.

Laurel frowned suspiciously. "What's that?"

"Deer meat," I answered, cutting her steak for her. "Give it a taste."

She chewed cautiously at first, then nodded. "Good!"

"Atta girl," said Olin.

"Mommy?" said Laurel.

"Yeah, sweetie?"

"I heard her again."

"Who's that?"

"Tinkerbell."

My heart stuttered in my chest. I set down my knife and fork.

"Not now," I murmured, handing her the breadbasket with a warning shake of my head. "Here, have a slice."

Olin looked intrigued. "What's this?"

"Nothing at all," I said.

"Tinkerbell," said Laurel. "She's up there."

She twisted in her seat and pointed high on the Mountain. Olin squinted, trying to make something out.

"It's nothing," I repeated.

Laurel pressed her lips in a stubborn line. "She was barking again," she insisted. "I *heard*."

"Is this your pup, hon?" Jessie asked her. "The one that run off?"

Laurel nodded. "I looked and I hollered, but she never came back."

"Now, that's a shame," said Jessie.

"Mommy, we gotta go get her."

"Please stop, Laurel."

"But, Mommy—"

"Laurel! Stop! Now!"

She was shocked to silence. But I could see the fury brewing, every ounce of it plain on her face, until she broke into howls of misery.

I took a deep breath and tried again, this time without the snap in my voice.

"Tinkerbell got lost a long way from here," I said. "She couldn't have walked this far. In fact . . . In fact, I bet some other family took her in by now."

A lie is forgivable, I figured, if it hides a wicked truth. And I had enough to handle as it was, without the worry of that poor, wretched dog.

Olin smiled at Laurel. "Why, that's very likely," he said. "Folks would take in a lost pup, quick as that."

Laurel didn't look convinced, but the howls were trailing off to wet hiccups, and she wasn't fussing anymore. She wiped her eyes with her sleeve.

"Simon," said Olin, "I hear you got yourself a new horse out at your place."

"Four-year-old gelding," said Simon. "Underweight at the moment, but good form. He'll fill out fine."

"Bring him over when he does."

"Or come see him yourself. It's been a while since you and Jessie were up. And, Joanna, you haven't seen my place yet. You and Laurel."

Before I could answer, Olin accepted for all of us. "You'll need a corral, though," he said. "Got any help?"

Simon hesitated. He glanced uncertainly at me before answering. "Davey's been lending a hand."

Olin and Jessie traded a queer look and fell silent. I'd never heard them—or Simon—ever mention anyone by the name of Davey before.

Simon cleared his throat. "Till the corral's finished, the horse boards close by. Grazes behind the cabin."

Laurel was looking curiously at Olin and Jessie. Even she could sense the shift in the air.

"Who's Davey?" she asked.

More silence. Finally Olin spoke.

"Why, a local boy," he said lightly. "Lives on a ranch outside town. Takes on odd jobs to help out his folks. Smart as a whip. Good with his hands."

Jessie was nodding in agreement. From the description, I couldn't see why the mention of the boy's name would scupper the conversation. None of them offered more than that.

I turned to Simon. "Do you have other horses?"

"This is my first," said Simon. "He'll be a handful when he's filled out. Do you ride?"

"I took lessons one summer when I was a kid. English style. I had what they call horse fever—read every book on horses I could get my hands on. But I can't say I'm a rider. Lessons ended before I got the hang of it."

"Why didn't you keep it up?"

Ending the lessons hadn't been my idea. The summer I turned thirteen, I was living—yet again—with my Oma in her little house outside Taos. Every time my mother took on a new man, sooner or later she'd pack me off to my grandmother's, which suited me fine. I guess when I was younger she meant to spare me the sight of strange men at the breakfast table. But as I grew older, she started to see me as competition.

That particular summer, my mother and I were living in a town in west Texas, and the new man was an assistant city planner who laughed too much and drank too much and had sweaty palms that he liked to drape over my shoulder in a friendly sort of way, casual, as if he weren't trying to run his fingers down the curve of my breast. One day my mother caught him at it, and the next I was on a Greyhound to Taos.

There was a small stable near Oma's house, and she signed me up for riding lessons. I took on babysitting jobs to help pay for them. It was a wonderful summer, until my mother's affair flamed out, as they always did, and she packed a cooler with six-packs and drove up to fetch me—at first because she wanted someone to comfort her in her latest hour of need, but eventually because she needed somebody to blame.

After that, we moved to another new town where my mother could put the booze and the past behind her. Start fresh. One more time.

"Riding lessons . . . they're expensive," I said finally.

"They are," said Simon. "But there's horse people round about that could help you take up where you left off. Olin here was a real rider."

"Good enough," said Olin.

"More than good enough," Jessie said affectionately.

Olin squeezed her hand. "A tale for another day. But if you're up to it, Joanna, I could make a real cowgirl out of you."

. . .

One morning not long after, I woke to the sound of whinnying. I belted my robe and headed to my bedroom window. There was a man on horseback below, speaking with Olin at the open gate of the corral.

And the corral was no longer empty, but held four horses. I pulled on jeans and a shirt and hurried outside.

"Mornin', Joanna!" Olin called. "This here's an old friend—Morgan Begay."

The man looked to be in his sixties, with a barrel chest, graying hair to his shoulders and deep brown eyes magnified by bottle-thick glasses. He wore a work shirt with a black vest and dungarees. Around his neck was a fetish necklace strung with polished stones carved into bear shapes.

"Are these your horses?" I asked him.

"From my herd." His voice was deep, with a clipped accent.

"They're beautiful."

"Begay's from the other side of the Mountain," Olin said. "He'll be leavin' these horses awhile. Wanna try one?"

"Now?" I asked.

"Which one you like?"

It had been so long since I'd sat a horse, I wasn't sure I wouldn't just mount up and slide off the other side again. I took a step back.

"Buck up, now," said Olin.

I looked the horses over. The first three were a handsome blood bay, a pinto and a big roan.

But the fourth horse was a sleek liver chestnut—a hand or two smaller than the others, with the swan neck and small, shapely head of an Arabian.

When I was thirteen, this had been my dream horse, like Lula's Eldorado.

"He's a beauty," Olin said, following my gaze. "Name's—what's he called, Begay?"

"Nastas."

"That's right—Nastas. What's it mean in Navajo? 'Leg-Breaker'? Or 'Never Been Rode'?"

I laughed. "Sure it doesn't mean 'Call an Ambulance'?"

"Atta girl," Olin said. "Actually, it means 'Curve Like Fox-tail Grass,' for that neck of his. Come on over and I'll make the introductions."

Begay had already dismounted and was leading Nastas to the gate where I stood. The horse seemed much bigger up close. His ears swiveled at the sound of my voice.

"Good boy," I murmured nervously, running my hand down the firm muscles of his neck. Olin handed me a carrot, and I held it to the horse's muzzle until he snorted and grabbed it in his teeth. All the while, Begay was settling a blanket on the horse's back, then a saddle. He cinched it snug.

"His mouth is soft, so easy on the bit," Begay said as he worked. "Ask him—don't tell him. He knows."

"Okay, boy," I murmured. "I'll go easy on you if you go easy on me."

"All set?" Olin asked, gripping the bridle. "Don't worry—he likes you."

"Yeah?" I said shakily. "Let's see him show it."

I stepped to the side and slid my left foot into the stir-rup, grabbed a handful of mane and pulled myself into the saddle. While Begay adjusted the stirrups, I ran through those old riding lessons in my head—*back straight, toes up, heels down.*

"Take the reins in your left hand—this is Western style, not English," Olin said. "Grip 'em in front of you. Not too tight. That's right."

Begay led the horse forward at a slow walk. We moved halfway around the corral like that, till he let go and moved to the side. Then it was just me and the horse making a circuit all by ourselves.

"How's it feel?" Olin called out.

I smiled. "Like riding a bicycle. A really big bicycle."

"Doin' good," Olin said. "Ready for the lesson?"

"I thought this was it," I said.

He and Begay laughed.

"Aw, now, you can do better'n this," said Olin.

Begay approached again. He patted the horse's neck and said something in a language I couldn't understand. Then he looked up at me.

"Listen to Olin," he said. "You can do better."

He stood back to give the horse a light slap across the flank, and Nastas set off at a hard trot that jarred every bone in my body. In desperation I tried to post, which I knew wasn't Western, either. Olin called out for me to sit and relax. Find the rhythm.

Instead, I pulled on the reins to make it stop before I could fall off. Nastas shook his head, his mane flying. He was disappointed; he wanted to run. I had a feeling this wouldn't end well.

"Whoa, boy." Olin was grabbing the bridle again as Nastas ground to a halt. "You're fightin' 'im, Joanna."

"I wouldn't fight anything that outweighed me this much. Maybe this wasn't such a great idea."

"Now, now, I can tell you rode before," Olin said. "You just don't trust your horse—so he don't trust you. And you're too afraid to fall off."

"I don't think that's unreasonable."

Olin chuckled. "Say you do. Then what? You climb back up and try again." He stepped back. "Ready? Kick with your heels. You can do it."

Nastas needed only another grazing swat to break into another trot that had me sliding to the side, grabbing for the saddle horn with my free hand.

"Keep goin'!" Olin called out. "That's it! You ain't bouncin' near as much as you think!"

I grit my teeth. I was still landing hard, fighting the urge to call it quits and yank on the reins again.

This was grim—not at all the joyful experience of my childhood. The horse's ears had flattened out; he was miserable, too.

I willed myself to try to locate some rhythm, but my entire body had clenched like a fist and refused to unknot. I wasn't just bouncing in the saddle, but sliding all over it. I knew I couldn't keep my seat much longer.

Frantic, I bent my knees, pulled up my heels and pressed hard—

And suddenly I wasn't bouncing anymore, but flying—cresting on rolling waves, up and down, up and down. Nastas had exchanged that punishing gait for a springing gallop.

Olin was shouting as if I'd managed to accomplish something, beyond not getting pitched to the ground.

We circled the corral several times before I reined in again.

The horse slowed to that awful trot, but I reined more firmly and he curbed to a walk.

Olin and Begay were outside the corral now, leaning on the top fence rail.

"A good start," said Olin. "Before you know it, you'll be stickin' to him like a burr and won't need those reins near as much. A good horse and rider—they're like one animal. You lean and turn, press with your legs, and he'll read you right enough."

"So when I bent my knees and pressed—"

"You were tellin' him, 'Let's hightail it!' So he did."

"And here I thought I was just hanging on for dear life. Can I give it another go?"

Lesson over, Begay rode off toward Morro, leaving me and Olin to ready four stalls in the barn for the new horses.

The others from Begay's herd were Kilchii, Yas and Tse.

Kilchii, the blood bay, and Yas, the pinto, were no strangers to the farm—Begay apparently would bring them over now and then for trail rides; Olin and Jessie had given up their own horses a long time ago. Kilchii means "Red Boy," for his deep copper coat. He was Olin's mount. Jessie's was Yas, which means "Snow," because he loves to roll in it.

The third horse, Tse, was the big roan mare, intended for Laurel. Tse was unflappable and solid, Olin said, so her name meant "Rock."

"They'll mean a lot more work around here," I said. "I'll take it on, in exchange for the lessons."

"Fine idea," said Olin.

"I know what you're doing," I said.

Olin blinked at me, but said nothing.

"First the café, now this. You're nudging me out of my rabbit hole."

"That right?"

"But you have to understand—there are reasons I jumped in there in the first place. And pulled Laurel in with me."

"I'm a fair listener."

I shook my head. "Don't nudge too hard. Just know . . . there are bad things out there."

Olin gave me a smile. "Don't forget," he said. "There's good things, too."

The Periwinkle House

The grade school in Morro is a one-room wood-frame structure that came from a mail-order catalog, just like Jessie's sewing machine. It arrived by boxcar in the 1920s in pieces by the thousands—from the lumber, siding, roof shingles and nails right down to the paint cans and varnish—ready to be assembled on-site. The men of Morro put it together over two days on an acre of land at the edge of town.

It was painted white, and stayed that way for years. It was Bree's idea to repaint it lavender, with shutters and trim a shade darker, and the front door darker still. Someone called it the Periwinkle House, and the name stuck. It was even printed on a brass plaque by the door.

The schoolhouse took in younger students, and there was a second school with its own teacher for older ones. I learned all this from Bree after Jessie dropped me off one morning to get Laurel formally and finally enrolled.

The big room was bright and colorful—with maps, photographs and posters, children's drawings and paintings, a mobile of the solar system and shelves filled with books. There were a dozen children studying at desks, grouped in a reading circle, working math problems on a whiteboard or gathered around a terrarium feeding whatever was inside. No different from a classroom you might find anywhere.

Laurel twisted her hand from mine and ran off to join the group at the terrarium. Before I could call her back, Bree stopped me.

"Let her make friends."

"I don't know how you handle so many grades under one roof," I said.

"It wasn't that long ago that schools like this were commonplace in rural areas," she said. "Besides, when you mingle the grades, older students encourage the younger ones."

She pulled a folder from a pile on her desk and leafed through it.

"I've already started a file for Laurel," she said. "I'll give her a few placement tests to see where she stands."

"I guess you have forms for me to fill out."

Bree closed the folder and tossed it back on her desk with a smile. "Nope."

Of course not. Why would she?

I watched Laurel at play with the other children; she was oblivious to me.

"It's pretty painless, isn't it?" I said.

"She'll be fine," said Bree. "And so will you. By the way, I told Reuben how you helped with the wedding quilt, and he'd love to meet you. I'm cooking dinner next Friday night—can you make it?"

Before I could come up with an excuse, Bree took my arm just as she had at the bee and walked me to the door.

"I'm not the greatest cook, but I do know wine," she said. "Come around six. My place is on the second floor here. The entrance is on the side."

She opened the door and ushered me through, then closed it firmly behind me.

The Dog That Didn't Bark

"*Mommy!* Come quick!"

Laurel ran into the living room to grab my arm, her small fingers digging in. She was burning with excitement, eyes wide.

I dropped my broom to snatch her by the waist for a quick once-over, top to bottom: no cuts, no bruises, no blood.

"What's wrong?" I demanded. "You okay?"

Before she could answer, before I could even think clearly, an awful thought hit me: *Jim.* He'd tracked us down. He was outside even now, heading for the door.

I rushed to the front window, where the curtains were open and the view was clear. There was no vehicle in sight, aside from Simon's yellow pickup at the café, same as always.

Laurel pulled my arm even harder, this time with both hands, desperate to get me to the door.

"Hurry! Before it stops!"

I stared down at her. Before *what* stops?

I let her tug me onto the porch and down the front steps. In the yard, she dropped my arm and turned toward the Mountain, wiping stray strings of hair from her flushed face.

She pressed a finger to her lips. "Ssssshhhh."

Then she pointed.

I looked where she was directing me—at a point near the crest, just below the tree line. Yet again my stomach lurched.

I knew very well what Laurel was so anxious for me to hear. I closed my eyes with a shiver, and listened.

And heard nothing. Nothing but the birds, the running creek and Laurel's quick, expectant breaths.

Simon's Cabin

After the horses arrived, it became my routine to lead them from the barn every morning and put them to pasture. Their range was the stretch of valley that started at the barn and ran due east. It wasn't fenced, but Olin said Kilchii and Yas knew the area well and never wandered far, and Nastas and Tse would keep close by.

While they grazed, I would get out the wheelbarrow, grab a pitchfork and muck their stalls. I carted the soiled bedding to the compost pile and laid down a fresh layer of straw. Olin taught me to clean their hooves, then groom them with curry-combs and brushes. Sometimes Laurel helped, standing on an upturned bucket to braid Tse's mane.

While Olin gave Laurel lessons in the corral, I rode Nastas in the pasture, practicing leg pressure and shifting movements.

Then, one morning after lessons, Olin saddled Kilchii and suggested he and I take a trail ride. Rather than head along the valley, though, he led us south on the hardpan road into Morro.

We cantered until we reached the town limits, then slowed to a walk, past the welcome sign and onto the smooth asphalt.

From Nastas's back, I could reach the lowest branches of the big elms, their leaves now turning a vivid gold. For all the notice we drew, a trail ride through town was nothing unusual.

We passed the Wild Rose and the general store, the gazebo, the library, the town hall and every door and shingle in between. We passed a cluster of boys huddled in an alley, fascinated by the contents of a small container.

"What's in the cigar box, boys?" Olin called out.

The boys looked up guiltily. "It ain't cigars, Mr. Farnsworth," one said.

"I'm sure it ain't. Best set it loose before long, or I'll know why not."

"Yes, sir," the boys replied.

"How'd you know they had something in that box?" I asked him.

"I didn't," he said. "But I do know boys."

I hadn't seen this side of Morro before—I'd never ventured this far. The asphalt stopped at the town limits and the hardpan picked up again, veering left into the Mountain. But there was a narrow secondary road splintering off to the right.

I reined Nastas to a firm halt. Olin pulled up, then circled back and drew alongside me.

"Somethin' wrong?" he asked.

The pull of the Mountain had grown more intense the closer we came, and now we were right at its feet. Resisting was taking real effort, and my head was throbbing as if the barometric pressure had plummeted.

"Are we going up there?" I asked warily. Nastas took several steps back.

Olin shrugged. "Figured to," he said. "Trail's good, and your mount knows it. You can trust 'im."

Nastas pulled at the reins and snorted, his eyes wide now. "Whoa," Olin murmured, and the horse steadied himself.

I gripped the reins tighter, staring at the fork in the road, struggling to steady myself, too.

"Courage," Olin said softly, "is a kind of salvation."

"What?"

"Somethin' an old Greek said once. Long time ago."

"Right."

He shifted in the saddle to take in the Mountain with me. "It's a far piece to the summit," he said. "Ain't never been myself, but I know some who trekked it. I don't figure to go anywhere near that far today. Just up a ways." He looked at me and smiled. "Then back down again."

Nastas was motionless now, his ears pricked as if awaiting instructions. I stared at Olin, willing him to say something that would buck me up, too, but he only sat in his saddle as if he had all the time in the world for me to make up my mind.

I drew a deep breath and tapped Nastas with my boot heels.

We moved forward.

Olin led the way, taking the narrower road to the right—a wide dirt track with a low incline for a mile or so before it began to climb. As it climbed, it wound through thickening forest. Sunlight sifted through the trees, and I could hear birds, the rustle and snap of twigs, the distant rush of water.

If I'd been afraid that this Mountain would rear up and

swallow me whole, it wasn't happening. There were no bogeymen in these woods, no fires, earthquakes or floods. My nerves began to settle.

We leveled out again and Olin, still riding ahead, turned in the saddle and called back, "Let's pick it up."

"I'm game," I replied shakily.

Then he was off at a canter, Kilchii on his long legs disappearing down the road. Nastas chewed his bit and bobbed his head, nearly pulling the reins from my hand.

"Okay, boy. Think you can take him?"

I tucked my legs and pressed, and Nastas lunged after them. Of the two, he was the smaller horse but not the slower, and he was eager to prove it. We drew up on them fast, Olin glancing at us as we overtook and passed them. Now the road ahead of us was wide-open.

Half a mile on I reined in and could hear Olin and Kilchii coming at a fast clip. They pulled up level, and Olin looked pleased.

Both horses had worked up a lather, so we set them at a walk to cool down. Nastas was still straining at the bit, snorting hard.

"He has more steam to blow off," I said.

"We'll set 'em loose up the road here," said Olin.

We rode on in easy silence. After another mile the forest began to clear on the left, opening onto a broad meadow. As we neared I could see the meadow wasn't empty, but held a small cabin, painted slate blue, with black shutters and white trim, a table and chairs on the porch.

And there in the narrow drive was a familiar yellow pickup.

Behind the cabin, two figures were sawing and hammering on a corral that was nearly finished. By then, I wasn't surprised to see that one of them was Simon. The other was much slighter, wearing a tan cowboy hat.

Simon straightened as we approached. He spoke to the person with him, who looked briefly in our direction. Then he headed toward us across the meadow, Pal hard at his heels.

Simon's hair shone nearly blond in the bright sun. He was bare chested, his work shirt knotted around his waist. As he walked, he loosened it, swung it around his shoulders and pulled it back on, but left it open in the heat.

"Come on up to the house!" he called. "I'll get us some cool water."

"Corral's comin' along," Olin said as we dismounted.

"Couple more days, I figure." Simon wiped his sunburned neck with a bandanna. "Sorry I'm not too presentable."

"You're a workin' man," said Olin. "Don't apologize for lookin' the part. We was out for a ride and figured to drop in."

"Glad you did."

Olin led his horse to a patch of shade on the far side of the house, then headed for the porch. I started to do the same with mine, when Simon fell in beside me.

"Here," he said. "Let me."

He took the reins from my hand and led Nastas to the same patch of shade. When he returned, he examined me curiously. "Your hair's different, Joanna. Very becoming."

I'd left it hanging loose this morning, held back with a band of ribbon. I could only imagine what a rat's nest the ride had made of it.

"It could use a good combing," I said.

"Looks better this way."

"You're an easy man to please, then. All a woman has to do is throw away her hairbrush."

He laughed. Then he called out to Olin, still waiting for us on the porch: "Go on in, have a seat."

The idea didn't appeal to me. None of this did. I knew Olin meant well—pushing me out of my comfort zone, challenging me to be brave. But this was too far, too fast. This felt like an ambush.

"Olin, we can't stay long," I said.

"At least rest awhile on the porch," said Simon. "I'll get some water. The horses could use some, too. Davey can see to that."

So that was Davey working on the corral—the boy whose very name at the barbecue a few weeks ago had stalled the conversation. From a distance he looked wiry and slim.

Simon called out for the boy to take the horses around back to the trough; then he brought a water pitcher and glasses to the porch table. Olin sank back in his chair. "All I need now's a smoke," he said.

"Can't help you there, my friend," said Simon. "Promised Jessie."

"She's right," I said. "She's worried about your health."

Simon and Olin traded smiles, and I realized my foolishness—in Morro, did Olin really need to worry about the afflictions of tobacco smoke?

"What gets her is the smell," Olin explained. "Says I should stick with a pipe. But she really took against cigarettes the night I burnt down the ol' outhouse."

"You didn't."

"It was years ago—burnt clear to the ground. Folks saw it from miles off and come to watch. Then they took to speculatin' as to what caused it, and I said it all started with Jessie's bean chili. She ain't quite forgive me for that."

I chuckled despite myself. "I can't blame her. You insulted her cooking."

"There's chili cooks would consider it a compliment."

"We use her recipe at the café," Simon said. "Now you know why it's called the 'house' chili."

"No! Poor Jessie."

"Naw, she thinks it's a humdinger," Olin said. "Just too proud to admit it."

Simon drained his water glass. "Would you like to see the new horse? He's out back."

The meadow behind his cabin was covered with thick blue grama grass and wildflowers past our knees. It was an easy slope to the tree line, where the Mountain started to climb again. There was a raised vegetable garden and a small grove of apple trees, stacked rows of honeybee hives and a tall smokehouse on a stone foundation.

Davey stood at an outbuilding with our two horses, a water bucket at his feet.

Simon pointed toward the apple grove, and I could see nothing at first. But when he whistled, a horse emerged from the trees.

He was tall—as tall as Tse. And you could tell he must have been beautiful once.

Now, though, his gray hide stretched across sharp hip bones and jutting ribs. His broad back swayed as if it carried an oppressive weight.

"Mind if I take a look?" said Olin.

"He's gun-shy," Simon cautioned as Olin headed toward the grove. Then he turned to me. "Well," he asked quietly, "what do you think?"

I didn't know how to answer him. Certainly Jim had proven

just how wretchedly an animal could be abused, but I'd never seen neglect like this. Still, I knew Simon wasn't fishing for compliments.

"He looks awful," I said. "What happened?"

"He was a racehorse once. Not a good one, I guess. Or his owner didn't think so. He was sold for dog food to some outfit down in Florida. Since he wasn't worth the cost of feed, they let him starve. He was just skin and bones when I got him."

"Worse than this?"

"He's improved quite a bit. And he'll get better still. Watch."

He whistled again and gave a call. The horse broke into a canter along the tree line, apparently unwilling to get too close. He pulled up and shook his big head, then finished his circuit across the field.

"There, now. See?" said Simon. "They didn't break him."

It pleased me to hear him say it. Most people wouldn't see much worth in salvaging an abused creature like this.

"He'll make a good trail horse one day," I said.

"No—thoroughbreds don't do well out here for trails or cattle. Their legs are too fragile; the country's too rugged."

"So you'll race him?"

"Oh, no."

"Then what on earth will you do with him?"

Simon hesitated, watching the horse turn and bolt back toward the grove.

Then he shrugged. "Let him run."

The horse was moving at a speed that seemed wholly unsupportable for his gaunt frame and gangly legs. But he tore up the distance with little effort, disappearing again in the apple trees.

"Almost like he has wings," said a voice behind us. "Like Pegasus."

We turned to see the boy, Davey, a few yards away in dungarees and a damp T-shirt, his cowboy hat shading most of his face.

"Pegasus, huh?" said Simon. "Could be a fine name. What do you think?" He was asking me.

What I thought was that even if that horse had actual wings sprouting from his withers, he looked barely fit enough to carry a child, much less Zeus's thunderbolts. But I had to admit he had spirit.

"I like it," I said. "Some names you just have to grow into."

Simon made the introductions, and Davey stepped forward to shake my hand. The boy pulled off his hat, and for the first time I could see his face clearly . . .

The slight arc to the bridge of his nose . . . the squared-off chin . . . and the hair—a deep mahogany brown.

The resemblance to Jim was uncanny.

I snatched my hand from his. It was then that I noticed the eyes looking up at me from that eerie, familiar, terrible face were the same quartz green as Laurel's. As mine.

"Joanna . . . ?" Simon sounded concerned.

I was staring at the boy with open revulsion. I couldn't help myself. I stared as he flushed a deep red, then ducked his head in confusion. He took a step back . . . recoiling from me.

The rational part of my brain was struggling to intervene. *This is only a child*, it said. *We don't choose the features we're born with.* And yet . . .

"I—I'm sorry," I managed to say. "I thought . . . we'd met before."

"No, ma'am," said the boy.

"No," I said. "I'd have remembered."

I dragged my eyes away from that face and turned toward the apple grove. I cleared my throat.

"How'd you come up with a name like Pegasus?" I asked finally. "Do you like Greek mythology?"

"Sure, I like stories about the old gods," Davey said. "Olympus and the Underworld."

"I did, too, when I was a kid," I said. "I discovered them when I was eleven. How old are you?"

"I turned nine in June."

I swallowed hard. "Nine in June."

The boy nodded. "I write my own stories, too."

"Best grades in his class," Simon said. "Davey, can you go water Pegasus?"

The boy bolted off, eager to please Simon. And no doubt just as eager to escape the crazy woman with the Medusa stare. When he was gone, I turned to Simon: "Tell me about his family."

He hesitated. "They have a little place on the other side of the Mountain."

"I remember," I snapped. "From the barbecue—ranch folk, respectable people. And he's their only child?"

"They have a couple more. Older boys."

"But he's . . . their *natural* child?"

Simon didn't answer, but watched Davey refill the water bucket, Pegasus at his side. Olin joined them and was running his hand over the horse's bowing back, then down each reedy leg.

When Simon spoke again, I could see what a careful, neutral mask his face had become.

"Davey was a foundling," he said. "They took him in as a baby. His natural parents—they've never been part of his life."

"They *found* him? On their doorstep?"

"I'm not sure what you want to know, Joanna."

I wasn't sure, either. How do you say, without sounding like a lunatic, that a boy you just met looks like a child version of your husband, but with your eyes? Like he could be your natural-born son?

A son that, in point of fact, had never actually been born.

I'd been about ten weeks along when Jim gave me that punch to the stomach. The fetus had barely been an inch long—it hadn't even registered a heartbeat. But I knew from pregnancy books that all its organs were in place. That it had ears and eyelids and a nose . . . a tiny body cabled with muscles and nerves. That it was distinct down to its fingerprints and hair follicles.

I'd never had an ultrasound and could never have asked the doctor, but I knew—in my heart I knew—he'd been a boy.

And for years I'd been imagining him: his features, his temperament. I'd been dreaming him up out of whole cloth, like Laurel with her rain boots. A boy who wouldn't inherit the malice of his father, but a finer, sweeter spirit.

And every year he grew older—a presence that only I felt. Only I missed.

If I'd carried him to term, he would have turned nine this past June.

And the name I'd chosen for him all those years ago—but never told a soul—was David.

Tea and Empathy

Back from Simon's cabin I withdrew again, hunkering down until it was almost like the bad old days under Jim's boot. I couldn't buck the feeling I'd stumbled onto something I shouldn't have—a glimpse of the baby I couldn't save . . . the boy he might have become if I had. I couldn't stop picturing his face—every line, every curve, every inch of it. I was floundering in grief and guilt.

Olin had said Morro could be a Place of Truth for me, but that nugget of wisdom should have come with a warning label. Truth wasn't just something that could set you free—it could kick you in the gut ten times over. In its way, truth could be as brutal a bastard as Jim ever could.

I kept to my room, just like the early days when we'd first arrived. Jessie brought me meals on a tray again and didn't ask what was wrong or where it hurt. At night, Laurel climbed up on my bed and slipped under the covers.

This was new territory. With Jim, it was constant survival mode—every morning armoring up for one more round. I could never have surrendered like this around him, or he would've eaten me alive.

But here . . . here, I could shut down. I could lie in bed—neither asleep nor awake—and just *drift.* Aimless and mindless as a dandelion seed. And know with utter surety that if I only let go, let go for good and all, I could rise and rise . . . a sweet, numbing *nothingness* sluicing over me, through me, warm and solacing . . . until I dissipated at last, like the cloud that day in the vegetable garden.

Courage is a kind of salvation.

It was Olin's voice.

Olin's words in my ear, so close he might have been drifting on the wind beside me. I could smell the tang of cured tobacco . . .

My eyes flew open, and instead of a blank, open sky above me there was only the bedroom ceiling. I concentrated until the light fixture slid into focus.

Courage? Forget it—wouldn't know it if I tripped over it.

And what's courage, anyway, but delusion? You pick yourself up only to get beat down all over again. That doesn't make you brave—that makes you a punching bag. I stayed ten years with a sadist because I was too witless to see him for what he was. And when I did, I was too big a coward to get the hell out.

And yet . . .

I focused again on the ceiling. On its vast, vacant depths.

And yet . . . I did get out, didn't I?

. . . a kind of salvation.

I *did* get out. And brought Laurel with me. We broke free of him. Whatever else, we were in a good place now, with good people. And after all this time, he still hadn't found us. Hadn't managed to make his own way here, for all his threats to never let us go. *Ever.* That was something, wasn't it?

Whatever else Morro might be, at least it was getting that job done. Even a rabbit hole can keep a wolf at bay.

I pulled myself up and leaned back against the headboard. My body felt leaden and sluggish, as if it had been weightless for a while and needed to acclimate.

There was a food tray on the nightstand. The tea was still hot.

Night-light

Later, I grew restless in the wee hours and got up. Laurel had slipped into my room again and lay fast asleep on the far side of the bed. I slid into my robe and headed down the hallway to the stairs, then down to the living room. Jessie hadn't drawn the front curtains—they were still wide-open to the darkened café and the empty road. The room felt exposed. I hadn't sat vigil on the porch in a while.

I unlatched the front door and stepped out. The narrow valley was hushed except for the pulsing chirp of crickets. I headed to the railing on the far side of the porch where I could see the Mountain clearly. And, no surprise, that tenacious light. Anywhere else, that light might be nothing more than a cell tower. Here, it was more likely a burning bush.

It was a riddle, but there were others—the stars here were strange, too. *Strangers.* For weeks now I'd been trying to trace the Big Dipper, the Little Dipper. The Lion, the Hunter, the Big Dog, the Hare . . . any of them. But they just *weren't there.* My constellations were gone. The stars here kept to their own patterns, their own boundaries, and I didn't know their names. Old ship captains used to orient themselves by the stars. Celestial navigation, they called it. If they tried that here, where would these stars lead them?

A cold wind gusted through, and I pulled my robe close and headed back inside, latching the door and drawing the front curtains. Then I turned.

Across the living room, a light emanated from the kitchen.

And there in the open doorway was the dark shape of a man.

Years of reflex kicked in and I yelped and stumbled back, hitting the wall with a painful thud.

"Whoa, Joanna, it's me."

Olin's voice.

I gasped, clutching my throat. "You scared the life out of me!"

Then he was beside me, taking my arm, steering me toward the kitchen. "I just made some cocoa," he said. "Come sit."

On the table, a teapot was steaming on a serving tray. He fetched a mug from the cupboard and filled it, then settled across the table. Jessie's half-moon reading glasses were perched on his nose and there was a magazine in front of him—a *Farmer's Almanac.* He gave me a rueful smile. "Better?"

"Yeah," I said. "It's just . . . I guess I still startle easily."

"What're you doin' up this time of night?"

"Couldn't sleep. Guess I had my fill lately. I'm sorry."

"Sorry?" he said. "What for?"

"Leaving Laurel to you and Jessie. And the horses—all the work."

"Don't you worry—some days I'm not fit company, neither."

He took off the glasses and laid them on the *Almanac.* I examined the cover more closely—even upside down it was easy to make out the year.

"Olin," I said. "That magazine is from 1938."

"A good year," he said, wiping cocoa from his mustache. "Got more of 'em in my den. We visit now and again."

If he sounded absurd, who was I to judge? I hid scraps of paper in a tea tin under a floorboard.

"Penny for your thoughts," said Olin.

"They aren't worth that."

"Seems to me you saw somethin' from the porch just now. Ain't a coyote, was it?"

"No," I said. "Not an animal."

I might have left it at that, but I was picking up the faint scent of tobacco again, just as in my room earlier when I was ready to give up and scatter to the four winds, until it latched onto me like gravity . . . like a rescue . . .

Olin's hair was lifting in white tufts all around his scalp, as if he'd just come from bed without bothering to comb it into place, and for one wild second, backlit by the lamp behind him, it seemed to glow.

"Olin," I ventured. "That light on the Mountain—what is it?"

"Well, now, that's been there so long, I don't think about it no more. It just is."

"But who put it there?"

He shrugged. "Always been there, far as I know."

"Nobody ever checked it out?"

"Sure did."

"And what was it?"

"I never asked. They never said."

I shook my head in frustration and looked down at my mug. I could feel Olin's eyes on me for a long moment before he braced his arms on the table and leaned in.

"Laurel's got a night-light," he said finally.

"Yes . . ."

"Makes her feel safe."

"I guess."

"So if she wakes in the dark, scared maybe, she knows it's just a light, but she feels better. Watched over."

"Olin," I said slowly, "you're telling me the Mountain has a night-light?"

"It pleases me to think of it on the same principle."

I frowned down at the *Almanac* again—at the cracked and curling corners, the yellow cover filled with gourds, twining vines and sheaves of wheat, sketches of spring, summer, autumn and winter frozen in time. It read, *146th year. Price: 15 cents.*

I picked up Jessie's reading glasses and turned them over in my hands. "You two have the same prescription? I guess you really are a perfect match."

"Me and her was meant for each other."

The phrase was cliché, but he made it sound like truth.

"Soul mates?" I asked. "What an awful thought."

"How you figure?"

"I don't mean you and Jessie—you're happy. But when you're not—when you're with someone who makes your life hell—the idea of being bound for eternity . . . God, I'd go insane."

"And I wouldn't blame you—but that ain't it. The one you're meant to be with ain't always the one you end up with."

"What . . . ?"

"I figure if soul mates find each other right off," he continued, "that's best. But if they don't, they can still make a good life—with somebody else or on their own. But sooner or later, if you're meant to be, you find each other."

"Olin, you're a romantic. And how do they manage that?"

He snapped his fingers. "I forgot. The ol' woman'll skin me."

He stood and headed for the butcher-block table by the stove. When he returned, he handed me a small parcel in brown wrapping.

"Simon heard you was under the weather," he said. "Left this for you."

I pulled off the wrapping, and inside was a book of poetry—selected works of Yeats. It was the same volume I'd had in college, only mine had fallen apart over the years. This one was pristine, the spine still stiff.

I opened to the cover pages, and there Simon had written in surprisingly fine penmanship: *Joanna, for inspiration.*

Inspiration? To do what?

As if in answer, Olin turned to pull open a drawer and fish something out. When he returned, he set a blank notepad and a pen in front of me.

Dinner at Bree's

The next afternoon I stood at my bedroom mirror and for the first time in ages was pleased with what I saw. I wore a light cotton cardigan of buttercream yellow with short sleeves and shell buttons, and a tan pencil skirt. I pulled on flat pumps for the short hike into town for Bree's dinner.

I ran my hands down my arms, feeling the firm cords of muscle under the skin. Even after lying in bed for days, they felt strong. I leaned toward the mirror and stared hard. The old scar along my eyebrow—the one Jim sliced open with his pinkie ring with a sharp backhand—was fading. In fact, I could barely make it out now.

I ran a brush through my hair and noticed my little finger—the one Jim had broken when I dropped a dish—was limbering up, starting to bend. That bone had never been set, and the finger had healed crooked and stiff. Now here it was, straight as a pencil. I flexed my fingers. Even the twinge in the knuckle was gone.

What was it Olin had said? *Get straight and strong inside.* And apparently outside, too.

Jessie called up the stairs. "Joanna! Best set out now!"

I smoothed the skirt over my hips and gave myself a last once-over. Jim would never have approved of these clothes—not the cardigan that flattered me, not the skirt sized to fit, not the sleek pumps with their pointed toes.

But Jim wasn't here.

I undid the top button of my sweater and headed downstairs.

The Periwinkle House had a tiny landing at the top of the side stairwell, with a lavender door under a striped awning.

I'd never met Bree's fiancé and knew nothing about him other than his name and that he worked on a ranch. So I expected a polite and reserved young man sunburnt to beef jerky. But when the door opened, it was a young Navajo standing there, flashing white teeth in a handsome, round, inquisitive face. He wore cowboy boots, black jeans and a silver-tipped bolo with his dress shirt.

"Joanna, right?" he said. "Reuben. Let me help you with that."

He reached for the cheesecake I'd brought as Bree called from inside. "Sweetheart, don't leave her standing there."

Reuben stepped aside, and I could see Bree at a little gas stove in a pink sundress and thick oven mitts.

"Look at you!" she said. "You should wear yellow more often. Reuben, honey, put that in the fridge."

"Sure there's room?" I asked.

The refrigerator was sized to fit the tiny apartment, which was a half story with sloped ceilings. The main room was an open kitchen and living room with a white couch and chair spaced around a Navajo rug. Off the kitchen was a small round table that was laid, I noticed warily, with four place settings.

Bree hadn't mentioned another guest.

"Can I help with anything?" I asked.

"Just grab a wineglass," said Bree. "Sweetheart, can you pour? Tell me what you think of the Riesling, Jo. It's from Virginia. And the fish"—she lifted the lid off a narrow steamer pot—"the fish is domestic, too. The boys caught them."

"The boys?" I asked.

She pulled off the oven mitts. "Reuben and Simon. He should be here any minute."

And that explained the fourth place setting.

"How about some music?" Bree said.

There was a small stereo on a console behind the couch. Reuben switched it on and turned the knob, catching station after station. When he hit soft jazz, Bree smiled.

There was a knock at the door and Reuben answered it. It was Simon, and he didn't look the least surprised to see me. He stepped in, kissed Bree on the cheek and handed her a small paper bag. She opened it and began to set cucumbers and tomatoes on the counter. Simon wasn't wearing jeans this time, but a dark sports coat and slacks.

"Evening, Joanna," he said as Reuben handed him a glass of wine.

"Why don't you two have a seat?" said Bree. "Dinner won't be a minute."

Simon pulled out a chair for me and waited.

I found myself unsure how to act with him. This wasn't a

Saturday supper at the farmhouse, so what was it? A double date? A setup? I felt blindsided.

This was also the first time I'd seen him since the trail ride to his cabin. Since Davey.

Altogether, it left me feeling vaguely bruised and resentful.

"How's Laurel?" he asked as I took the chair he offered. "Does she like her new school?"

I nodded.

"She making friends?" he asked.

"She's my little helper," Bree called from the kitchen.

"I want to thank you for the book," I told him a little stiffly.

"Not at all," he said. "Maybe it can help you find your voice again."

Before I could answer, Bree was standing over us with a platter.

"All set?" she asked. "I hope y'all have an appetite."

She and Reuben brought more food dishes, nearly overwhelming the little table. Reuben uncorked a second bottle of wine.

"My father says you're getting to be quite the rider, Jo," he said. "He's not an easy man to impress."

"Your father?" I asked blankly. As far as I knew, I'd never met the man.

"Morgan Begay—he brought the horses."

"Oh, yes," I said. "But I haven't seen him since."

"He must get updates from Olin. They're tight."

"Reuben's been teaching me, too," said Bree. "I have more room for improvement than you, Jo."

"You didn't ride back home?" I asked. "Virginia, right?"

"Hampton Roads. Very old family. My parents are both at NASA Langley. I, on the other hand, always wanted to teach."

"But not in Virginia . . ."

"Oh, I did, for a while. After I graduated William and Mary, I taught for a bit in Norfolk. Third grade. But one night . . ." She frowned as if trying to pull up a faded memory. "One night, that all changed."

She sounded oddly wistful.

"What happened?" I asked.

Bree concentrated harder. "I was out with friends at a concert at the Coliseum. Little Phish. I was heading home right after, and there was a trucker talking on the cell with his boy, saying good night. The phone slipped. He went to catch it and jerked the wheel just enough to cross the center line. Hit me head-on."

"Oh, God," I said. "I'm so sorry. Were you hurt bad?"

"About as banged up as you can be. I'm fine now, of course. The poor trucker, though—I doubt he's gotten over it."

"I don't know if I could be so forgiving," I said.

"I bet you would," she said. "Anyway, I needed a change. That's how I ended up in Morro—just felt drawn to the place. And after I met Reuben, I knew why."

Drawn to the place? I wondered if she had the same reaction to the Mountain as I did.

Bree took Reuben's hand and squeezed it, and Reuben gazed back at her with every ounce of heart and soul right there in his eyes. I felt a pang of envy—no man had ever looked at me that way.

"How'd you two meet?" I asked.

"She stabbed me," said Reuben.

Bree groaned. "I *didn't*. It was a little dart and never touched a lick of skin. It hit your *boot*!"

Simon noticed my confusion. "The pub down the road has

dartboards," he explained. "And, well, some people have better aim than others."

Reuben pointed to the toe of one worn cowboy boot. "I still have the hole."

"I'll buy you another pair," said Bree.

"I like these just fine," he said, pulling her hand to his lips to kiss her fingertips. "Even if they do leak when it rains."

That was when my old habit kicked in, and I began to watch them over my wineglass for telltale cracks in those happy, shiny surfaces. For a note too sour, a look too sharp . . .

But I could detect nothing wrong. Nothing rang false or out of place between them—not a single, solitary fraudulent thing.

And I felt thoroughly ashamed of myself.

"Joanna," said Simon, "you and Reuben have something in common. You both studied in Albuquerque, right?"

"Another Lobo, eh?" Reuben asked.

"It was years ago," I said. "Only three semesters."

"Double features at Don Pancho's . . ." he said with a smile. "Ice cream at the Purple Hippo . . ."

I smiled back. I knew those places well. "Cinnamon buns at the Frontier—that's where I packed on my freshman ten," I said. "The Living Batch Bookstore . . ."

Memories that had been long dormant came rushing back in an instant—familiar, yet foreign, too. As if they were from somebody else's life. It didn't seem possible it had once been mine.

"I had no idea those places were still around," I said. "But they must be—you couldn't have graduated that long ago."

"I didn't graduate, either. A couple years, I was back home. I missed my family. I missed—" He shrugged. "I missed my father. And by then I was drinking. My uncle in Shiprock took me to help with the ranch. Herding ponies on motorcycles, whipping in and out of arroyos . . ." His eyes began to shine. "That was a good year. But even that wasn't enough. We'd go to Wheeler to drink our paychecks—no alcohol sales on the rez. I started to hate the idea of going back to the ranch. And one day, I didn't."

I understood. Wheeler used to be notorious for weekend bar traffic—thousands pouring in from reservations or rural towns. A core group of alcoholics never left. At night, cops would round them up and haul them to the drunk tank at the edge of town to sleep it off. Come morning, they'd be sober enough to straggle to the nearby soup kitchen run by Catholic nuns. After that, they hit the streets again—panhandling, petty theft, pawning their blood—to score more alcohol.

When the weather was good, the system worked—even when officers couldn't find everyone who'd passed out in the bed of a pickup or collapsed in a dark doorway.

But in winter the temperatures could drop to freezing at night, and it wasn't that unusual to find someone dead of hypothermia by sunup. The city kept a running tally. Jim called them popsicles.

Reuben leaned close. "You know Mother Teresa?"

"Of course," I said.

"She came to the mission once. One morning we were sitting there with our cheese sandwiches and heard a ruckus. I looked up and there was this shrunken little woman in white robes, face like a walnut and the saddest eyes. My first sober thought that day was, 'Holy shit, it's Mother Teresa.' She was walking through, nuns at her heels. Photographers, TV cameras. An hour out of the drunk tank, this is the last person you expect to see, right?"

I knew about that day—Mother Teresa had come to town several years before Jim brought me to Wheeler. It was her Sisters of Charity that ran the soup kitchen. People still talked about that visit.

But that happened—what, fifteen years ago? Twenty? If Reuben had seen her in town, he would've had to be around Laurel's age at the time . . .

"So she's passing my bench," Reuben continued, "and I stagger to my feet. Then I drop to my knees, holding my arms up like I'm a referee and somebody just nailed a field goal. And I'm not even Catholic. She totters over and for a second or two lays her hand on mine. Then she goes on her way."

He shook his head slowly. "It was one of those moments, you know?"

I nodded. "Life-changing."

"Hell, no! I went out, pawned some stolen hubcaps, bought myself a bottle—business as usual. Things didn't change till that winter. I was in an alley one cold night, massively stoned, thinking how strange it was that I couldn't feel my arms or legs anymore. And that if I wasn't careful, I could lose everything. *That* was my wake-up call."

Bree was giving him a small, consoling smile.

After dessert, Bree suggested a walk to Schiavone's bakery down the block to cap off the evening with genuine Italian coffee. It was mid-September by my best guess and the air had chilled considerably. It felt like the first bite of autumn, and I chafed my arms against the cold.

Simon peeled off his sport coat and, before I could object, draped it over my shoulders. It was warm and smelled of cedar wood.

"But now you're in shirtsleeves," I protested.

"I'm fine. We mountain men defy the cold."

"I thought mountain men defied the cold by wearing animal pelts, not by shucking their clothes."

He chuckled and fell in beside me on the sidewalk.

Bree and Reuben were a few paces ahead, arms linked. Bree was leaning into Reuben, whispering in his ear. Now and then she glanced back at us, her expression conspiratorial.

Lampposts were lit all along the main street and strings of lights were wound around tree trunks and branches. Most stores had already closed for the day, but others remained open: a fifties-style malt shop, its counter packed with young people; a steakhouse and saloon, the kind with swinging doors and frisky piano music inside. The Wild Rose had a candle burning in each window, and the pub looked like it had been transported stone by stone from an Irish village. I imagined it was there that Bree had punctured Reuben's boot with the dart.

Schiavone's had a half dozen café tables on a patio, and most were taken. Bree and I found an empty one while Reuben and Simon went inside for the coffees.

The lights were still on at the town hall across the street, and Bree explained it doubled as a community center for plays and concerts; some evenings they hung a screen for a movie projector.

At the next table sat three older men with intense, angular features, wearing worn cloth coats and drinking from espresso cups. They were deep in conversation in a language I couldn't begin to place.

"This is like nothing I've ever seen in Wheeler," I murmured.

"I've been to Wheeler, so I know what you mean," said

Bree. "Me, I prefer farther afield. Reuben and I just trekked through Scotland. Next summer, we're hitting the Amalfi Coast." She laughed. "My Reuben may come from a desert people, but he loves the sea."

Reuben was approaching with a tray, Simon close behind. He placed four foaming glasses on the table, along with four forks. I thought he'd made a mistake in the cutlery till Simon set down a small plate: on it was a huge cinnamon bun—exactly like the ones from my late-night binges in college.

Simon handed me a fork. "They even warmed it," he said. "Shall we?"

They waited for me to take the first bite. It tasted just as I remembered, down to the sweet, dripping butter.

"They make these here?" I asked.

"Not ordinarily," Simon said vaguely. "You have to know who to talk to."

Later that night, Simon insisted on driving me home. He opened the passenger door of his truck and offered his hand to help me inside. I ignored the hand and climbed in on my own. The bench seat was upholstered in soft cowhide that warmed my legs, despite the deepening chill.

Simon started the engine, then turned a knob on the dashboard. "Doesn't take long for the heat to kick in."

"I'm fine."

I slid his coat from my shoulders and folded it neatly. I laid it on the seat between us.

"Are you?" he asked. I knew he wasn't talking about the chill.

The evening had been surprisingly pleasant, but now that Simon and I were alone, the resentment was back and doubling down. Just how was he expecting this lift back to the farmhouse to end? With the two of us parked in the driveway steaming up the truck windows? Sloppy kisses on the porch?

Besides, I couldn't look at him without seeing Davey pulling off his cowboy hat, exposing that face . . .

I turned toward the side window and watched as Morro swept past. The truck left the asphalt and hit the dirt road with a faint bump. As we drove on toward the farm, I shifted in the seat to look behind us.

Tonight the snowcap on the Mountain shone with a kind of phosphorescence. And there near the top was Olin's night-light.

If I climbed up and found that light, if I touched it, would it burn like fire? Or like ice?

Simon was reaching for the knob on the dash again.

"Corral's almost finished," he said as warm air fanned my legs. "Pegasus has even jumped the rails a few times, but he always comes back. I wouldn't have thought he could hurdle that high—not in his shape. Maybe he's got wings after all."

I dragged my eyes from the Mountain and straightened in my seat. "You're keeping the name?"

"Wouldn't want to disappoint Davey," he said.

"He seems like a nice boy."

"He is."

"Yes," I said tonelessly. "And he looks *exactly* like a nine-year-old version of my husband." The words tasted bitter as rue on my tongue. "Except he has my eyes. Didn't you notice?"

I turned to stare at the window glass. I could feel Simon studying me, but he was silent for a long while. Then, "I knew there was something."

We were almost at the house now; the drive from town

wasn't long. Despite the warm air in the cab, I was shivering all over again.

"Yes," I said. "There was something."

Simon didn't answer. He kept his hands level on the wheel, his eyes on the road. And just . . . *waited.*

I felt no demands from him. No expectations. No judgments.

I knew we could ride the rest of the way without another word being said—we could drive clear up to Canada as silent as two monks—and it would be perfectly fine with him.

But this time the truth sat painfully in my throat, straining to burst free. This time there was no one compelling me to speak.

And that meant no one to resist.

"I was pregnant once before," I began quietly. "Before Laurel, I mean. I lost the baby early. If he'd been born—" I shook my head. "His name was David. At least, that was my name for him. His due date was in June. Nine years ago. Sound familiar?"

I was startled to realize my cheeks were wet. I wiped at the tears, then stared at my fingers.

We were drawing up on the farmhouse, pulling into the drive. The porch light was on; a single lamp shone through the front window. The rest of the house was dark. It wasn't late, but Olin and Jessie kept farm hours.

Simon switched off the engine and made no move to exit or to help me out. Instead, he rested his left arm on the steering wheel and eased himself in his seat, angling in my direction. Still he said nothing.

If he'd questioned me then, I couldn't have gone on. I would have shut down, just as I'd done with the doctor in the clinic and with Alicia from the prosecutor's office. It wasn't from obstinacy or defiance. It was just that some wounds run so deep, they can cut you all over again in the telling.

But almost before I knew it—there I was, telling Simon. It helped that it was too dark to see his face well, or for him to see mine.

I told him about Jim's jealous rage that day, and the punch to the stomach. About the emergency trip to the clinic two days later. I even told him something I'd forgotten till that very moment—about rushing to the bathroom in the clinic before the exam because I was bleeding through my clothes. And somehow there was my blood all over the bathroom floor, the walls, and I panicked, pulling paper towels from the dispenser, frantic to clean everything up before anybody found out I'd made such a mess.

Then, after the exam, the curettage, with Jim hovering and the doctor advising us to go try again, we stood in line to pay the bill, just one more couple like any other in the room. An office assistant was soothing a fussy toddler, holding him over a machine to copy his tiny hands till he laughed.

As I stood there watching them, it was the first time—the only time—I shed tears over the baby. A nurse pulled us out of line and hustled us to a desk in a quiet corner to handle the payment in private. Jim went through the motions of a man comforting his wife, his hand a vise on my shoulder.

Once home, he warned me never to mention the baby again.

And so I hadn't.

"Joanna, I'm so sorry." Simon reached for me, but I shrank from him.

"I appreciate it—I do," I said apologetically. "But I don't think I could handle a single bit of kindness right now. Does that make sense?"

"It does."

"I always thought I'd break into a thousand pieces if I ever dared tell anyone about Jim. Like there'd be some punishment—from Jim or, I don't know, from God, for all I knew. As if the two of them were one and the same. Crazy, right? I mean, if one of them existed, the other couldn't possibly."

"It's hard to make sense of the world when people do terrible things."

"And get away with it—don't forget that. *And get away with it.* If God protects fools and drunks, he sure as hell protects bastards, too. Where's all that righteous anger of his, anyway? I've seen plenty of anger out there, but never his. If he hears the smallest prayer, he sure as hell can hear a scream."

Simon was looking off in the distance. He had an earnest grip on the steering wheel.

"It can seem that way sometimes," he said, his voice low. "In our darkest hours, it can seem like there's nothing out there. When you're fighting for your life, weeks into a battle—outgunned, outmaneuvered and so exhausted you don't know if you're awake or just trapped inside your own nightmare. Watching your buddies disappear one by one in a blast of shells—just *gone*—or ground up like raw meat under tank treads."

His voiced trailed off. I was watching him then, mesmerized by his profile, by the strain in his voice—so unlike him. I waited for him to go on.

"Artillery, mortar fire, tanks raking you from all sides . . . explosions so close your ears bleed. You wipe at the mud and the blood, knowing there's nowhere to run. *Nowhere.* So scared all you want to do is crawl up inside your own helmet. And you hear the screams. You hear the prayers, too. Impossible to miss." He turned and gave me a thin smile. "Trust me. Impossible."

"Simon . . . I'm sorry. I had no idea."

"No reason you should."

"You make me ashamed."

He cocked his head. "Why on earth?"

"I forget other people have scars, too. Where were you? Afghanistan?"

He didn't answer.

"No," I continued slowly, "that couldn't be right. We haven't had battles like that over there. Weeks and weeks, against tanks . . ." I waited for an explanation, but he wasn't offering one.

"You know," he said finally, "maybe some prayers aren't answered right away. Maybe we have to wait for it. Or *work* for it."

"A bootstrap theology."

"Not quite," he said. "We don't always have to go it alone, you know."

Suddenly I was remembering Bernadette.

"There was someone who helped me once," I said. "And for no good reason I know of. She said it was because I asked her, but even so, I don't know many people who would've done that. Jessie and Olin would have. *You* would have."

"Joanna, listen. When you first came, you could've knocked on any door and been taken in. That's just the way it is. I believe that's how most people are, given a chance."

"I wish I could believe that," I said.

"Give it some time."

I drew a deep breath; the choking knot in my throat was gone.

"Better?" he asked.

"I feel empty," I said. "But in a good way—lighter, cleaner. You're a good listener."

"Happy to lend an ear. Anytime."

"You must be kidding. Why in the world would you want to hear about the hot mess that is my life?"

He pulled on his door handle. "It's late. I'll see you to the house."

Olin's Kachinas

I was raking oak leaves in the yard when Laurel bolted outside with a shout. She ran up and latched onto my leg. "Mommy! Mr. Olin plays with *dolls*!" She chortled.

Olin had followed her onto the porch, looking tickled.

"Honey," I told her, "I'm sure Mr. Olin doesn't play with baby dolls . . ."

"No!" she said. "With little wooden Indians."

I understood then what she meant: kachinas. They were in every souvenir shop in Wheeler—cheap, clunky carvings decked out with gaudy paint and feathers, glued to wooden stands.

"Those aren't dolls, sweetie. They're—" I fumbled for something inoffensive. "They're special figures in Indian culture."

"That's near the point, punkin'," Olin told her. "But there's more to it than that. Come on—I'll show you."

"You, too, Mommy."

"In a minute. You go on—I want to get this done before Simon comes."

I was finishing up when Simon and his dog rounded the café, heading for the house. I waved, and he raised his arm in turn. Pal must have thought I was giving him a signal because he put on speed and bulleted right at me. I dropped the rake just as he reared up, his front paws ramming my shoulders. I staggered from the impact.

Simon whistled and Pal jumped down and swung around, waiting for his master to catch up.

"Sorry. Did he get dirt on you?"

I brushed at my sweater. "No harm done."

Simon gestured. "Missed a spot."

"Where—here?"

"No." He hesitated, then picked a crushed leaf from my shoulder. "There—now you're perfect."

"And you're full of it."

He laughed. We climbed the porch steps together, and I leaned the rake against the house. He glanced around curiously. "Where's my little lookout?"

"Inside. Playing with Olin's kachinas."

"Ah. That could take a while. Have you seen them?"

"Not yet. Thought I'd look in when I was more presentable."

His eyes swept over me again, this time down to my capris and bare feet. I'd kicked off my sneakers while I raked.

"You look just fine," he said. "I should . . . go on upstairs."

I nodded.

He took one final glance before disappearing inside. I followed soon after, checking in with Jessie in the kitchen to see if she needed help with supper.

"Not a thing," she said. "What on earth are you smiling about?"

"What?"

"Child, you look right pleased with yourself. What's going on?"

"I don't know what you mean. I'll get Laurel washed up. Olin's showing her his kachinas."

"Those?" Jessie muttered. "I hope he doesn't frighten the poor thing."

She pulled off her apron and dropped it on the butcher block, then headed for the living room.

I hadn't seen Olin's den yet—I knew it was his personal retreat, but could only imagine what it looked like: deer heads mounted on the wall, a gun safe in the corner, a cracked leather sofa by a fireplace . . .

The door to the room was open and I followed Jessie inside. Olin was bending over Laurel, his palm outstretched.

"And this here they call the 'Priest Killer,'" he was saying.

"Land's sake! Don't show her that!" Jessie snapped.

Olin was holding a figurine so tiny I couldn't make it out from the doorway. Laurel was staring at it, her eyes wide.

"Can I touch it?" she asked.

"Olin!" Jessie growled.

Before Olin could reconsider, Laurel snatched up the figurine. It was impossibly small—two inches, if that. And she looked mesmerized.

"Is that a knife with *blood* on it?" she asked. "Is he holding somebody's *head*?"

I drew closer. It was a stocky figure in a leather cape, loincloth and red moccasins. There were two red squares where his ears should be and an orange ruff around his neck. He had a black wolflike snout. In one hand he was clutching a decapitated head; in the other, a knife tipped with red.

"Why did he kill the priest?" Laurel asked.

"Well," said Olin, "Indians didn't much appreciate other folks sayin' their ways was no good, tryin' to make 'em follow theirs. So one day they up and went to war. Attacked a mission."

"They didn't want to believe in God?"

"They did believe—in the Great Spirit. Believed other things, too. In the Earth Mother, in balance and cycles to life. And spirits everywhere—not just in people, but in trees and animals and every God-made thing."

Laurel looked thoughtful. "I like that."

"Me, too," said Olin.

"I think the oak tree outside has a spirit."

"I often thought that myself."

"Why do people fight over things like that?" she asked.

"It'd take a wiser man than me to figure it out. Till a man goes to his reward, he don't know nothin' for sure. Till then, arguin' over it is like blind men arguin' over the color blue."

Gingerly, Laurel handed the figure back to Olin.

"Mommy," she said, "look at these."

She pressed her face against a display case filled with carved figures of every size—from miniatures like the Priest Killer to others topping two feet. All were made of cottonwood root. Some were very rough, very old. Others were large and resplendent, finely sanded and painted, dressed in real feathers, soft fur and leather. None looked anything like the knockoffs in those tourist shops in Wheeler.

Olin explained that the older, plainer carvings were Hopi—

the pueblo tribe that originated the kachinas. The Zuni and Navajo had adopted them later.

By tradition, he said, there are hundreds of kachinas, each representing a supernatural being that protects, teaches, amuses or disciplines. They're also messengers to the spirit world.

Just before spring, the kachinas leave their ancient home in the sacred mountains to live among the Hopi, to help with the hunt and the harvest. Then in midsummer they hold the Home-Going Dance before they return to their mountains.

Some appear in animal form, while others are mudheads, or clowns, with fantastical headpieces. Ogres teach children right from wrong. And still others, said Olin, aren't strictly kachinas, but dancers. Many are revered for their virtues—their wisdom or healing, their skill as hunters or warriors. Some help the rains come.

Laurel found a tiny Warrior Mouse that Olin said saved a village from a hawk that was gobbling up all its precious chickens. The mouse taunted the hawk till it dived and impaled itself on a sharpened greasewood stick.

"What's 'impaled'?" Laurel asked.

"A fine thing to have to explain," Jessie muttered, heading for the door. "Supper in fifteen minutes."

She left just as Simon entered. "Impaled?" he murmured, so close that his breath brushed my ear and I could smell the Lifebuoy soap on his skin.

"Some story about a Warrior Mouse and a hawk," I said.

He nodded.

"Well," Olin began slowly, rubbing his chin, "when the hawk dove to the ground, that greasewood stick was stickin' up just like a little spear, see? And the hawk, he flew smack into it before he even knew what happened."

Laurel looked intrigued.

I pointed to a nearby figure. "What about this?"

Olin smiled. "Now, that's right special—and not just to Hopis. He's the Hummingbird."

He picked it up—a figure less than a foot high, with a straight body painted aqua and yellow, arms crooked at the elbows. It was dressed in a white leather skirt, a green mask and green moccasins, and crowned with a ruff of Douglas fir. It didn't look any more remarkable than the others; in many respects, it looked much less so.

"The Hopis, they send the Hummingbird up to ask the gods for rain so the crops can grow," Olin explained. "One time, when the whole world caught fire, it was the Hummingbird who gathered all the rain clouds to put it out."

A colorful legend, I thought, but I wasn't sure why a Hummingbird that could summon rain was any more special than, say, the Antelope or the Long-Haired kachinas, which could do the same.

"And the Apaches, they got a story about a warrior named Wind Dancer who saved Bright Rain from a wolf," Olin said. "He died and Bright Rain took to grievin', and the whole world settled into a long winter. Bright Rain, she set out on long walks, and a hummingbird took to flyin' with her, whispering words of comfort in her ear, restorin' the balance. Turns out, that hummingbird was Wind Dancer. And after a while, Bright Rain stopped her grievin', and winter broke and spring come again."

Laurel was tracing the crown of the Hummingbird kachina. "Too bad Bright Rain didn't turn into a hummingbird, too, so they could be together."

Olin smiled down at her. "When her time come, maybe she did," he said gently. "Maybe heaven ain't all harps and halos."

But he wasn't finished with the lesson. "Go back far enough," he said, "the Mayans thought the hummingbird was the sun in disguise. And the Aztecs—to them, hummingbirds was warriors that died in battle."

He was eyeing the figure thoughtfully. "And out of all of the kachinas, only the Hummingbird ever flew high enough to see what was on the other side of the sky."

That intrigued me. "What did he find?"

Olin shook his head. "As the story goes—nothin'."

Jessie's voice rang out from the kitchen: "Supper!"

The lesson was over. We put the figures away and headed for the dining room.

"Mr. Olin," Laurel asked, "do all old people know as much stuff as you?"

He chuckled. "Li'l gal, I been thinkin'. I figure 'Mr. Olin' is a mite formal for good friends like us."

"But what should I call you, then?" she asked.

"What'd you like to call me?"

"Can I call you Opa?"

I shushed her. "Laurel, no."

Olin looked puzzled.

"*Opa* is German," I explained. "It means 'Grandpa.'"

He considered for a moment. "Sounds easy enough to pronounce, for bein' German. You call me Opa anytime you want. What should I call you?"

"My name's Laurel."

"True enough. But how 'bout I call you Honey Bunny?"

Laurel giggled.

"Only sometimes I might call you Honey for short, and other times just Bunny. But Honey Bunny for more formal occasions."

Laurel took his hand. "What do you think heaven is, Opa?"

He looked around the room—from his wife to the hearth to the table set for supper.

"Well, Bunny, I think heaven is whatever, wherever and whoever makes you happiest."

After supper, Olin and Jessie began clearing the table and Laurel headed upstairs to get ready for bed, leaving me to see Simon off. From the porch, I could hear bluegrass music on the radio inside. I pulled one of Jessie's woolen shawls around me as Simon turned to leave.

He hesitated on the porch steps.

"It occurs to me you haven't been to the pub yet," he said. "I wonder if you'd care to rectify that."

"What?"

"I mean, with your interest in Irish poetry, and the proprietor of the pub being Irish—it just makes sense."

"You're trying to set me up with the pub owner?"

He laughed. "I'm not trying to set you up with anyone. I'm asking, in my clumsy way, if you'd care to go to the pub some evening. With me. The pub owner's married."

"Simon, there are so many reasons to say no, I couldn't begin to list them all."

"Then don't say no. Say you'll think about it. Then think about it."

I hugged the shawl tighter. "Laurel's waiting. I told her I'd read to her before bed."

"Night, then."

He turned and headed to his pickup truck. I waved as it pulled away, certain he was watching.

As I entered the house again, I noticed the door to Olin's den still ajar. I could hear him and Jessie puttering in the kitchen, so I slipped inside for another look, pausing just inside the doorway.

I looked around at the sage green walls and white molding. His rifles and shotgun were mounted on a far wall, along with an old-style cavalry carbine. No deer heads, though, and no leather sofa. Instead, there were two overstuffed club chairs slipcovered in yellow flowers; both looked comfortable and well used. There were shelves lined with books flanking a deep stone fireplace, and on the mantel a display of Indian pottery, pewter mugs and candlesticks, and an enameled tobacco box.

As I turned to leave, I spotted a photograph in a silver frame on a small table. It was an old black-and-white of cowboys in slouch hats, kerchiefs knotted at their necks. They were surrounding a standing figure that looked remarkably like Teddy Roosevelt. As I read the caption, I realized it *was* Teddy Roosevelt: *Rough Riders, 1898.*

Several of the men were on their feet while others knelt on one knee or sat cross-legged on the bare ground. The landscape looked like Southwestern desert.

I scanned the faces—the young and cocky, the stern and worldly-wise. Kneeling in the foreground was a youthful cowboy with dark hair and a bristly mustache, grinning into the camera, cradling a carbine very like the one now mounted on the wall.

I leaned closer. The cowboy looked like a young Olin Farnsworth.

"See the resemblance?"

Olin was behind me, gazing over my shoulder at the picture.

"I didn't hear you come in," I said. "What a time you must have had . . . storming San Juan Hill."

Olin paused. "Well, that ain't exactly the case. Not all Teddy's boys made it to Cuba. When orders come, they wasn't enough room on the transport ship." He nodded at the picture. "Some had to stay behind in Florida. Most of the horses and mules did, too, which wasn't an ideal situation for a crack cavalry outfit. And that's why the Rough Riders took San Juan on foot."

I looked over the kachinas one last time. All those intermediaries between people and their gods. All that blind faith in the unknowable. Faith that something better was waiting, just out of sight. And spirits ready to step in, if asked. To guide and protect. To fend off mortal enemies.

And what of those enemies? Do they have their own spirit champions? And when they die, do they ever get to see what's on the other side of the sky?

"What about someone who does bad things?" I asked finally. "Does he deserve to be happy? Does he deserve heaven?"

"I figure a man can't be all that happy if he does bad things. And it ain't up to me to say what he might deserve. But I figure when he passes on, he's where he oughta be."

"Some people . . . some people don't believe in Judgment, a reckoning. Any of that."

Olin shrugged. "I figure it ain't up to them."

Red Bird

This is a dream

I wade through wet cement . . . straining to *run* . . .

A scarlet bird flies in my face, wings flapping like a Fury. My head explodes like shattered glass and I fall and fall until I can't fall anymore

I smell heat rising from red rock . . . I taste grit . . .

This is a dream

My mouth opens to scream, but no sound comes. I scream again and again until my throat is scoured raw. But no sound comes

I know this is a dream

I fight like a demon to *wake up wake up wake up* but can't move . . . only my mouth moves, gaping like a canyon, mute as rock

. . .

I bolted upright in the dark, gasping for breath like a drowning woman breaching the surface.

Like a cornered animal, I threw wild eyes around me at every shadow.

There was no cement, no scarlet bird.

I was in my own bed at the farmhouse. My nightgown was drenched with sweat and I couldn't suck in air fast enough.

No cement. No scarlet bird. No explosion inside my head. I groaned and buried my face in my hands.

The nightmare still gripped me like a claw. Every smell, every taste. Every fresh stab of fear. I could even hear it—the screams that wouldn't come. But they were coming now, high-pitched and howling . . .

. . . and down the hall.

I threw off the quilt and ran toward Laurel's room. I burst in to find her kicking and thrashing on her bed, eyes clamped tight, moaning and shrieking. I ran to gather her up, hugging her against me to quiet her, to stop the thrashing.

"It's all right, sweetie," I crooned over and over. "It's all right."

It was a long while before she could hear me, before she opened her eyes and looked at me, staring as if she hadn't seen me in forever. She reached out and fingered my hair as if I were some foreign thing.

Then she burst into sobs and flung her arms around my neck. I let her cry it out, holding her close, walking the room with her as if she were a baby again. Olin and Jessie were watching from the doorway.

"I'll heat up some milk," Jessie murmured, and headed for the stairs.

Laurel's face was buried in my neck and she was mumbling

something over and over that I couldn't make out. I stroked her hair. "What is it, honey? What are you saying?"

She shifted her head until she could speak more clearly.

"He's coming," she whispered.

"Who's coming, sweetie?"

She buried her face in my neck again, but this time when she spoke I could hear her plain enough:

"Daddy."

The Ravenmaster

Jim didn't come that night. Not the next night, either, nor the one after that. It was painfully obvious that my daughter dreaded her own father the way other children fear monsters under the bed. But in her case, she had every right to.

Laurel insisted she didn't remember much about her bad dream, but it was a while before she settled down to sleep. For the rest of that night, though, and for several nights after, she slept with me.

I didn't mention to anyone my own nightmare that had coincided with hers—the last thing I wanted was to compare notes. But I wanted very much to understand what it augured. Was it her own fears manifesting? A premonition?

Or had Olin's kachinas and his stories of life and death and spirits sparked something in her? In me?

Her dream didn't repeat itself, and in no time she seemed to have forgotten it.

I didn't.

Soon enough, for the first time since we came to Morro, there was frost on the ground when I set the horses to pasture. The days were growing short, and Laurel grumbled about waking in the dark. She dressed for school as I packed her lunch, then bundled her in a jacket for the walk to town with Olin.

I was working the café that morning, and when I arrived there was already a stranger sitting quietly at a window table—a tall man with a bottlebrush mustache wearing a green tweed coat; a slouchy tweed cap sat on the table in front of him. There was a canvas knapsack at his feet and a walking stick propped against the wall.

When I greeted him, the man turned and blinked as if he'd just noticed where he was and that someone else was with him. He nodded.

In the kitchen, Simon was tying on his butcher's apron.

"Who's the early bird?" I murmured.

"Showed up just after I did," he said. "Told him I wasn't quite open, but he said he'd wait."

"I'll start the coffee."

"Better make it tea—he's English."

Earl Grey steeping at his elbow, the man examined the menu. "Let's try something exotic," he said. "Spanish omelet. When in Rome, eh?"

He handed back the menu, and when I returned with the order Simon came with me.

"I'm just getting my sea legs, as it were," the man said as

he ate. "This . . . traveling takes getting used to. You know, we'd always talked of moving to the American Southwest one day, the wife and I. Running a bed-and-breakfast."

"Oh, is she with you?" I asked.

"No—back in Surrey. Keyes, by the way."

"Pardon?"

"My name. Albert Keyes."

"Joanna. And this is Simon."

"Delighted."

Simon took a seat at the counter. "You're far afield, aren't you?"

Keyes nodded. "I'll be returning before long, once I've seen a thing or two. Like your town here—Morro, is it? And your desert." He gazed wistfully out the window. "And, perhaps, the Northwest."

Pal rose from his quilt and headed for the window, his ears pricked, his eyes trained like gun barrels on something outside. In the growing light I could just make out a huge black bird perched on a signpost across the road. It seemed to be staring back.

"Look at the size of that crow," I said.

"Raven," Keyes replied. "A very old friend, and now my traveling companion. His name is Gruffydd." He spelled it out. "It's Welsh. After a prince who fell from the White Tower in a failed escape, a very long time ago."

Simon smiled at my confusion. "I believe he's talking about the Tower of London," he said.

"That's right," said Keyes. "I was a yeoman warder there a number of years, after service as a regimental sergeant major. Began as deputy to the ravenmaster. He retired some years ago, and I took over."

He nodded toward the black bird.

"That's how we met. Raised him from a fledgling. Named him as well. At one time, all the birds were named for the Queen's regiments. Now they're often named for old gods, or for those who find them. Or rescue them. I named Gruffydd there for the prince that couldn't fly."

Simon leaned back against the counter, crossing his arms. "I remember the ravens," he said thoughtfully. "I was in London a few weeks before shipping out. Took a tour of the Tower. The ravens were *something*. Six of them. Bigger than you'd think. Must be a huge responsibility, taking care of them. What is it they say? If the ravens ever leave the Tower, the empire will fall?"

"That's the legend, anyway," said Keyes. "But there have been episodes when the ravens have been absent—toward the end of the war, for instance—with no detriment to the monarchy."

"How do you keep them from flying off?" I asked. "You don't keep them caged, do you?"

"They are, indeed, caged at dusk. I whistled them in for bed, but at dawn they were out again, roaming the grounds. I fed them from my own hand—raw meat from Smithfield Market. Boiled egg every other day. Bird biscuits soaked in blood—a delicacy. The odd roadkill. And they don't fly off because their wings are clipped—or one wing, at least—every few weeks. They can still fly a bit, but no appreciable distance."

There was affection in his voice, but it still seemed a cruel fate for such wild creatures.

"They are wild," Keyes said thoughtfully. "But they're natural mimics, and very intelligent. And they do have their fun. Gruffydd was always my favorite. Every day he tells me, 'Good morning.' When I fill his water bowl, he says, 'Cheers.' He used to stake out a particular doorway at the Tower, lying in ambush for tourists. If you wore a hat, he'd try to grab it. And if he made off with it, he'd be off to a restricted area and battle that hat like billy-o."

Pal plopped his rump down heavily on the tile floor, still training on the bird. He licked his chops and whined. Simon tapped his leg. "Here, boy." Ever obedient, Pal rose and moved to sit next to him.

"Don't worry about Gruffydd," Keyes said. "He can manage, should the dog get out."

I wondered what sort of bond this man and that raven could possibly share. If Keyes whistled, would Gruffydd come? Perch on his shoulder, clutching the nubby tweed? Say "Good morning" and "Cheers" on cue for a boiled egg or beef?

Keyes sighed. "Twenty-five years—he was getting on, you know. After his de-enlistment I brought him back to Surrey. My wife is still there—did I say?—puttering about the garden."

When he was ready to head out, I rang the man up as he pulled on his cap and gathered his things. I cleared his breakfast dishes and delivered them to the back. By the time I returned, Keyes and Gruffydd were gone.

For the rest of the day, I couldn't get that raven out of my head—picturing him perched on weathered stones in high places, buffeted by winds that would never bear him away.

The Parting Glass

The librarian, Jean Toliver, arrived at the farmhouse one morning dressed in the long skirt, velvet blouse and squash blossom necklace I now took to be her uniform. I imagined she'd come to press me to attend her club meetings, but soon found it was to invite me to a poetry reading set for the following week. Amateur poets, most of them local.

Then she asked where I'd like to appear on the program, and somehow by the time she left she'd inked me in for a slot.

I'd never enjoyed reading in public, and had only ever done so twice: at a student event in college, and a small community reading by a pair of unknowns—myself and a coffeehouse barista.

Both times, I'd nearly backed out. But for the first reading, Terri had been there to make sure I made it to the podium. I managed the second only after a shot of vodka from a hip flask the barista had stashed.

This time, I not only lacked the nerve, but the material as well.

That night I sat in the rocking chair in my room and opened the notebook Olin had given me—I'd been using it as a journal, after many failed attempts at poetry. Apparently Yeats no longer had the power of inspiration over me. Or I was no longer a likely vessel.

I came to the notebook that night with fresh purpose and not a little desperation, but with the same result: after a good hour, the page was still empty. There was nothing for it. Words weren't failing me—I was failing them.

I slapped the notebook closed, capped my pen and returned it to the nightstand, the blank page just another white flag of surrender. Tomorrow I would withdraw from the reading. The decision came as a relief.

And a vague sting of disappointment.

Over the years I'd grown keenly aware of risk, and adept at avoiding it. The risk here, it occurred to me, wasn't in standing before a roomful of strangers to read my own work. It wasn't even the struggle to find my own voice.

It was finding out if I had anything worth listening to in the first place.

And the only one who could determine that was me.

I looked down at the notebook in my lap. I opened the cover and leafed through the pages—the journaling I'd been doing nearly every day since I'd received it. The pages already filled with words.

My words.

By the night of the reading, I had two poems in hand. If I wasn't ready, I was at least resolved.

Jessie enlisted a girl from town to sit with Laurel; then Olin washed and waxed the old Ford pickup he stored in the barn and drove Jessie and me to town. He opened the pub's heavy oak door and I hesitated in the doorway until Jessie did just as Terri would have, and urged me inside.

The Parting Glass was a series of small cozy rooms strung together, and it was just as I imagined an old pub should be—coal fires and pipe smoke, beamed ceilings, odd recesses and crooked corners.

"There you are!"

It was Jean near the entrance, checking names off a clipboard. "Your table's in the second room, through the archway," she said. "Name's on the placard. Simon's already there."

Then she broke into a broad, dimpled smile. She had tiny round teeth, barely bigger than seed pearls.

"Who else is reading?" I asked.

"Only seven tonight. Don't look so worried—people at these things are ready to like everything they hear. You're"—she consulted the clipboard—"sixth up."

Through the archway, the second room was much larger than the first. One side was lined with booths, and on the side opposite was a small stage and podium. In between were tables, nearly all of them occupied. Bree and Reuben called out from one of them.

"How wonderful," said Bree. "You're a poet."

"That remains to be seen," I said.

"Jean says you're good."

How would Jean know any such thing? I hadn't written these poems until a few days ago, and she'd never read them.

Jessie tapped my arm. "Honey, we're off to say hello to Liz and Molly. Meet you at the table."

The sisters Liz and Molly were there, with Liz's husband, Faro, from the general store and a second man I'd never seen before. He was lively and middle-aged, dressed in a brown suit with a windowpane pattern and wide lapels. He had an infectious laugh—head thrown back, Adam's apple bobbing. From the way Molly was smiling at him, eyes glistening, she was clearly smitten.

So this was George, from Bristol.

Simon was sitting at a corner booth. In front of him was a tall beer, and at his side was a young woman, unreasonably pretty, her blond hair pinned back on either side to fall in a soft wave to her shoulders. She was leaning toward him, her pink lips moving. Then they were both smiling, as if at some shared joke.

"That's your table," said Bree, watching me.

I hadn't thought much about Simon attending the reading tonight. Still, when Jean had mentioned him, it hadn't been a surprise. Part of me had expected him to be here, as a gesture of support.

I just hadn't expected him to bring a date.

I'd never thought of Simon with a woman. Certainly Jessie and Olin had never mentioned him seeing anyone. Not even casually. Maybe this was someone new in Morro. Newer than me. Or maybe she'd had her eye on him for a while now and was finally making progress.

Had she been up to his cabin yet? Gone for rides in his pickup? Cooked him dinner? Shared pastry under the stars? Had he invited her to the pub because I'd turned him down?

As I approached, I pulled a smile that felt forced, and too big for my face.

"Hey!" I said.

"You're here!" Simon looked pleased, and not a whit embarrassed. He stood. "There's someone I'd like you to meet. Joanna, this is Meg."

To my dismay, Meg was even prettier up close. "I've heard so much about you," she said. Her voice was warm, her smile sincere. "I'm glad we could meet."

I took a seat across from them. "I'm glad, too. But I have to say I never heard—"

"Simon never mentioned me? No surprise. He's off in his own world sometimes." She shook her head at him affectionately. "You're settling in, are you? At the farm?"

Before I could answer, a big man appeared, shirtsleeves hitched above his elbows.

"This the new one, is it?" His Irish accent was thick, and he was gesturing at me with a toothpick. "You can call me Mahenny. You like Italian food, do you?"

"I . . . adore Italian food," I said.

"Lovely, then. I'm an old mick, but my wife's from Firenze. She's the cook. I recommend the lasagna."

He glared, as if daring me to refuse.

"I'll have that, then," I said.

"Brilliant. I usually only take orders at the bar, but on this particular occasion, I'll make an exception. Understand?"

No, I didn't understand. But I wasn't about to tell him that.

"I appreciate it," I said.

"Now, for wine you got two choices: red or white."

I was sure any pub owner—married to an Italian, no less—knew what to serve with lasagna. Mahenny was playing with me.

"Surprise me," I said.

The glare softened. "That I will, darlin'. Lasagna all 'round, then?"

"Not for me," said Meg. "I'm off to rejoin my husband."

Husband? I smiled with relief.

Meg smiled back with what looked like—understanding? Apology?

"His name's Will," she said. "You can meet him later."

Then Meg and Mahenny were gone, leaving me sitting across from Simon in an awkward silence. Simon broke it first, but not on the topic I'd hoped.

"He seems gruff, but he's a sweetheart," he said. "Not that he can't toss a guy out on his ear if he has to. His wife—she's the sister of Schiavone, the baker."

"And Mahenny's not from these parts, either."

"County Armagh."

I nodded. "Meg seems like a sweetheart, too," I said lightly, trying to strike the right note of disinterest.

"We've known each other for years. She's the kid sister of an old friend. Back then, she was just a tomboy, trailing me like a puppy. Then one day I turned around and the tomboy was all grown up."

Mahenny swooped past, setting a wineglass in front of me. Then he was off again. I took a sip and smiled—Chianti. I focused on its rich red color, the better to avoid Simon's eyes.

"A long time ago," he continued, "Meg and I were sweet on each other, but . . . things didn't work out. She and Will are very happy. Five kids."

"Five?" I stared at him in disbelief. "With that figure? That has to be . . . physically impossible."

He laughed. "You can meet them someday. Meg and Will are heading back to Colorado tomorrow."

He reached for my poems, and I slapped the pages back on the table.

"Sorry," I said. "I'd rather you didn't. I can't explain it—"

He didn't seem offended, but amused. "Artistic temperament," he said. "I can wait."

Jessie and Olin joined us—Jessie already pink cheeked from the sherry in her hand, Olin nursing a bottle of Rio Grande beer. Lasagna arrived for the four of us; Mahenny was right—his wife was an excellent cook.

Soon, Jean stepped to the podium with her clipboard, tapping the microphone to test the sound, then introduced the first of the poets. One by one, they took the stage, reading from note cards, from paper or from memory.

A tense older executive type in horn-rimmed glasses went first, followed by an academic with white hair and precise diction. I was surprised to see Faro take the stage next. He closed his eyes and clasped his hands behind him, just as he'd done before he produced Laurel's yellow boots, and let loose with a love poem that had Liz looking cross, then pleased. After him, Jean read three works—compact and clipped works that reminded me of Emily Dickinson. Then a young woman with multiple piercings on her pretty face read fierce free verse about an ill-fated love affair.

Then it was my turn.

Olin was beside me on the bench seat, and stood to let me out. He squeezed my shoulder encouragingly.

As I made my way to the podium, I was suddenly very grateful for the Chianti—I was sure it was giving me the courage to go through with this and not bolt for the exit. It nearly steadied my hand as I adjusted the microphone. I was grateful for the darkness of the room that blurred the faces all around me, and for the many brands of beer Mahenny stocked to loosen up the audience.

I stared down at my papers and cleared my throat.

"This is for a woman I met in the café," I said. "Lula told me about a cemetery back home in Mississippi—a black cemetery, mostly forgotten now, being farmed over. It's called 'Brother Stones.'"

I couldn't stop my hands from shaking. I drew a deep breath and began:

Brother stones rise to the plow,
crack the topsoil
in a catch of breath
audible only to the blue boneset
and the Quaker ladies.
A barren harvest of white stones,
then seed is thrown back:
soybean and cotton.

This gravel road between Dunleith
and Long Switch runs past
an empty space
where the Baptist church
once stood, dug up by its roots
twelve years ago to become
another wide load rumbling
across the Mississippi Delta,
a far piece from empty sockets
in the fractured earth where
uprooted metal markers lay,
one by one.

"There was no cemetery there."
There was a child, seven,
cradled his head and rolled
to the kitchen floor
of the shotgun shack.
There was the child's brother.

There was a young man, drowned
in the River, his great-grandmother,
dead of the "sugar."
A hundred others or more
planted in this earth,

a quiet population
under a blowing field of cotton,
a disjunction of bones and teeth
rising like smooth stones
through the earth,
a terminable progress

from this place where they are not,
up toward the cotton in fruit,
toward the topsoil, sunbaked to fissures,
toward the vigorous light,
to break the fresh furrows finally
with a gasp.

I could hear murmuring as I switched papers, smoothing them under the bright podium light, still struggling for control.

"And this is for Keyes, an Englishman who passed through

Morro with a raven named Gruffydd. I call this 'Six Ravens at the Tower of London'":

They are the darlings of the Yeoman Warders
who named them after regiments
of the Queen, who feed them
eggs and bread and meat,
who clip their wings, jealously pinch back
their bold growth
toward the sky.

They perch regal and wild and wary
on the wrought-iron gate, dwarfed
by the thousand-year stones
of the White Tower.
Here, a captive Welsh prince once leapt,
spread his arms and
did not fly.

If these creatures fly off,
England will fall.
By royal decree, then,
they will never leave.
For four hundred years these stones
have been their keep.

Their black, bottomless eyes
stare at a silence worn smooth
by a river of centuries,
restless as the London mist,
tameless as Cuchulain's
horses of the sea.

A thousand voices speak to them
each day in every tongue
but their own.

I gathered my papers. Without daring to look at the audience, I left the podium.

As I stepped from the stage, the applause began. The other readers had had their share of applause, of course, but this applause—this applause was for me.

This was mine.

And it felt . . . *wondrous.*

At the booth, Jessie and Olin hugged me in turn. Then Simon was standing in front of me, looking unsure. I laughed breathlessly. "I'd better sit before my knees buckle," I said.

Back in the booth, Simon leaned across the table. "You were marvelous," he said.

"I was okay. But I appreciate it."

My head was spinning so fast I still can't recall the last reader of the night—for all I knew, it could have been Yeats himself.

The readings didn't close out the evening. Mahenny removed the podium, and three Irish musicians took the stage. The lead singer had ferocious red hair and a bird's nest of a beard, and the three didn't just sing their songs—they attacked them. Tables and chairs were pushed aside to clear a dance floor.

George threw off his jacket and swung Molly around in a bucking polka, and the young poet with the piercings paired off with a cowboy in a starched shirt and handlebar mustache.

Bree stopped by with Reuben. "Jo, you were terrific." She had to shout to be heard above the reel blasting from the stage.

Reuben leaned close. “The family’s throwing a shindig in a few weeks for my brother’s birthday. You’re all invited.”

“How old’s he now?” asked Simon.

“Turning sixteen,” Reuben answered as Bree pulled him back to the dance floor.

Olin stood and offered his hand to his wife. “Honor me?”

Jessie’s smile as she took it dropped decades off her.

“You know,” I told Simon as I watched them on the floor, “they dance like this more nights than not. Turn on their old radio and off they go. I don’t know where they get the energy. I’m starting to wonder what he packs in that rolling paper of his.”

Then it was Simon who stood and stepped to my side. “May I?”

I stared at his open hand.

“Simon,” I said, “I haven’t danced in years. And I’ve never tried a reel in my life.”

He glanced toward the stage, then back at me. “This song’s about over. If the next is a slow one, will you dance?”

The Irishmen had been playing only jigs and reels. They could read the crowd, and the crowd wanted to *move.* I felt safe in agreeing.

“Sure,” I said.

Almost as soon as I said it, the reel was over. There was a pause, and the three musicians exchanged a look. Without a word, one of them took up a penny whistle, the second an electric guitar and the third an electric bass. The bass beat a deep, rhythmic thrum while the flute broke into a slow, melancholy tune.

“What are the odds?” I murmured.

Simon was gazing at me steadily now, arm outstretched.

I laid my hand in his and he pulled me gently to my feet.

Even after a decade, I still managed to remember whose arms went where. What I'd completely forgotten was the initial thrill of stepping into a man's embrace—the feel of skin against skin, of warm breath against my temple.

I moved stiffly at first—for so long, physical contact with a man was something I'd tried very hard to avoid. And I was painfully aware that I was just as skittish as I'd been at my first junior high dance. But if Simon was aware of it, he didn't show it.

He didn't pull me tight or let his hand roam, nor could I ever imagine he would. Not like that. He pressed his palm lightly against the small of my back, and the warmth of it seemed to percolate through my clothes, through my skin, down to my core.

The music was almost primal—a minor bass chord, over and over, like the beat of a drum, the flute raveling against it like a keening voice, prickling every hair on my arms.

I closed my eyes and there were images of landscapes I'd never seen before—immense, ragged mountain ridges carved by receding glaciers. Deep valleys exploding with yellow gorse and purple thyme. Lush lowlands sweeping down to the North Sea, waves pounding against the rocky coast, so close you could breathe in the cold salt spray . . .

The scenes were so intense, so vivid, that when I opened my eyes again it was disorienting not to see the surf crashing on the rocks right in front of me . . . to feel the salt water on my face, or taste it on my tongue . . .

And there was Simon, watching me with the slightest smile, and those knowing, careful, hooded eyes.

Climbing a Mountain

It took a while to identify what I was feeling lately. I ran through the usual roster, but nothing fit.

At last, I put my finger on it: I was *happy*.

It had been so long. Jim had taken so much—lopping away bits and pieces until there was nothing of the essentials left. Till Joanna was gone, boiled down to baser elements.

Now here she was again in the mirror, gazing back at me. Not quite what she had been, not yet. But no longer the lump of potter's clay on Jim's wheel, either.

The feeling persisted until I filled up the notebook, then started another. I had so much to say, and every word on every page felt like a victory. A battle won. I reveled in it.

But there was a part of me that didn't trust it. A part that knew better.

And she wasn't wrong.

Late one afternoon I stepped out back to call Laurel in for supper. I heard nothing in return but the cluck of hens and sheets snapping on the line.

It was a peculiar, yawning silence, and I could feel the skin on my arms prickling to gooseflesh.

I called again.

Olin appeared in the open barn door, wiping his hands on a red bandanna. He was alone. He latched the door behind him and headed toward the house.

The sun was close to setting, shadows slanting low.

My heart skipped a beat. An alarm was clanging in my brain.

"Where's Laurel?" I demanded. "Not with you?"

Olin shook his head. "Not for a good while. Said she was headin' inside to help with supper."

I swallowed hard. "When was that?"

"Oh, nigh on a couple hours."

I swiveled and started to round the house at a fast clip, scouting the landscape for signs of her. Not by the creek. Not in the fields. She wouldn't have gone so far as the foothills, would she?

I turned one corner, then another, till I'd nearly circled the house, calling her name over and over.

Jessie swept through the front door onto the porch. "Somethin' wrong?" she asked.

I turned and stared, incapable of speech.

Wrong?

There were lots of reasons a curious seven-year-old might slip off and disappear for a while. None of them meant a thing to me in that cold-blooded moment.

By then, Jim had finally shrunk down from monster-sized

to something more manageable—a toothless jackal prowling the perimeter. I could go entire days without his name, his face invading my thoughts. Weeks without sitting sentinel on the porch, watching the road.

Stupid, stupid, stupid.

I ran up the porch steps, pushing past Jessie into the house. I took the stairs by twos up to the second floor and Laurel's room at the end of the hall. Empty. I ran to mine. Empty, too. The bathroom, Jessie and Olin's room, back downstairs to the den, the kitchen, calling Laurel's name in a ragged voice.

I pulled up in the middle of the living room, my heart thumping so hard it made my chest ache. Jessie was back inside by then, watching me gravely as I began to tick off Laurel's movements like a trail of bread crumbs that would end with her smiling up at me as I reached the last one.

"She came home from school . . . then with Olin in the fields . . . then heading inside . . ."

Then what? Then Jim intercepted her? Bundled her up, threw her in his Expedition? Drove back to Wheeler? Daring me to come get her?

Is that even possible?

Laurel's nightmare came back to me: *He's coming . . . He's coming . . . Daddy . . .*

Olin was inside now, too.

"I need your truck keys," I said, brushing past him to the cabinet where he kept his ammunition. I slid open a drawer and grabbed two boxes of shotgun shells.

"What on earth?" Jessie murmured.

"I'll need your 12-gauge, too."

I didn't wait for permission. The shotgun was still mounted on the far wall of his den, next to the pair of Winchesters and the antique carbine. I took it down, broke open the breech, mastered my trembling hands long enough to slide a cartridge into each barrel, then snapped it to.

Olin was watching from the doorway. "Keep the safety on."

"Not for long," I said, pocketing the boxes of shells.

He followed me as I made for the barn and his truck sitting inside. It might be old, but it sure as hell would get me three miles over the break of hills and thirty miles due west.

In the barn, I opened the driver's door and slid the shotgun behind the seat. Finally I turned to Olin, my hand out for the keys.

But Olin was looking toward the far wall of the barn, at the row of horse stalls. They were empty—the horses were still pastured outside.

"Hold on . . ." he said, moving away.

"Olin, there's no time to waste," I said.

"Hold on now," he repeated, more firmly this time.

Then he was standing by the tack, eyeing bridles, halters, reins, martingales hanging from wall hooks, leather saddles slung side by side over a broad beam.

"Olin," I barked.

"Her saddle's gone," he said. "Looks like she tacked up."

He turned and left the barn, making for the pasture. I followed, and we both stared at the three horses grazing there.

Three horses. Not four.

Tse—the big roan, Rock, Laurel's horse—was gone.

"She couldn't have," I said.

"She knows well enough how to do it," said Olin. "It'd take some effort for a mite like her, but she could do it."

Relief pulsed through me till I thought my head would burst. I tried to laugh but I huffed instead, catching my breath.

So Laurel hadn't been kidnapped after all. Jim hadn't snuck in while my guard was down and snatched her up.

"But why?" I said. "And where?"

Once more I scanned both ends of the valley, east and west. Then north at the foothills darkening under the setting sun, this time looking for a rider.

But Olin was peering up.

Up at the Mountain.

"I figure," he said, "she went a-lookin' for that little dog of hers."

Simon arrived by the time we'd saddled the three remaining horses, but supper would have to wait. It was decided Jessie would stay behind in case Laurel came home on her own. Simon would take Yas.

The three of us made for town at a canter, pulling up once we hit the asphalt. There we could see another rider waiting in front of the general store, watching us approach. It was Faro LaGow on a big Appaloosa.

"Heard your little gal went up the Mountain," he told me as we pulled up. "Figured to help out."

I didn't ask how he'd heard—he was one more pair of eyes on a good horse, and a cold night was falling fast.

"Thank you," I said.

At the far end of town where the main road and the secondary splintered off, we stopped to carve out a plan. While the men briskly sorted it out, I glared up at the Mountain, impatient to be off.

This time there was none of the old, fearful reluctance. Its magnetic pull was just as sharp, but this time I wasn't resisting it. This landmass was a barrier between me and my daughter, and as far as I was concerned it had lured her there under false pretenses. Played on her affection for a dog that was long gone. This time I couldn't assail it soon enough.

It was decided that Olin and Faro would take the steeper main road that switchbacked up the side, while Simon and I took the narrower one that rounded it at a lower pitch and led to his cabin and beyond. I knew both routes also had any number of trails leading off into the forest.

I half expected someone to raise an objection about the futility of searching in the dark, especially with no clear sense of where to start and so much ground to cover. I thought someone might even suggest waiting to fetch some hunting dogs to try to sniff out a proper trail. If I'd been in my right mind, I might have suggested such a thing myself.

Olin wheeled Kilchii around to fall in beside me. His slight smile was meant to be comforting.

"Young'uns have lit out on their own before, up the Mountain or down the valley," he said. "And we always find 'em safe and sound. We'll find your girl, too."

There was a choking lump snagged in my throat. I nodded.

Then Olin and Faro trotted off to the left without a backward glance, disappearing into the gloom and the first bend in the road.

I turned to Simon, who was watching me with sympathy.

"Ready?" he asked.

Again, all I could do was nod, flick the reins and kick off.

Simon rode ahead where I could barely make him out in the darkness. But I could hear him plainly enough, calling Laurel's name. I called, too, our voices carrying into the dim woods on either side of us. Now and then I'd hear a dry rustle in the distance or the call of some creature or other, but never Laurel's voice calling back.

After an hour or so, Simon pulled up and handed me a canteen. It was coffee, still hot. He offered a sandwich Jessie had packed, but I had no appetite. Laurel was out there somewhere. Likely hungry and scared. Had she taken her jacket with her? Her mittens? Had she even thought that far ahead? Or had she just figured to point Tse in the general direction of that barking dog and be back with Tinkerbell in time for supper?

"How cold is it expected to get tonight?" I asked.

Simon was tucking his canteen back in his saddlebag. "Try not to worry."

"Freezing?" I continued, ignoring him. "Even if it doesn't drop that far, hypothermia can set in well above freezing."

I ran a guilty gloved hand down the arm of my warm sheepskin coat. The moon was slipping out from behind a bank of clouds; it was still a few days from full but bright enough now that I could make out my breaths hitting the chilly air in puffs.

I heard a voice then, calling from farther up the road. But deep—the voice of a man, not a child. "Hello up ahead!"

Simon and I turned as one toward the sound. "Hello!" Simon shouted in return.

Out of the darkness appeared two riders at a hard trot. They were nearly upon us before I recognized them—Reuben and his father, Morgan Begay.

They reined in as they reached us. They didn't offer pleasantries or explanations about how they, too, had joined the search.

"Nothing on the road this side," Begay said in his clipped voice. "We'll double back. Hit some trails."

Simon nodded. "We'll take some trails, too. She's headed up—we know that."

"She kept hearing a barking dog," I said to Begay. "Any idea where it might be coming from?"

Begay shrugged. "Hard to tell. Lots of dogs here."

"You find her, fire off three shots," Simon advised him. "And we'll come fetch her."

He said it as casually as if they were talking about a child who'd wandered off in a supermarket: *You find her in aisle three, give a holler.*

"She won't be lost long," Reuben said gently, watching me. "Tse has a mother spirit."

A mother spirit? What on earth did that mean? That made as much sense as Simon telling me to "try not to worry."

I wanted to light into both of them, kicking and punching. When your daughter runs off God knows where into the freezing cold, lost and alone, *you* try not to worry.

We divided again, each pair returning the way we'd come. Except this time we didn't go far before Simon pulled up beside the barrel-sized trunk of a nearly leafless oak tree. It stood next to a narrow path I hadn't noticed the first time we passed.

"Started out as a deer track," Simon explained. "Hunters use it mostly."

My heart dropped.

"We must have passed dozens of these," I said. "We don't have time to check them all."

"Farther up the Mountain, a lot of them join together, like a big tangle," he said reassuringly. "But the layout makes sense, once you know what you're dealing with. And I've been here awhile. I know what we're dealing with."

The track cut up the Mountain at a steep, snaking incline—so steep in places that Nastas and Yas had to strain to climb as we stood in the stirrups, leaning forward for balance.

On either side, trees towered over us, many of them bare and black as woodcuts, others shaggy pines; together with the clouds snuffing out the moon, they made it impossible to see far in any direction. Now and then we'd stop and call, then keep still for a response, ears pricked, the horses under us panting from their effort in the thin air. Morro already sat at high altitude—more than a mile high. This mountain was taking us higher still.

Finally we stopped to call out again, and this time I heard something in the distance.

Not a voice. Not a human voice, anyway.

But a whinny.

I held my breath and waved for silence.

There it was again.

"Over there!" I said excitedly.

"I heard it," said Simon. "Wait here. I'll check it out."

"Like hell," I said, wheeling Nastas toward the sound and kicking off.

The forest was thick, and Nastas had to maneuver carefully, picking his way on slim legs through a natural obstacle course of dead tree trunks toppled at weird angles, over brush and limbs and large rocks. I could hear Simon and Yas close behind. But Yas had surer footing in rough terrain and soon lunged around us, Simon urging him on. I tried not to think Simon was worried about what I might find if I got to the source of the whinnying first.

But soon there it was, in a clearing some fifty yards off.

It was Tse.

Riderless.

Her saddle was empty and slightly askew, as if it hadn't been cinched tight enough; the reins hung loose from the bridle. She stamped and whinnied again as we neared.

Simon was well in front then, and I could hear him murmuring, "Whoa, girl," as he got to her and reached from Yas's back to gather up the reins.

It was then that Tse—gentle Tse—reared up, lashing out with her hooves. It startled Yas, who reared up, too, then landed and bucked.

It wasn't a hard buck, but it caught Simon just as he was leaning to the side, off-balance, and pitched him to the ground. He landed with a cry of pain.

I dismounted and ran toward him. He waved me off.

"Get the horse," he said with a gasp.

I saw that Yas had turned to launch himself back through the brush, leaping and hurdling toward the track we'd just come from. Fleeing faster than I could possibly manage, even on Nastas.

"No!" Simon cried. "Get Tse!"

I turned in confusion toward Tse, who wasn't hurdling headlong anywhere, but standing almost motionless at the edge of the clearing. She appeared to be watching me.

I approached carefully, murmuring, unsure if she would rear up again. But this time she was her familiar gentle self. I took the reins and led her back toward Simon, who had propped himself up to a sitting position but seemed unable or unwilling to get up. I tied Tse's reins around a low branch and went to him.

"It's my leg," he said as I knelt down. "Twisted a bit. Not broken, though."

"Can you stand?"

"We can try," he said.

"Here—put your arm around me."

He slung one arm around my shoulders and pushed off with the other, and together we managed to get him back on his feet.

"Son of a—" he muttered with a grimace.

"Can you put any weight on it?"

"Not without doing some serious damage to your eardrums," he said.

"Hang on."

I left him balancing on his one good leg to search the ground for a branch straight and strong enough to bear his weight. When I found one, I helped him limp to a seat on a nearby boulder.

"Wait here," I told him.

"I'm not going anywhere."

I hitched a deep breath and walked deliberately to the edge of the clearing, nearest the spot we'd first seen Tse. I scanned the dark undergrowth for a flash of color, of pale skin glowing in the shank of tepid moonlight. Then I began to call Laurel's name.

I circled the clearing as I scanned and called. I heard nothing in return. When I ventured deeper into the woods, Simon called me back.

"You won't see your hand in front of your face in there," he said. "You'll only get lost. Then we'll need two search parties."

"You can't ride," I said. "And I can't just stay here."

He patted a spot beside him on the boulder. "Sit down," he said. "Let's think this through."

Even thinking seemed like a luxury of time I couldn't afford.

"I can't sit," I said, gazing almost longingly at the dark woods. "I have to do something."

"Then get me some coffee. Jessie packed some in your kit."

I stared at him, mutinous.

"Please," he said firmly.

Nastas was still under a tree branch I'd hitched him to, chewing on his bit. I dug around in the saddlebag and pulled out a thermos. I returned and tossed it to Simon.

"You can't understand," I told him as he caught it. "You've never had a child."

"True enough," he said.

"You can't—" I stopped short.

He couldn't possibly know—the guilt, the loaded gun with a hair trigger that always seemed trained on your daughter. And all you could do was try to keep her, if not absolutely safe, at least blissfully ignorant.

"I failed her enough," I said. "I won't fail her this time."

"I believe you."

"This . . . *Mountain* can't have her."

Simon gave a slight smile. "You talk about it like it's alive."

"I know—it's crazy."

He didn't answer.

"How rich," I said, suddenly deflated. "If all that time with Jim she never got a scratch, but a few months alone with her mother she ends up—"

"Here's an idea," Simon said abruptly. "Take Tse and give

her her head. Let her go wherever she wants. There's a chance she'll go back to where she left Laurel."

"Simon, there's an even better chance she'll head right back to the warm barn. Why would she take me to Laurel?"

"You might ask her to."

I shot him an angry look, expecting he was making light of an unspeakable situation. But even in the thin moonlight I could see he was dead serious.

Tse stood quietly while I readjusted the loose saddle and tightened the cinch. I lowered the stirrups to fit me. I leaned in close to where Tse could hear, but Simon, still seated on the boulder, could not.

"Come on, girl," I whispered. "Take me to Laurel."

I mounted up.

"I'll be back," I called to Simon.

"I'll be here," he said.

The climb began in earnest as Tse—the reins slack, no guidance from me—picked her own path up the Mountain. There were moments when, just as Simon had said, I could barely see my hand in front of my face. But Tse seemed to move as if she were on a mission.

As the way grew steeper, the trees began to thin out. They were mostly pine by then, and aspens with their slim white trunks and quavering yellow leaves. A half hour or more we climbed, till I was standing almost steadily in the stirrups and Tse was grunting from the effort. Soon her hooves began to slide out from under her.

I dismounted and led her to a young aspen, knotting the reins about its banded, chalky trunk. I patted her neck.

"I'll take it from here, old girl," I said.

Before I left, I took the signal pistol from the saddlebag and slipped it into my pocket. I had no idea where I was headed, only that Tse had tried to get me to some fixed point on the Mountain. She hadn't tacked back and forth to make the way easier. She hadn't turned and headed for the warm barn. She'd plowed on with what looked like purpose. And so would I.

The snowpack didn't start till much higher on the peak, but the air already felt glacial. I was panting from the climb, and my lungs felt chilled, too. The effect wasn't debilitating, but oddly bracing. On the ground, thin patches of snow glistened almost preternaturally bright in the moonlight.

What had felt before, from far below in the valley, like the magnetic tug of the Mountain had become at this altitude not just a *pull*, but also a *push*. As if now there were also a wind at my back, like an unseen hand.

But this time, I wasn't resisting. Not a whit. Not if it might get me closer to Laurel.

Suddenly I caught a flash of movement out of the corner of my eye. Something small and nimble darting through the trees. I turned toward the movement, and it was gone.

I held my breath and listened, and heard nothing but the rasp of aspen leaves.

Still, I'd seen something. I was sure of it.

I changed direction, heading toward the movement. It hadn't looked big enough to be a seven-year-old child, but then again, I hadn't caught a good, full-on look. And if it was a wild nocturnal creature, I expected to either flush it out or make it scurry off.

"Laurel?" I called tentatively, scanning the woods as I moved.

No response.

"Laurel!" I shouted, then paused, listening harder.

Snap.

I swiveled at the sound, and there it was again to my right, vanishing behind a giant ponderosa pine—a flash of what looked like fur. Four legs. A tail. It might have been a large raccoon, but for what looked like patches of white on its body. White fur, maybe. Or snow crusted to the animal's hide.

Either way, I could feel the hair bristle on the back of my neck.

As I stepped toward the pine, I stripped off my gloves and felt for the signal pistol in my pocket. I drew it out and switched off the safety.

The pine trunk was so big it would have taken two of me to wrap my arms around it. Its scaly bark was the color of oxblood in the dark and had that familiar faint scent of vanilla.

I rounded it carefully, eyes pitched toward the ground.

But there was nothing on the other side of the tree trunk. Nothing but a thin, crusty patch of snow. I knelt and looked closer. The snow was unbroken. No paw prints.

I glanced around. I had the uncanny sensation I was being led somewhere. Lured.

A copse of aspen trees, white and reedy as ghosts in the moonlight, lay up ahead, snow gleaming at their deep roots.

And there it was again among the trunks. A flash. White and dark together, in a quick, sylphlike movement.

Then it was gone.

My heart began to race, and it had nothing to do with the altitude or the thin air or the cold. Even under my wool sweater and my warm coat, the skin on my forearms was contracting painfully. My palms were so slippery with sweat, I had to rub my gun hand against my jeans to get a dry grip.

I knew—*somehow I knew*—there was something in those trees that I didn't want to see.

Just as I knew I had no choice but to see it.

This time the Mountain was no help. It neither pulled nor propelled me. It waited for me to choose to walk the thirty feet, then twenty, then ten to the stand of aspens, which clumped together almost protectively in a rough circle.

And inside that circle was a small dark shape curled on the ground, motionless.

The back was to me, so I couldn't make out the face. But I could see the hair—honey blond and splayed loose upon the snow.

My breath caught and held. Hot tears spilled down my cheeks. My mouth opened, but no sound would come.

I dropped to my knees beside Laurel and the gun fell from my hand. I reached out to stroke her soft, cold hair. Then her cheek.

And her cheek was warm.

Her skin was flushed with warmth. It felt hot against my trembling fingers.

I leaned close and saw the warm breaths puffing from her parted lips.

I moaned and gasped with relief, convulsing into dry sobs.

Between the sobs, I managed to gasp out her name again.

Laurel.

She stirred then, and yawned.

And then I saw it. What her little body had been curled

around. What her arms had been embracing as she lay fast asleep at the base of the trees.

A furred head popped up and blinked at me with brown eyes lined like Cleopatra's. It had foxlike ears, a white ruff and a lush caramel coat.

It was Tinkerbell.

Back Again

Laurel sat on the kitchen floor stroking Tinkerbell so tenderly it made me wince. Jessie had given the dog a little hook rug to lie on next to the warm stove. It was resting, eyes closed, its pretty, perfect head buried in its paws. A food dish and water bowl had been licked clean.

I sat heavily in a kitchen chair and watched them. All it had taken was three signal shots of the pistol to bring Olin and Faro, Reuben and his father right to the aspen trees. In no time at all. We'd gathered up Simon and Nastas on the ride down, and found Yas on the road, waiting right at the trailhead.

Laurel was none the worse for wear, despite a tumble from the loose saddle and a few hours in the cold. She was as unblemished, as unmarked, as the dog.

Wordlessly, Jessie brought me a cup of hot tea and squeezed my shoulder.

Dark Night

Olin worked the root vegetable beds. Jessie hung laundry in the thin autumn air. The dog would trail behind one, then the other. They both spoke to it, patted it, filled a water bowl for it from an outside spigot. It licked their hands gratefully. It stretched languidly, stealing quick naps in shafts of sunlight.

For whatever reason, it never came to me. Small favors. I couldn't look at the creature without reliving that wretched afternoon behind the shed all over again—the object lesson that broke the last of me.

For everyone else, something wonderful had happened. A little dog was lost, but now was found. Laurel said it even remembered the rollover trick she'd taught it last year.

The first night, and the next, I refused Laurel's pleas to let it sleep in her room. So when she begged the third night, I could tell by the surprise in her face that she wasn't expecting me to answer as I did: *yes.*

That night, Laurel bathed and dressed for bed. From the kitchen, I could hear the dog scramble up the stairs as Laurel took it to her room.

Hours later, when the house was dark and hushed, I dressed in jeans and a jacket and took my boots in hand. I tiptoed in stocking feet down the stairs.

In the kitchen, I eased open the catchall drawer and drew out a flashlight. Out the back door, I sat on the stoop and pulled on my boots. The moon was full now, and so bright I made my way easily to the barn, unlatched the door, slipped inside and waited for my eyes to adjust to the darkness.

Nastas nickered softly. I switched on the flashlight to make my way to his stall. He nuzzled my shoulder as I saddled him, then led him outside. I latched the barn door and mounted up.

The bedroom windows of the house were still dark, the curtains drawn. I nudged Nastas to a walk to the dirt road, then reined him south at a canter toward Morro.

We cast a long, loping shadow all along the road, the air so biting it made my teeth ache. The snow on the Mountain stretched halfway down its hulking side now, so deep that the serrated ridge at the crest could barely punch through. And still that burning beacon shone. Fixed and watchful.

As we hit town, we slowed once more to a walk, Nastas's hooves falling with a dull rhythmic *clomp.* I'd never seen Morro when it wasn't bustling with life. Now all its windows were dark or shuttered, but for a few random panes still softly glowing. Many were strung with orange Halloween lights and cutouts of witches and ghosts.

At the fork at the end of town, I took the smaller secondary road on the right and nudged Nastas back into a canter.

After a mile or so, just as before, the road began to climb through thick forest before leveling out again.

It was only then that it occurred to me Simon might not be awake by the time we reached his cabin. That he was surely in bed by now and sound asleep. Why wouldn't he be? He started work early. It was already past midnight.

I reined Nastas to a halt.

I pictured myself on Simon's porch, pounding on his door in the dark, Pal raising a ruckus. Then Simon blinking at me from the doorway, groggy and confused.

And then what? Asking him if this was a nice time for a chat?

Just ahead and still out of sight was the clearing where I knew his cabin sat, with the new corral and the orchard behind, the smokehouse and the little stable. An hour ago, this had seemed like a good idea. No—a *necessity.* Now it felt more like lunacy.

Nastas stamped hard, shifting to the side. He yanked his head, trying to turn us both around. He wanted to be back in the barn, in his warm stall. At that moment, there seemed no sensible reason why he shouldn't.

I patted his neck. "Sorry, boy."

I started to rein around, glancing one last time at the road ahead.

Wait . . . Had that glow been there before?

It was faint and seemed to be coming from the clearing on the left. I nudged Nastas forward.

As we neared, the glow grew more distinct. Brighter.

Then, as the trees began to clear, brighter still.

We broke the tree line into the clearing, and there was Simon's cabin. And there I could see where the light was coming from.

The oil lantern on the porch was lit, casting flickering shadows over the table and chairs there.

Something stirred in one of those chairs. A slim figure rose, moved to the porch steps and paused at the top.

My heart leapt. Had Simon been expecting me?

I didn't have to guide Nastas to the porch—he moved in all on his own. I jumped down, looped the reins around the saddle horn and let him loose. I knew he wouldn't wander far.

Nearer the steps, I could make out Pal sitting at the bottom, gazing calmly in my direction as if seeing me ride up in the middle of the night was nothing out of the ordinary. I moved past him and up the stairs. Simon was still waiting at the top, now with his hand outstretched. When I was close enough, I took it.

Then I burst into tears.

I couldn't tell how long I stood there, gathered in his arms, leaning into him, my face buried in his shoulder, shaking with sobs that I was both embarrassed and relieved for him to see. He didn't ask why I was there, or why I was crying. He just kept murmuring that everything was going to be all right, his lips now warm against my temple, now brushing my cheek.

It felt so safe, so lulling, I didn't want to pull away, even after the tears had subsided. If I could have pulled some lever then, releasing us both from time and space, I would have.

When I finally did pull back, wiping at my eyes and nose, the only thing I could say was, "You're not wearing a coat."

He shrugged. "I've got a fire going inside."

He paused as if considering what he'd just said. Then we both laughed.

"Come on in," he said.

This time there was no hesitation. The cabin had a great room with fireplaces on either side, one of them already lit and crackling before a deep sofa. On the opposite side was a dining table and chairs. In between was a stairway to the second floor.

Simon led me to the sofa, only the slightest hitch in his step from his fall a few days ago on the Mountain. An end table was set with a bottle of whiskey and two empty glasses.

"I was about to have a drink," he said. "Like one?"

I don't usually drink hard liquor and was about to tell him so. Then I realized that whiskey sounded exactly like what I needed. I pulled off my jacket and threw it over the back of the sofa before taking a seat.

"A small one."

He poured them both out, handed me the smaller, then settled in beside me.

"How's your leg?" I asked.

"Nearly good as new. How's Laurel?"

I sipped the whiskey carefully; it was bracing, not burning. "I've never seen her happier."

"You don't look happy about that."

It was an invitation to open up. All I had to do was take it: *No, not happy. Not happy at all. Here's why . . .*

"Why are you up so late?" I asked.

He gestured in the general direction of the meadow out back. "Checking up on Pegasus. He was restless tonight." His voice was low and familiar, perfectly pitched for firelight. "He isn't the only one."

Another invitation. I focused on the glass gripped in my lap. "I couldn't stay at the house tonight."

"Talk to me, Joanna. That's why you're here, isn't it?"

I drained the glass and handed it to him. "Can I have another?"

He smiled. "Irish courage, eh?"

"I'll take any kind I can get."

The refill he returned with wasn't as small as before. I had to down half of it before I was ready to begin. Even then it wasn't soon, and in little more than a whisper.

"That dog back in Laurel's bed right now?" I said. "It didn't just run away—that's only what I told her. That dog is . . . Jim killed it with a shovel. Made me bury it in the yard. I can't . . . I can't even bear to look at it. It's ghoulish."

I paused and glanced at him, but he said nothing.

"There's so much I don't understand," I continued slowly. "Olin has told me a few things. The rest he said I need to figure out for myself. But I don't know the rules." My voice began to rise. "I don't know what's real or not. *Who's* real or—"

Simon raised his hand, cutting me off. "Do you feel safe here?"

The question caught me off guard. "What?"

"Do you feel like you belong?"

I shook my head at him, still confused.

"Belonging can mean a lot of things," he continued. "As for me, I was born not far from here, on a little ranch my father built. This is where I grew up, so I know this country. This is where I *fit.* Where I want to be. This is new terrain for you, and I don't just mean the landscape. You're bound to have questions."

"New terrain . . ." I repeated. "Yes."

"You don't know how you ended up here, beyond me finding you wandering around lost, holding on to Laurel for dear life. You see things you can't explain. You sense things, but don't know how."

"Not everything," I said. "Laurel used to tell me she could hear the dog barking on the Mountain. Even when I couldn't."

"The dog," he said. "What else?"

He was coaxing me, guiding me. And at once in my mind's eye I could see the Mountain—the way it loomed over me that first day at the breakfast table, and every day since, urging me to come . . .

"That was no mistake," said Simon, and I knew he was seeing the Mountain with me, feeling its gravitation. "You were heading for it when I found you. Do you remember?"

I shook my head.

"It's got a will of its own, hasn't it?" he asked. "More intense at first. I've seen people traveling through and they're single-minded. They want to hike right to the top, and no mistake."

"Simon, I don't want to hike to the top."

He smiled. "You've got a will of your own, too."

"Free will . . ." I murmured. "Really? Even here?"

"Even here. Nobody brings anything here they didn't already have. The good, the not so good. The idea, as far as I can tell, is to keep *trying*."

"Trying what?"

"Not exactly clear on that one myself," he said with a small chuckle. "Maybe to follow our better natures till we get it right. Or maybe it's different for each of us. But the thing to bear in mind when Morro confuses or frightens you is that it's a community like any other. And the people here, they're just *people*. And you . . . you've got time to figure things out."

"How much time?"

He hesitated. "As long as you need to make a choice."

"You know about that, too."

"Yes."

"Olin told me—'Stay and get strong,' he said. 'Then decide.' Simon, did you have a choice? When you first came?"

His expression shifted. There was a fixedness to it—the mask was back.

"No, Joanna," he said finally. "Few people do."

"This is a good place," I said. "I feel like it fits me, too. Olin seems to think I should go back. And face my husband."

"Did he say that?"

"Yes. Well, no—not exactly. He said I should consider this like a Place of Truth for me. To think of the things I'd done. Or failed to. And what I'd do with a second chance."

"A second chance . . . sounds tempting."

"You don't understand. Neither does Olin. It would mean going back to . . . a monster. Jim wasn't just a rotten husband and it wasn't just a rotten marriage. *Even here* I've had nightmares about him. Laurel, too. She dreamed he was coming for her. She was terrified."

Simon was watching me steadily.

"Do you recall the day I found you?" he asked.

"I don't. Not everything."

"Try. What do you remember?"

I tried to oblige him. To dig deep. Like Bree when she was remembering the trucker who had hit her head-on as she drove back from a rock concert.

"We were on the way to Albuquerque," I said. "Running for our lives, really. Jim had threatened to kill me so many times. Even showed me how he'd do it. How he'd get away with it." I downed more whiskey, my hand shaking now. "I remember looking in the rearview at his police unit. The flashing lights. The siren."

Simon shifted on the sofa. His face was averted, but I could still make out the furious cast of it.

"Why'd you stay with him?" he asked.

"God, that's a cruel question."

"I'm sorry," he said. "Don't answer it."

But it was the obvious question, too. And now it was the bell he couldn't unring.

"Because it wasn't so bad in the beginning," I managed finally. "Because I did love him . . . once. Because I was weak. All of the above."

"Joanna—"

"Really, the first six months, the first year, it was great—or that's what I thought. And I wanted so much to make it work, even if I didn't have a clear idea how. I'd seen my mother fail at so many relationships, and I didn't want to live like that. Jim was like the ideal husband at first—charming, attentive, handsome. So when things started to go bad, I thought it was *me.* That I was doing something wrong. Failing somehow. I thought all I had to do was change *me* and everything would be all right again.

"By the time I realized what was really going on, it was too late. I was alone, cut off. He had me trapped and wasn't about to let go. Till death do us part . . ."

I tipped my glass in toast, but didn't drink. Simon took my free hand and held it.

"It's all right," I assured him. "That's all over. He'll never do anything like that again. I'd kill him first."

The words were out of my mouth before I realized they were ever in my head.

And I meant every one.

"Oh, God," I said. "Does that shock you?"

He smiled. "Honestly, Joanna, it would take more than that to shock me."

"That's good. Because if Jim is unfinished business . . ."

I hesitated, and Simon waited for me to continue.

"This thing with Jim, a part of me knows it's not over," I said. "I get the feeling, even as I'm sitting here, that I'm still running. Sometimes when I try, I can almost feel the hard rocks under my feet, the dry wind on my face—I'm literally *running*. And I . . . I don't know how to stop."

Simon squeezed my hand gently.

"And to think I came here to talk about Tinkerbell," I said.

"Aren't we?" he asked.

"Simon . . ."

"All right—Tinkerbell. Is she the same dog you remember?"

"To the smallest detail."

"And this dog was up there on the Mountain, sticking to your daughter when she was alone and scared."

"But not in danger . . ."

"There are real dangers here, Joanna. Not always the kind you expect. So Tinkerbell stuck right with her. Till you came to the rescue."

I shook my head. "No . . ."

"That's right. Till you rescued them both."

Rescued them both. Hot, grateful tears sprang from nowhere. "Yeah," I said wryly. "I was the cavalry riding over the hill."

"Hey, now. That's just the booze talking."

I laughed, and he smiled back. The whiskey was bolstering me, true enough. Its warmth was soothing. But it wasn't only the drink.

Suddenly, as if for the first time, I was aware of Simon's nearness on the couch, and it seemed to unstitch me. He was so close I could feel his breath on my face as he spoke. So close that, if I leaned toward him, I could kiss him without any trouble.

The image was so clear in my mind that I could feel the heat rise in my face. I also found myself wondering if he was entertaining any such thoughts about me.

As if in answer, Simon slowly, purposefully turned my hand over in his grasp. I couldn't help but stare in fascination, as if his hands were disembodied things, acting independently of the man they were attached to.

His fingers traced their way lightly, slowly, along my palm. A thrill surged through me far stronger than the whiskey. Then he brought my palm to his warm lips, kissing the places where his fingers had just been.

I wasn't sure I could speak even if I wanted to. His lips felt branded on my skin.

He took my glass and set it on the table, then drew me to my feet. Then he drew me into his arms.

He didn't try to press or persuade. I could feel his lips move like a caress over my cheeks, my closed eyes. Then they were on my mouth, kissing me over and over . . . And once more I was leaning into him, and his arms were around me, pulling me to him, to his beating heart.

His lips slid to my neck, the stubble on his cheek scraping my skin. When they moved back again to my mouth, I wrapped my arms around his neck and pulled him tighter till he sighed deep in his throat, still kissing me, and drew himself up till my feet left the floor.

I'd never felt so giddy, so breathless. His body against mine was a foreign country, but at the same time as familiar as the bay rum I could taste on his skin. As if holding him were the true muscle memory, and every moment that had ever come before only a waste of body and soul.

Forgiven

I raced the dawn back to the farmhouse that morning. The house was still asleep as I slipped Nastas back into the barn. I stripped off his saddle and set it back on the railing. He returned of his own accord to his stall, and I swung the door closed; it latched with a click.

I stood in the yard and watched the sun crest, wishing Simon were there to see it with me. Leaving him had been hard, even knowing I'd see him again soon at the café.

But before I got ready for work, there was something I had to do.

Inside the house, I returned the flashlight to its drawer and climbed the stairs again in stocking feet. From the top landing, I didn't head for my bedroom, but for Laurel's. Her door was ajar, a night-light glowing in an outlet near her headboard. I stepped inside and heard a rustle on the bedding. A small, furry head popped up near her pillow, peering in my direction, followed by the rhythmic thump of a tail against the quilt.

I could hear Laurel's deep, regular breaths before I was close enough to brush stray streaks of hair back from her face and tuck the quilt close. Her forehead was cool when I kissed it.

As I straightened, the tail thumped more energetically. I skirted the bottom of the bed to where the dog still lay—she was stretching a bit now, dark eyes blinking, tongue darting nervously in and out. As I approached, her head sank to her paws and she burrowed into the covers as if she wanted to disappear.

As gingerly as I could so as not to wake Laurel, I sat on the bed, then drummed my fingers against my leg. Tinkerbell leapt to her feet at the signal and climbed into my lap, her tongue licking at my face. I stroked her soft coat and scratched at the base of her ears. Felt the firm muscle and bone beneath my fingers, the pulse at her throat. She curled up in my lap, her fox tail wrapped around her body, and sighed.

I leaned down and kissed the top of her head, then buried my face in her fur.

"I'm sorry."

Kindred

"I learned about the Big Dipper when I was a little girl," I said. "The Little Dipper, too. The Seven Sisters."

"Mmm," Simon murmured sleepily.

We were stretched out together in a sleeping bag in the field next to his cabin. I adjusted my head on his shoulder, the better to examine a million brilliant stars in a perfect black sky.

"The Seven Sisters are a star cluster," I explained. "Pleiades. Look at them straight on and they're just a blur. But look off just to the side and you can make them out. Peripheral vision. I figured that out when I was a kid."

"Show-off," he mumbled, stroking my hair.

"It ain't braggin' if it's true." I could feel the rumble of his chest as he laughed. "But no matter how hard I look," I continued, "I can't find the Big Dipper anymore. Or the Little Dipper. Or the Sisters. I haven't seen them since I came here."

Simon's laughter faded. "Does it bother you?" he asked quietly.

"Would it make a difference if it did?"

When he didn't answer, I raised my hand, gesturing overhead. "So tell me about *these* stars."

"That's easy," he said. "Those over there? That's the Spatula. And those? Ten-Gallon Hat. And those five grouped together over that way? Bluebeard and His Wives. But you have to squint and cross your eyes at the same time or you can't see them right."

"Ass." I tucked my arm back inside the sleeping bag, nestling against him with a shiver.

"Sure you don't want to go inside?" he asked.

"No. This is nice. You cold?"

"I'm fine. I've been colder."

"Tell me."

He paused. "A long time ago. Winter. A forest in Germany."

"Ah. One of those trips to far-flung places? Was it beautiful?"

"Used to be."

His tone was light, but there was a finality to it. Like a door closing.

"So, tell me more about when you were a little girl," he said. "Did you have pigtails?"

"Pigtails?" I laughed.

"Sure. The kind boys dip in inkwells."

I raised my head from his shoulder to gape at him. "Inkwells? Just how backward was the school system when you were a kid?"

"We were lucky to have slate boards and chalk. We rode dinosaurs to school."

I kissed him. "Poor boy."

"If I tell you about the outdoor privy, do I get another kiss?"

"Don't you dare." I kissed him again, this time lingering. When I raised my head again, I stroked the hair springing from his temples.

"How'd you manage to stay a bachelor so long?" I asked.

"It takes commitment."

"Seriously. Meg's been married for a while. You must have had . . . other opportunities."

He ran a finger lightly down the bridge of my nose to my lips.

"I didn't want opportunities. I was waiting for you."

"Stop it. I'll believe every word you tell me right now."

"You should." His hand was cupping my cheek, his face solemn.

I nestled back on his shoulder. "Tell me something you've never told anyone before. From when you were a boy."

"Let's see. There was the time my dad and I were driving back from Santa Fe. On Rural 14, through Madrid. A coal town."

"Used to be. They're turning it into an arts colony now."

"Hey, who's telling this story?"

"Sorry."

"Anyway, it got dark and I fell asleep in the front seat. Next thing I knew, my dad was shaking me awake. He wanted me to see the moon."

"The moon? I think I like your dad."

"It was a full harvest moon, on the night of the autumn equinox. Hanging so low over the piñon pines you could almost reach out and touch it. So we sat there on the ground, backs against the truck, drinking Nehi Wild Reds till the moon went down."

"That's a nice memory."

"I remember something else, too."

"What's that?"

"I remember the Big Dipper."

Night Chill

A dull *thunk*, like an ax splitting cordwood.

Spasms of exquisite pain . . .

I woke in my bed with a moan, my hand flying to my skull. To ward off, to stanch—I wasn't sure which. It took a while for the throbbing to go away.

Nightmares had been coming on more often lately, although when dawn came I could remember them only in snatches. Sometimes vague impressions lingered, like a bad taste in the mouth or a heaviness of spirit. But by breakfast, I was usually myself again.

I was learning to see them as clarifying. Like visions that focus the mind. Giving it direction.

But that night, as the pain ebbed, something else took its place. Like a voice, but not quite. It was giving me direction, too.

Get up, it urged. *Get up*.

I did as it told me. I opened my bedroom door and headed down the hall.

Laurel's door was cracked, her night-light glowing. I stepped inside and there she was, asleep in bed. She was curled on her side, peaceful, both hands tucked under her chin.

Tinkerbell was there, too, but awake and crouched protectively against Laurel's back. The dog was growling low, a relentless rumble deep in her throat, her white teeth bared. It shocked me, until I realized Tinkerbell wasn't looking at me.

She was looking at Jim.

Jim was standing over Laurel's bed. Or, at least, some version of him was. There was no real substance to him, nothing to equate flesh and blood. The form was there, with all the right lines in place, but it was colorless, translucent.

I stepped into the room, and Jim turned toward me. His movements were slow and impassive. His face a blank, an abyss. A beam of light slanted steeply through the bedroom window. Not the moon—there was no moon that night. The light had to be coming from the top of the Mountain. And it glinted off an object in Jim's hand. Long, flat, tempered steel. Machete.

A cold, contained fury erupted inside me.

Jim turned again, back toward Laurel, and Tinkerbell snarled and half rose to her feet, primed for attack. I moved then, too. It was only a few steps to where he stood, and I was on him in an instant.

I overtook him in midstep . . .

. . . and he dispersed like fog gusting from dry ice, until there was nothing to grapple with but a clammy chill.

Just like that . . . he was gone.

Into a Fogbound Moon

The night before the birthday party for Reuben's brother came the first snow of the season. We had a dusting just after Thanksgiving, but it didn't last long. This time the snowfall was four inches at least, and it stuck. It was even deeper on the Mountain, where the Begays lived, so we had to get there on horseback.

That morning, Olin and I saddled the horses while Jessie buttoned and zipped Laurel into warm boots and a parka. Tinkerbell had built up a thick coat for the winter, but I wasn't sure if her paws could handle the trail higher up, so I slung an army blanket across my saddle in case she needed to hitch a ride.

We packed up the birthday gifts. I wasn't sure what a sixteen-year-old boy might like, but Liz LaGow had assured me a fleece-lined hackamore was just the thing, because the main present from the boy's family was to be a saddle horse.

As I mounted up, I tried not to stare at Jessie, who was wearing belted woolen trousers—so different from her usual matronly attire that she seemed almost a different woman. Olin winked at me before he gave Jessie a leg up. Jessie reined the pinto into a fast clip toward the road.

"She's a firecracker on horseback," Olin said admiringly. "Even did some barrel racin' as a girl."

"What's barrel racin', Opa?" Laurel asked as Olin swung her onto Tse's broad back.

"That's expert ridin', Bunny." He tucked her boot into the stirrup. "I'll show you come spring."

He swatted Tse's flank as Laurel dug in with her heels, and the big horse took off after Yas, who had slowed to an easier pace toward town. I waited for Olin to mount up; then we cantered after the others, Tinkerbell loping behind.

The broad avenue through Morro was strung with pretty plastic snowflakes—huge ones that lit up every night now. Garlands of ivy and red holly berries were wrapped around each lamppost. Doors and lintels were hung with evergreen wreaths and swags decorated with pinecones and fruit, ribbons and bows. Inside the gazebo was a Christmas tree with handmade ornaments.

We headed past homes where kids were scraping together snow to build snowmen. Others were sliding down the foothills on wooden sleds. Past the Wild Rose, the general store, Schiavone's, the library, the pub. The town hall, according to the sign out front, would be showing *It's a Wonderful Life* this weekend. It didn't strike me as ironic.

Just outside Morro, we bore to the right to climb into the forest on the access road. The snow was still a dry powder, so the horses kept their footing with ease.

I glanced at the spreading snowcap overhead. Ever since that night when I'd found Laurel and Tinkerbell, the Mountain and I seemed to have reached an understanding. Maybe it had lost interest in me and loosened its grip. Or maybe the prospect of getting caught up in its orbit had lost its menace. I'd made my peace with it—like going from a bone-jarring beginning to finding the right rhythm at last.

At Simon's cabin, Pegasus was corralled out back pacing the fence. He'd filled out into a powerfully built animal—nothing like the emaciated creature I'd seen that first day.

But in front of the cabin was a handsome bay I'd never seen before. Simon was snugging the saddle cinch as we approached.

Tinkerbell raced ahead and onto the porch, stretching out beside Pal. Laurel called out, waving her arm like a flag, and Simon returned it. He was wearing a brown cowboy hat and sheepskin coat.

"I'll see if he needs any help," I said, leaping from Nastas's back.

"Fine, fine," Jessie said. Then to Laurel: "Why don't we ride 'round back and visit Pegasus?"

As I headed toward Simon, I watched the three of them disappear behind the cabin.

"Mornin', cowboy. Need some help?"

"Always."

He leaned over as I moved in for a kiss; then another. "You're beautiful," he murmured.

"Your nose is cold."

"You know what they say: 'Cold nose, warm heart.' "

"That's 'Cold *hands*, warm heart,' " I said.

"In that case, I'd better get these off." He was pulling at his gloves.

"Stop that!" I grabbed his hands with both of mine. "You'll freeze."

He tugged me to him. "With you here? Not a chance."

Olin's voice rang out: "Don't forget the saddle, Simon! The boy'll be disappointed if you do."

He and Jessie and Laurel were returning. Simon patted a large lump wrapped in a thick blanket strapped tight behind his saddle. "Right here!"

"Best get started, then," said Olin. "It's a ride."

The Begay ranch lay on the other side of the Mountain. The access road would take us to it, cutting around the Mountain rather than over. Laurel rode ahead with Simon. She had always taken to him, from that first night he came to dinner; perhaps that's why she seemed to accept our being together now without hesitation or fuss. He was pointing out the places he'd gone hunting or fishing as a boy, or where he and his uncle hunted mushrooms or dug up sassafras roots to make tea.

"What's sassafras?" she asked.

"A tree," said Simon. "Deer eat the leaves and twigs, and rabbits eat the bark in wintertime."

"What's it taste like?"

"You like root beer? It tastes like that."

She gave him a look that said she didn't just fall off a turnip truck. *"A root beer tree?"*

He reached for his canteen. "Here," he said, unscrewing the cap and passing it to her.

She took a sip. "It's a little like root beer," she said. "But no bubbles. It's warm, too."

"Like it? Then drink up."

In time, the road hit a steep incline, which the horses took at a slow, methodic pace in snow that was well past their fetlocks. When the road leveled off again, we were high up on the Mountain's south side, breaking free of the forest and overlooking a deep, sweeping valley so spectacular it took my breath away.

I reined in. The others did the same.

The late morning sun hit the slope at an angle that made the snow shine as if every inch were dusted with crystals.

And moving along the deep slope were bison—hundreds and hundreds of them, massive and shaggy, pawing at the ground, blowing out steaming breaths like bellows. Tinkerbell and Pal began to bark, but the bison ignored them—all but one great bull that raised his huge horned head, his muzzle white with rime ice, and heaved a huge snort. The dogs quieted.

Along the valley floor, a river was whipsawing through. Scattered along its banks were buildings of various sizes and shapes. You could smell wood smoke from chimneys and fire pits.

"And over there," said Olin, pointing to the opposite slope, "those are Begay's sheep. Some of 'em, anyway."

A faint jingling noise erupted farther down the mountain road, growing louder by the minute. Finally I could make out a red sleigh on runners, drawn by a horse with silver bells on its harness.

We sidled closer to the Mountain to make way for the sleigh to pass. Seated inside was a woman in a silver fox coat and hat and a man in a wool overcoat and Russian-style fur cap. They were rosy cheeked and giddy, and the woman waved and called as they passed: *"Gruss Gott! Wie geht's?"*

I sputtered after them: *"Gruss Gott—gut, danke!"*

Then I burst into laughter. "Who on earth were they?"

"That looked like Santa's sleigh," said Laurel. "But that wasn't Santa."

"No, sweetie, that wasn't Santa," said Jessie. "Santa's busy at the North Pole this time of year."

I wouldn't have contradicted her.

By the time we made it to the ranch on the valley floor, it was past noon. Morgan Begay met us as we rode up and directed some of the many children on the premises to tend to our horses as Simon unhitched the bundle.

"I'll show you where to put that," Begay said, gesturing for us to follow. A few curious children trailed after us.

He led us to a long stable that was nearly empty; his main herd was out to pasture. Begay nodded toward one of the stalls. "What do you think?"

As we neared, a head popped up and slung over the stall gate. It was the prettiest pinto I'd ever seen: a quarter horse with dark brown and pure white markings, brushed and curried till he glowed like polished wood.

Laurel stretched up to touch the horse's muzzle; he dipped his head so she could reach. "He's beautiful," she said. The children who'd followed us inside giggled.

"Think my son will like him?" Begay asked her.

"I think so. What's his name?"

"The horse? His name is Shilah. It means 'Brother.' My son's name is Trang."

The name of his son didn't surprise me. Simon had already explained that Trang wasn't Navajo, but Vietnamese—an adopted son. But he hadn't said how he'd come into the family.

"Tell me," Begay asked Laurel. "Have you ever seen a sheep up close before?"

When Laurel shook her head, Begay said something in Navajo to the children nearby.

"They will show you around, if you like," he told her. "Show you the cook shed, too, where the food is."

"Go have fun, honey," I told her. "I'll find you later."

Then Laurel and the children were gone, the dogs hard at their heels.

"I could do with some mutton stew myself," Olin said.

"Up to the house, then," said Begay.

The main house was large and rambling and stood out from the smaller structures on both sides of the river. Some of those structures were more modest homes and trailers; the rest were work buildings, barns or sheds.

There was also a hogan on the far slope, distinct for its rough, round shape. I'd seen them before on the reservation, but had never been inside one. I knew they were traditional Navajo dwellings of wood and mud, usually with six or eight sides. By tradition, the doorway faces east. Some Navajo still lived in them, but in more modern times they were usually used only for ceremonies.

Begay led us on, past empty sheep pens and corrals, past a volleyball net strung between two bare trees where teenagers lobbed a ball back and forth.

At the main house, we were hit with a wave of warmth and noise as Begay led us into rooms packed with people. The aroma of roasting meat made my stomach growl. Olin followed Begay to the food table, while Simon disappeared with our coats.

"Jo!"

Bree was moving toward us; she gave me a quick hug, then did the same to Jessie. "You made it! Met the family yet?"

"We just got here," I said. "I wouldn't know who's family and who isn't."

"Darlin', they're *all* family."

"All?"

"That's the clan system—everyone's your brother or your sister, your auntie or uncle, grandmother or grandfather. That's why you're not allowed to marry someone from your own clan—too close for comfort. Lucky for Reuben, I came along, huh?"

"Wedding all set, honey?" Jessie asked.

"Every bit of it. Just show up and have fun. Less than two weeks from now—can you believe it?"

Actually, I couldn't. Back at the quilting bee, I wouldn't have believed we'd still be here by now. That Laurel would be thriving like this. Or me.

"Come on," said Bree. "I want you to meet the newest member of the family."

She led us through the crowd to a small bedroom where a handful of young people had gathered. In the center of the room was a lean, angular man whose age I couldn't begin to guess. His wire-rim glasses made him look collegiate, but there was silver in the long black hair flowing down his back, bound loosely at the nape with a leather cord. He was cradling a newborn in the crook of one arm, rocking from side to side. Reuben was standing with him.

The baby began to fuss, and the father broke into a song that seemed half lullaby, half chant as he bounced the baby lightly in time to the music. By the end of the song, the baby was calmer, staring at his father with a frown of concentration.

Bree approached them with a smile, then motioned Jessie and me closer.

"This is Samuel, and he's brand-new. Yes, he is. Yes, he is!" The baby gripped her forefinger in a tight fist.

Jessie patted the man's shoulder. "Fine job, Jasper," she said.

"Want to hold him?" he asked.

Jessie held out her arms and Jasper eased Samuel into them. She handled the baby with a midwife's efficiency. There was warmth in her face, but I could detect an ache there, too.

This was, after all, a moment she and Olin had never been able to share. It reminded me of what she'd said when they'd first taken us in: *A ready-made family.*

Bree moved next to Reuben, who pulled her close. She hugged his waist, her thumb looped through the belt of his jeans.

"Jasper," she said, "tell them about the ceremony."

"Which one?"

"You know—the baby's-first-smile ceremony."

"Well," he began, "the Diné believe that when a baby's born he's still of two worlds: the spirit people and the earth people. So we wait to hear the baby's first laugh. That's when we know he's made the choice to leave one world and join the other."

The choice to leave one world and join the other . . .

For a second, Jasper's words rattled me.

"Then there's a party, with gifts," Bree was saying. "And people bring plates of food so the baby can salt it—why is that again?"

It was Reuben who answered: "To show a generous spirit."

"And how does a tiny little baby manage to put salt on food?" I asked.

Jasper held up his thumb and forefinger, barely an inch apart. "With a tiny little saltshaker."

We laughed, and Jasper took Samuel's walnut-sized fist

and waggled it gently in a pantomime. "Actually, with a little help from his father or mother."

Simon appeared at my elbow with two bowls of mutton stew. "He could start right now, if he likes."

"Don't rush him, Simon," Jasper said with a smile.

Simon handed me one bowl and offered the other to Jessie. She waved it away as she handed the baby off to his father.

"I'm off to find that man of mine," she said. "You two youngsters enjoy yourselves."

Simon led me to the back of the house, where there was a screened porch warmed by a wood-burning chiminea next to a sofa. We sat to eat, spreading a wool blanket across our laps. Through the screen we could see the river snaking past, and the earthen dome of the hogan. We could hear the faint sound of drums and chants.

"They're doing a Blessing Way," Simon explained, nodding toward the hogan.

I'd heard of the ceremony. "They do that for expectant mothers," I said.

"For others, too. Someone who's sick, for instance. Or a warrior going off to battle. Sometimes they hold one because it's been a while and it seems like a good idea."

"Who's this one for?"

He hesitated. "This . . . is to restore balance," he said vaguely. "Health. Strength."

"Did they have one for you, when you went off to war?"

He paused again.

"Not before I left, but when I came back," he said. "It's a different ceremony, though, when you come back. Called the

Enemy Way, and it's more . . . intense. Lasts about a week. It restores balance, too, but first you have to drive away the ugliness, the violence, of battle. Chase off the ghosts of men you've killed."

As he went quiet, I reached for his hand. "Whenever you're ready," I said, "you can tell me anything."

"I know, sweetheart. But not yet."

There was a movement in the doorway, and Reuben and Bree entered.

"How's the fire?" Reuben asked. He hiked up the sleeves of his sweater and laid a small mesquite log inside the wide mouth of the chiminea. Then he and Bree sank into nearby chairs.

"We were just listening to the chanting," I said. "Is it for your brother?"

"The Hozhooji ritual," said Reuben. "It should last a while yet. It's for him and . . . whoever might need it."

He was gazing at me frankly, his dark eyes suddenly unreadable, and it flustered me.

"For little Samuel, then," I said. "Who's his mother?"

"That would be Emmi, my sister."

"Actually," said Bree, "Emmi would be his cousin. But in the clan system, they're brother and sister. Or might as well be."

"Add it all up," I said, "and it makes for one huge family."

Bree laughed. "A real tribe."

"So," said Simon, "is Trang happy about the pinto?"

"Picked him out himself," Reuben said. "From Great-Grandmother's herd."

"He's got a good eye," Simon said.

"He's a long way from Vietnam," I said. "How did he come to be in your family?"

"Quite a story, actually," said Reuben. "When he was little, he lived in a village with his parents. Straw huts, the whole deal. One day his older brother took him fishing, and while they were gone soldiers came through, shot up the place, torched it. Killed his parents. Trang was six or so."

"God. The poor kid," I said.

"That's only the half of it," Reuben said. "After a few years, they made it to the States. His brother got a job on a shrimp boat off Louisiana and they lived there awhile. Then one day his brother was out in the Gulf when a big storm blew through. Swept him overboard."

"Did they find him?"

Reuben shook his head. "Lost at sea. Trang waited a week till the coast guard gave up the search. When the food and money ran out, he packed up one night and hit the road."

"Where did he think he was going?" I asked.

"West. He heard once that he had an uncle in San Francisco—it was all he had to go on. He walked, slept under overpasses and bridges. Hitched rides with truckers when he could. Some of them bought him meals. Then one morning my sister Angela—"

"*Cousin* Angela," Bree murmured.

"Angela," Reuben continued, smiling, "was tanking up at the truck stop—you know, the big one outside Grants—when she saw this skinny, scrappy kid thumbing a ride. She picked him up and brought him back here. It was supposed to be for a meal and a bed, then send him on his way in the morning. But the family took to him and he took to us. So he just . . . stayed."

"He must be resilient as anything," I said.

"He's having the time of his life now," said Reuben.

. . .

It was near dusk by the time the birthday gifts were presented. As the big family crowded outside the stable, I tried to pick out Trang from among them, but couldn't.

Teenage boys came running from the direction of the river, jostling and laughing; they were among the group we'd passed playing volleyball when we'd arrived.

They pushed one boy forward—smaller than most, skinny and dark, his glossy black hair shaped in a bowl cut, black brows arching over almond eyes. He grinned up at Morgan Begay, standing at the stable door.

So this was Trang.

Begay gestured for the boy to come closer, then spoke to him. I couldn't understand the words. Then Begay turned and entered the stable. He returned leading Shilah, by then decked out in a handsome silver-tipped leather saddle and full tack, including my hackamore.

I was surprised, though, to see the pinto's white mane and tail covered with dozens of streaming bows of colored yarn. He looked like a rainbow on the hoof. Laurel was standing nearby with Olin and Jessie, beaming.

With others calling out encouragement, Trang stepped to the pinto's side, slipped his foot in the stirrup and pulled himself into the saddle. He kicked off and the horse vaulted forward. Off they rode—down toward the river, then along its banks—hooves throwing up hunks of snow and mud.

Laurel ran to my side. "Did you see my ribbons, Mommy?"

"Honey, I don't think you missed a single color."

"You know," Simon told her, "that's the way they deck out their horses for special ceremonies. Then they all mount up and ride across the valley. It's a sight."

"When's the next one?" Laurel asked him.

"Don't worry—you'll see it."

A waning moon was rising, fogbound and hugging the Mountain. The stinging smell of wood smoke intensified as fires lit up along the riverbank. Laurel took my hand, then Simon's. We headed across the compound, taking our time, toward a white trailer where Begay had said a birthday cake was waiting for the kids.

The trailer door was wide-open, spilling yellow light and the voices of children. Trang sat at a kitchen table facing a big white cake with candles. A gold party hat was strapped to his head. Someone placed a toddler in his lap, and he slid a steadying arm around her.

"You two go on," I said. "I couldn't eat another bite."

Simon looked back quizzically as Laurel pulled him toward the trailer.

"Really, I'm fine," I insisted. "I just want to enjoy the quiet."

I found a seat on a tree stump near a stand of junipers. There was a fire crackling a few yards off, with three men hovering over it watching a skillet of meat and fry bread on a grill. Now and then the burning wood spat out a spark in a soaring arc that was hypnotic to watch.

I turned to the trailer again and the children playing inside, loud and giddy. Each of them had a story like Trang's; I was sure of it. Only—God willing—not so tragic. Stories that were cut short. They looked happy enough, all of them. But how many would choose to stay here, and how many would take up their stories again, if only they could? And Laurel . . . on her next birthday, would she be just as happy here in Morro? Would she turn eight years old, or would she be seven forever, here in the forever place?

That first day at breakfast, Olin had told me I still had something to accomplish. Laurel, too. He'd seemed so certain . . .

"It's the violet hour, isn't it?"

I started at the voice—female, coming from behind me. I turned, and there was a dark shape next to a juniper tree—a shadow within a shadow—not ten feet off. It shifted, apparently to reposition itself in a better light so I could make it out.

It was Jean Toliver, cocooned in a woolen blanket from neck to ankles.

"I didn't startle you, did I?" she asked.

"Well, no."

"Good. I always do like the dusk—don't you? I like to greet it alone when I can."

"Ah," I said, finally getting the drift of her remark. "Eliot's violet hour—'The evening hour that strives homeward, and brings the sailor home from the sea.'"

Jean rose from her seat and moved closer, settling on a fallen log. She drew her blanket over her head.

"Not quite," she said. "I was thinking more along the lines of DeVoto."

I wasn't sure if she was referring to a person or a car—the name meant nothing to me.

"Sorry?"

She turned toward me, and I could see the flames from the grill fire dancing in the round lenses of her glasses. She reminded me of an owl.

"Bernard DeVoto. Historian and author. 'This is the violet hour,' he wrote. 'The hour of hush and wonder, when the affections glow again and valor is reborn, when the shadows deepen magically along the edge of the forest and we believe that, if we watch carefully, at any moment we may see the unicorn.'"

Her voice was tremulous.

"That's lovely," I said. "A poem?"

"A cocktail manifesto. Would you like some?"

The blanket rustled and I looked down. She was holding a small silver flask, half buried in the folds. She put a warning finger to her lips. *"Shhh."*

I choked back a laugh. If the Navajo reservation was dry, apparently Jean would make do.

The flask was etched with Celtic knots. I uncapped it and took a sip. It went down with a scouring that made me shiver.

I handed the flask back to her. "What is it?"

"Rye whiskey," she said, stealing a quick sip before recapping it and tucking it back in the folds. "Chilled."

She murmured the last word primly. Then together we burst into snorting giggles that drew the attention of the men around the fire.

"Too much of that and you *will* be seeing unicorns," I whispered.

"Wouldn't that be charming?"

"And yet a unicorn wouldn't be the strangest thing I've seen since I came here."

"New place, new rules," she said.

"Excuse me?"

"I think the most important thing when you're a stranger in a strange land is to try to enjoy it while you're there. Besides, the farther back you go, there are no strangers, are there?"

I began to wonder how long she'd been tippling from that flask.

"Come, Joanna. You've noticed it—I know you have." Jean was nodding meaningfully at Trang, still framed in the open doorway. She waited.

She was trying to herd me toward something. But what?

I looked at Trang. At the toddler in his lap. At the faces of the other children gathered around the table. What was I seeing? Except for Laurel, nothing but dark eyes, dark hair on dark heads. Nothing unusual. I looked from one face to the next, sifting through . . .

Till I realized: this was precisely what Jean was talking about.

Nothing unusual.

Aside from Laurel, the faces were nearly indistinguishable from one another. Southeast Asian . . . Diné . . . hair, features, skin . . . so similar . . . so familial.

Cousin, kin, clan.

Jean sighed with pleasure and shifted on the log.

"Athabascan," she murmured.

I reached back to my U.S. history lessons and dredged up what I could about Athabascans. Crossed from the Asian continent thousands of years ago. Their descendants became the Inuits in Canada. Then much later some turned south and migrated again—latecomers, compared to other tribes. And their descendants became the Apache, Hopi, Zuni—and the Navajo.

"They crossed the Beringia on foot," said Jean, still watching Trang. "Followed the migrating bison south along the Rockies. They retain so much of the look of their Asian forebears, don't you think?"

In my mind's eye I could see with utter clarity what she was describing. The slow southward progression of clans at the end of the last ice age. If you stretched back far enough, Trang and the Begays could easily share common ancestors.

Unlike those first immigrants, of course, Trang didn't cross the land bridge into Alaska. He rounded the globe from a different direction entirely—to connect through sheer happenstance with cousins a thousand generations removed.

Millennia of separation until—a homecoming.

"It wasn't an adoption," I murmured. "It was a reunion."

"At any moment"—Jean nodded, uncapping her flask—"we may see a unicorn."

We were back in the great room saying our good-byes before heading out when Jessie led me toward the kitchen.

"Let's pay our respects to Begay's grandmother. She's old as they come, and all this"—her hand circled in the air—"all this is hers."

I knew the old Navajo tradition was matrilineal, and it was daughters who inherited livestock and land. But I didn't know it was a custom still followed.

The kitchen was crowded with women talking animatedly in English and Navajo. Seated in a chair against the far wall was a petite, wizened woman, her white wisps of hair twisted into a traditional bun. She wore a red velvet blouse cinched at the waist with a sash, a black skirt to her ankles and soft deerskin boots. Slung over her shoulders was a simple gray blanket with stripes of white and black. The lines of her face were so deep-set, they didn't seem so much the wrinkles of age as the fissures of natural erosion.

She turned in our direction as we paused in the doorway. Then she said something in Navajo and beckoned us closer, her face breaking into a delighted grin, her thin lips parting over teeth almost too white, too perfect. She watched as I approached, her brown eyes probing mine . . . just like Olin at breakfast under the oak tree.

"Yuhzhee," said Jessie as the room quieted. "This is Joanna."

Slowly, deliberately, Yuhzhee raised a wrinkled hand, stretching to touch my face. I had to bend for her to reach. Her fingers were thick, the tips as worn as weathered wood.

I'd never been around someone of such great age before. Jessie and Olin were old, certainly, and my Oma had been in her seventies when she passed, but this woman felt . . . ancient. She didn't seem weighed down by the years, but buoyed by them. Weightless as a cornhusk doll. Or a carving out of cottonwood root.

She said something in Navajo, and I shook my head. "I'm sorry—I don't understand."

I peered about the room for someone to translate, but no one seemed inclined to do so. Finally, a young woman stirring a pot on the stove spoke up:

"She said you shouldn't be here."

I pulled away from Yuhzhee and straightened. Shouldn't be here? I might be a newcomer, but I wasn't a stray cat scratching at their door.

"I was invited," I said stiffly.

Jessie laid her hand on my arm, shaking her head as if I hadn't understood.

"No," the young woman continued, not unkindly. "You're a welcome guest. She means there's somewhere you need to be. Something you need to do." She shrugged. "This is not a bad thing."

The old woman was urging me closer again. And again I leaned down, if more reluctantly.

This time, Yuhzhee fingered a lock of my hair, examining it curiously. She said something and the women in the room burst into laughter. I glanced around in confusion.

The young woman at the stove spoke up again. "She says you have pretty hair. The color."

My hair? Pretty? I never imagined I'd ever hear that compliment again. Especially from a Navajo grandmother in deerskin boots.

And then, of all things, Jim's snarling face flashed in front of me, hurling insults, threatening worse. The man might be invading my sleep or appearing like an apparition in night visions, but this felt different. This felt like an ambush.

Habit alone should've had me bracing for impact. For the familiar surge of panic to freeze me in my tracks.

Instead, I felt prepared. Strong.

My hands of their own volition curled into fists.

Slowly I straightened, Yuhzhee's eyes locked steadily with mine, and behind them I sensed a message she was trying to convey. A question, awaiting an answer.

I felt ready.

"Can you tell her I said thank you?" I said.

The old woman needed no translation. She nodded and gave me another pearly, perfect smile.

Have You Ever Heard of Little Orphan Annie?

Simon and Laurel were at the edge of the woods, cutting evergreen boughs for the mantels. I could see the two of them through the side window—Laurel pointing out the branches she preferred and Simon tackling them with a pair of loppers, then stacking them in the snow in a growing pile. It had snowed for real last evening, and Simon was wading knee-deep in powder that came up to Laurel's hips. Now and then, if she seemed to struggle in a drift as they moved from tree to tree, Simon hoisted her over his shoulder like a sack of grain, her long toboggan cap of red and green swinging down his back as he cleared a path. I could hear her peals of laughter from here.

By morning, the snow clouds had blown off to the east,

leaving behind a radiant blue sky and snow so blisteringly white it stung your eyes. Another shiny day.

Simon's cabin was already filled with the scent of pine from the blue spruce—an eight-footer we'd cut that morning and set into a cast-iron stand in the living room—and the wild turkey that was roasting in the oven.

I was sitting in the middle of storage boxes, rummaging through lights and ornaments to decorate the tree before dinner. I pulled out tangles of green cables strung with round bulbs. I peeled tissue paper from glass ornaments—balls of every size and color, stars with long spires and tails. There were delicate bird nests, toy soldiers, carousel horses, a tiny cuckoo clock.

At the bottom of one box was a cardboard container the size of a board game, orange and yellow, stamped with a green Christmas tree. It looked well used, but still in good shape. The printing on it read, *Cartoon Character Christmas Tree Lights* and *Made in Japan.* The design was outdated, antique. On the lid were drawings of each character and its name. Some I recognized—Dick Tracy, Betty Boop, Little Orphan Annie, her dog Sandy. As for the rest, I had no idea who they were. A bald man in a black vest and red tie named Andy Gump. Another man with a feckless expression named Moon Mullins. A surly boy in a blue-brimmed hat, his arms crossed, named Kayo.

I lifted the lid. Each figurine was in its place, like eggs in a carton. The paint was bright, but so roughly done it had to have been done by hand. And not very artfully, either. These figures looked like something a child would treasure, not a grown man.

I got up and peered through the window again. Laurel was

loading the cut boughs into Simon's waiting arms, higher and higher, laughing as he pretended to buckle and stagger under the weight. She saw me watching from the window and waved, still laughing. When had I ever seen her laugh like that?

Simon spotted me then. He stopped staggering and stood up straight, dropping the branches in a heap as he waved, too. Laurel cried out in dismay and began to scold him.

I went back to the box with the cartoon character lights. I picked it up again, brushed off the lid, then placed it at the foot of the tree. They could be a family heirloom, passed down from father to son. Simon could have found them in the general store, or special-ordered them. Maybe they were a gift from a friend who appreciated vintage things, and discovered them tucked away in some old shop.

But I knew none of that was the case. I knew those cartoon lights were Simon's. That, when he was a boy, he'd helped string Little Orphan Annie and Smitty and Kayo around his family's tree. That it was an experience close to his heart, a warm memory he'd carried with him since.

The way today would be for me.

The stamping noise on the front porch meant they were back with the evergreens. They burst through the door, and Olin, who'd been napping on the couch, sprang up to take the boughs and carry them to the fireplace, exclaiming how fine they were, while Laurel and Simon pulled off their boots and hung their coats on pegs by the door.

Simon padded over to me in thick wool socks, blowing on his bare hands to warm them. He was windblown, his cheeks ruddy. His tan was faded enough that a sprinkle of freckles showed through.

"Brrr. The frost is really biting today." He embraced me

from behind as I looked the tree over, and laid his cold cheek against my ear.

I rubbed his arms. "It got your nose pretty good."

"I think we even spotted Jack Frost in the woods out there. Isn't that right, Laurel?"

Laurel was at the fireplace with Olin, holding her hands to the fire.

"Jack Frost isn't real," she said. "That was a rabbit."

"Was it a *jack*rabbit?" Olin asked, his mustache twitching.

She pulled a face at him. "Ho, ho, ho."

Jessie called out from the kitchen. "They back yet? There's hot cocoa for those who want it!"

I turned and gave Simon a quick kiss. "You guys go on. I'll stay here and do the bough thing."

As Simon passed by the fireplace, Laurel planted herself in front of him and raised her right arm high. "Let's show her the fireman's carry," she said.

"The what?" I asked.

In answer, Simon leaned down, grasped Laurel's raised arm and swung it behind his neck. When he stood straight again, Laurel was slung around his shoulders like a fur stole, giggling, while Simon held her right leg and arm with one hand, anchoring her in place.

"The fireman's carry," Simon said before turning to head toward the kitchen.

Laurel's head popped up from his shoulder, her hair swinging. "They use it to rescue people," she called as they disappeared through the door.

Their low voices carried from the kitchen as I arranged the evergreens and pinecones on the mantels—the one in the dining area and the other in the living room. I'd found rolls of gold satin ribbon in one storage box, and cut and tied them into bows, placing them here and there among the boughs. I stood thick beeswax candles at either end of the mantels, and lit them. They smelled like honey.

I stepped back and studied the effect. Simple, but not plain.

Laurel padded out from the kitchen, a mug in her hand. "This is yours, Mommy." It was almost too hot to drink, but not quite. Exactly the way I like it. Topped with tiny, melting marshmallows.

Laurel stood in front of me facing the fireplace. She took my free arm and wrapped it around her, holding it with both her hands, which were warm now. I marveled at how much taller she seemed. As if she'd sprouted inches since the summer. I leaned over and kissed the top of her head.

"It looks happy," she said quietly. "I don't think I've ever seen a happier fireplace."

We'd never decorated a mantel for Christmas before, so I didn't doubt it.

"Me, either."

She tipped her head back to peer up at me. "I like it here."

"Really? What do you like about it?"

"I like Oma and Opa. I like Simon and the dogs. The horses." She paused, lowering her head again to look at the fire. "And I like you. You're not like back home, scared all the time."

I drew a deep, steadying breath.

Out of the mouths of babes . . .

So. Despite all my efforts, I hadn't been able to shield her. Not from everything.

Not from me.

"You used to be only two colors. Maybe three, on good

days," Laurel said, as if she were drawing me in crayon. "Now you're all of them."

I couldn't speak for a moment. And I couldn't disagree with a single word.

"I think . . . I think that's the nicest thing anyone's ever said to me. Thank you."

She tipped her head back again. This time she was smiling up at me.

"You're welcome."

I leaned over and kissed her again. "Want to help with the tree?"

We started with the strings of lights. Before long, Jessie, Olin and Simon came from the kitchen to join in, Jessie ordering Olin about to make sure the lights were well distributed around the tree.

The last string to go up was the one with the old cartoon figures. I handed the box to Simon. He stared at it thoughtfully, moving his hand slowly over the characters on the lid as if he weren't standing in that room anymore but in another one, at another time. A smile flickered. When he looked up again, I was still studying him, seeing the boy he'd been and the man he'd grown into. I reached to brush his cheek. He caught my hand as I pulled it away, and kissed it.

Then he turned to Laurel, who was fingering the yarn manes of the tiny carousel horses. "Look, Laurel," he said, holding out the box for her to see. "Have you ever heard of Little Orphan Annie?"

When every ornament was in place—every shiny ball and spired star, every wooden soldier and nesting bird—we stepped back, waiting for Simon to plug the lights into the outlet. Right before he did, he warned us that the strings were old, that if a light had burned out since last year it could break the circuit for an entire string. Maybe we should have tested them first, he said, before we went and put them all up. I wasn't sure if he was trying to lower our expectations or build the suspense. Probably both.

He plugged it in and the tree lit up at once. No light had burned out; no circuit was broken.

"Whoa," said Laurel.

"Wait till the sun goes down," Jessie said, making a small adjustment to an ornament. "Then you'll really see something."

It was time to set Simon's little table for dinner. Jessie spread a damask cloth and handed Laurel linen napkins to roll and slide into copper rings. I took the white plates she'd stacked on a kitchen counter and began to space them around the table.

When I was finished, I noticed something was off.

"Jessie," I said, puzzled, as she set a basket of cutlery on the table. "There's an extra plate here."

"Is there?"

"We're five, not six." I took up the extra plate.

"There's six napkins, too," Laurel said, counting them off.

"My, my," Jessie said absently. "What was I thinking? Well, just set 'em aside."

Finally Jessie called everyone to supper. Pal and Tinkerbell trotted out from the kitchen and slipped under the table.

The turkey was a deep golden brown, with cherry and chestnut stuffing, set on a platter of roasted vegetables. Laurel leaned into it before she took her seat, and sniffed.

"Can't wait," she said.

"You have a biscuit, honey, to keep you," said Jessie.

Simon took on the turkey, dismantling it as efficiently as if he did it every day.

"I do appreciate a man who knows his way around a carving knife," Jessie said.

"Then, ma'am," said Simon, "what you need is a short-order cook."

He was serving up the turkey slices when I heard it: a distant rumble that seemed uncannily familiar.

And utterly out of place.

It was so faint I thought I might be imagining it. No one else seemed to notice.

Until it came again—a faint roar now, but growing louder.

"Does anyone else hear that?" I asked.

Simon, Jessie and Olin exchanged glances. Laurel closed her eyes, frowning in concentration. The roar was growing even louder, coming even closer, until it was clear it was a powerful engine heading toward the cabin.

Laurel dropped her fork on her plate with a clatter. "It's the lady!"

She pushed off from the table and raced to the front window, wiping condensation from the glass to stare down the road.

The lady?

It couldn't be, could it? Here? Now? After all this time?

I left my chair to join Laurel at the window, wiping at the glass, too, staring out in disbelief. The road was empty, still packed with snow from last evening, lined with bare deciduous trees and bottom-heavy firs. Anyone trying to make it up this mountain in anything with tires and a motor, let alone a motorcycle, would have to be crazy as a wildcat.

So, yes, I thought: *Bernadette.*

In another moment, we saw her, her Harley breaking through the forest road at the edge of the clearing, moving steadily but not fast, tires skittering and sliding in snow that nearly buried them. It had to take considerable skill to keep the bike upright and plowing through two feet of powder.

"Oh, my God," I murmured as I watched her finesse it.

She still wore her black leather jacket with the zippers and studs. She had on black snow pants that, at the moment, looked more snow than pants, and her red bandanna was replaced by a red scarf. She had on black Oakley sunglasses—the wrap-around kind that mercenaries wear in Hollywood movies.

My mind raced, questions flying. What was she doing here? How had she found us? *What does this mean?*

With a last, snarling burst, the bike slid into the driveway behind Simon's pickup. The rear wheel sprayed snow in the front yard just as it had kicked up grass and dirt when she'd peeled out from the house in Wheeler that day back in June.

She checked out the cabin, adjusting her sunglasses. Then she dismounted and set the kickstand.

There was something else new: a leather saddlebag strapped behind her seat. She opened it and lifted out a small drawstring bag that looked filled to the brim. She slung it over her shoulder like a biker-chick Santa and headed for the porch.

Laurel ran to open the front door. Her eagerness astonished me. She'd seen this woman just once, months ago, and so briefly. She couldn't have known what Bernadette was doing at the house that day.

Or could she?

Bernadette stomped her boots on the porch mat as Laurel held the door wide-open for her. Then she stepped inside. She pulled off her sunglasses and looked me up and down.

"Good God, Jo! Look at you! You clean up fine!"

She was just as tall, just as striking, just as imposing as the first time I'd seen her in the Javelina Saloon, when the crowd had parted for her like the Red Sea for Moses. With the red scarf around her head and earrings of tinkling silver coins cascading to her shoulders, she was like some gypsy Amazon. I embraced her like a long-lost sister.

When I let go, I brushed the tears from my eyes.

"Hello again, *niña*," Bernadette said to Laurel. She pulled the drawstring bag from her shoulder and handed it to her. "Here—why don't you take this? Go ahead and take a peek—there's something funny inside."

Laurel set the bag down and pulled excitedly at the drawstring. She drew out a present wrapped in glossy yellow paper topped with a bow. She stared at the gift tag, then up at Bernadette.

"It's got my name on it," she said.

"See, that's the funny thing—I got these from a guy in a red suit on the way up here. I thought they were for me, but then I peeked inside and saw your name, so I thought I'd bring it by."

Laurel turned to me. "Can I open it?" she asked.

"Honey," I said, "Christmas is still a couple weeks away."

She screwed up her face, girding for battle. A spoiled evening was only a tantrum away.

"All right," I relented. "But just this one."

She tore at the wrapping as I made the introductions. Then Bernadette pulled off her jacket and boots and set them by the door. She unzipped her snow pants and stepped out of them to reveal slim black jeans.

"You'll stay for dinner," Jessie said.

I retrieved the extra plate and napkin Jessie had set out

earlier; now I understood why she had. I filled the plate to overflowing and set it before Bernadette.

Laurel's gift was a book: *Charlotte's Web.*

"I liked it when I was a kid," Bernadette told her. "Of course, all I could tell you about it now is it's about a pig and a spider."

"It's perfect," I said. "Laurel will love it."

"Hey, *niña,*" said Bernadette. "Why don't you go see what else Santa put in there?"

Laurel ran back to the bag, pulling out more gifts. "Mommy! There's a present for Simon, too. And Oma and Opa. And one for you."

I looked at Bernadette questioningly. She arched her eyebrows at me, then mimed locking her lips and throwing away the key.

I scanned her smiling face, searching for answers—how had she come here? did she know what Morro was?—but afraid of what I might find. Comprehension was trying to settle in, but I was beating it back.

Laurel ran to the table to pass out the rest of the presents, and Bernadette insisted they be opened at once. Simon's was a Leatherman knife. Olin's, a pipe of polished sandalwood. And Jessie's, a pair of fine kid gloves, dyed a deep scarlet.

I wasn't sure Jessie would approve of such a brassy color, but her eyes sparkled as she tugged one on, stroking the soft leather.

Bernadette shot me a look that seemed to say, *Every lady needs a little red in her life.*

Finally, I turned to mine—a box wrapped in silver with a silver bow. But as I began to unwrap it, Bernadette placed her hand over the box to stop me.

I looked at her in surprise. Her face was solemn. When she spoke, her voice was pitched low, for me alone.

"Not now. Open it before you go to sleep tonight."

How odd. I couldn't fathom why. But without a word I set the box on the floor by my chair.

Olin held up his pipe, admiring the slim black stem and the wooden bowl shaped like an old-fashioned corncob. "I'll break this in after supper," he said. "I thank you, Bernadette."

"Use it well," she told him. "And you can call me Bern—suits me better." She licked the tip of her finger with a hiss: *"Tsssss."*

Olin laughed.

"Where you from, honey?" Jessie asked, still wearing her scarlet glove. "Your people from around here?"

"Nope. Cuba. Not the island—the town north of here." She took a bite of cherry stuffing and moaned. "*This* is delicious. Did you make this, Jessie? Good God. For this, you deserve a little red hat to match those gloves. Think I'm kidding? Just wait—next time I come through."

Color sprang to Jessie's cheeks. "Have some more—there's plenty."

"My family has a sheep ranch outside Cuba," Bernadette continued, her nose wrinkling in distaste. "I grew up on boiled mutton, mutton stew, lamb stew. I lived with sheep, played with sheep, wore sheepskin and slept under it. Hell, till I was five, I thought I had a fleecy tail."

Laurel giggled.

"I got outta there when I was fourteen," Bernadette said. "A wild child—not that you can tell." She winked at Olin. "As for my people, they go back to the conquistadors, the Towering House Clan and the Irish Potato Famine. A real pedigree, huh?"

"Towering House?" Simon asked. "Our friends the Begays are part of that clan. One of them is getting married day after tomorrow."

"Mazel tov," said Bernadette.

"I mean, I'm sure they'd like to have you. Unless you have somewhere to be."

Bernadette set her fork down, frowning in thought. "Well, I was planning on a bike trip . . . *Whoa* there!" She leaned back in her chair, lifting the tablecloth and peering underneath. *"Hello,"* she said.

I'd forgotten Tinkerbell and Pal were still under the table, eager for scraps.

Bernadette looked at Olin. "You have dogs?"

"A couple."

"Good. No cause for alarm, then." She took two pieces of turkey from her plate and tossed them under the table. "Here ya go."

Simon rose from his chair and gave a low whistle. Pal darted out, Tinkerbell close behind. He gestured to a blanket by the fireplace, and the two dogs settled onto it, licking their lips.

"Sorry about that," Simon said as he took his seat again.

"No harm done," Bernadette said.

"Well, if your trip can wait a bit," I said, "why not come to the wedding? It's only two days. At the hotel in town."

"The big red one? I'm staying there tonight."

"Stay a couple more nights, then."

"Well," she said slowly, tapping her lips with a black-lacquered nail. "I guess there could be diversions." She glanced at Olin. "How's that saloon I saw on my way through? And the pub? Either of them disreputable?"

"No, no," he said reassuringly.

"Well," Bernadette drawled, shaking her hair back till her earrings tinkled like bells. "They will be when I get done with 'em."

Bernadette didn't stay long after supper—night fell early, and she wanted to make it back to the Wild Rose before then. We made plans to meet at the pub the next evening—there was so much I had to ask her, to tell her.

In the living room by the fire, Laurel settled on the couch between Jessie and Olin to read *Charlotte's Web* to them. Simon and I were in the kitchen washing the dinner dishes, the radio on the counter playing Christmas music. Sometimes we sang along, making up the lyrics we couldn't remember.

Before long, we'd saddle the horses and ride back to the farmhouse. Tomorrow, I'd help Bree finish up the hotel ballroom for the wedding. Simon would open the café early, and Jessie would help out for a few hours. The schoolhouse was on winter break, so Laurel would tag along with Olin at the farm.

In my mind's eye, I could see the day play out. And the day after that, and the weeks, the years after that—stretching like an unbroken winding road toward a chosen horizon.

I swished my hands in the warm water, staring down at the suds. Simon was at my shoulder, drying plates with a dish towel. I could feel his eyes on me.

"What do you see?" he asked.

I turned to him, blinking to clear my head. "Hmm?"

"You're staring so hard, like at a crystal ball."

"I don't believe in fortune-telling."

"No?" he said. "What do you believe in?"

I almost smiled, but the magnitude of what I believed at just that moment was too sobering. As were the consequences.

"Choices," was all I said. I pulled the rubber stopper in the sink and the water began to drain with a sucking sound.

His towel froze for the merest second. "You decided, then."

The window above the sink looked out on the meadow behind the cabin. In the dark, the trees had disappeared except for the snow coating their limbs, etching them in white.

"I can't tell you how much I love this place," I said. "But you know that." I turned to him. "Laurel, too, because here she has people who love her. Protect her. That's something I didn't do."

He moved toward me. "Sweetheart—"

"No, please. Let me finish." I took a step back, away from him. "I've been offered a rare thing, right? You said it yourself—not everyone gets a second chance, so there must be a reason. These things can't be random, can they? At the Begays', the birthday party, Trang turning sixteen . . . I think about Laurel, and what I want for her is *real* birthdays. Growing up, growing older. Learning about the world, making her way in it."

"That can happen here," said Simon.

"I'm sure. In its way. But it would always be . . . an imitation, wouldn't it? No—an *echo*." I shook my head. "No, that's not right, either—at least an echo begins with the real thing. She hasn't had that. She never will. And *she* had no choice in this. Any of it. This was . . . forced on her. Because *I* failed to make the right choices back in Wheeler."

I paused, struggling to untangle a knot of feuding emotions. Simon waited for me to continue.

"And Jim. He won't let us alone—not even here. He's invading this place, our dreams. It's like we're *fused* somehow. Or maybe we're bringing him with us because we can't let *him* go. I even saw him one night in Laurel's room—or a vision of him—standing over her while she slept. You said there are risks here—even here—remember? I'm her mother. I'm supposed to protect her. Maybe I do that by going back and getting it right. Doing what I should have done, or just doing things differently. Maybe that's what Olin meant. Maybe that's my truth."

Simon was watching me as if he was dealing with his own feuding emotions. I willed him to move, to speak, but he didn't. Or wouldn't. Above all, I didn't want to leave him. Didn't want to disappoint him. And I didn't want the three feet of empty space between us to turn into a chasm that couldn't be bridged, ever.

I moved to him and wrapped my arms around his waist, burying my face in his shoulder, holding on for dear life. The tears started, dampening his shirt.

After a moment, Simon coaxed my head up and brushed the hair from my face. He kissed the tears on my cheeks.

The truth was, I might not understand Morro—its physics or how we ended up here—but I did understand it was a sanctuary for us. But sanctuaries aren't forever—that's their nature.

"I told you I fit here, and I do," I told him. "I fit with *you*—I've never been more sure of anything. But not like this. Not . . . yet."

He kissed my lips, then leaned toward the radio and turned the dial.

"You asked me once about my favorite song," he said.

"And you said one day you'd tell me."

He stopped on a ballad, low and slow. A woman's voice. An old song from when crooning was popular.

His arms were around me again, and we began to sway to the music. The song was from the 1940s, but I knew it. Redone . . . how many times? It made me think of Manhattan nightclubs, swing bands and cigarette smoke, tear-filled good-byes at train stations, soldiers shipping off to war half a world away.

I pulled back just enough to look into Simon's face. And at last I saw none of the guardedness he could slip on like armor. No careful neutrality. His eyes shone the deepest grays and blues, and his whole heart and soul were in them.

"This isn't good-bye," I said. "I'm coming back."

"I know," he said. "I'll be here."

At the farmhouse, Laurel was tucked into bed, Tinkerbell curled beside her. Olin had ducked outside to the kitchen stoop, stealing his last cigarette of the day.

I stood outside on the porch, hugging my coat around me.

There was a slim fingernail of a moon. Not enough to cast shadows or illuminate much. I stared up at the Mountain, lying as quiet and still as a great hibernating beast. It was completely blanketed in fallen snow that filled and tempered its deep ravines and blunted the long, rocky ridge along its crest. It wasn't watchful anymore, or even restless in its sleep. The point of light near the crest was faint now and for the first time it was flickering, like a flame about to go out.

Behind me, Jessie opened the front door and stepped onto the porch. She was already in her thick bathrobe, her bun undone for bed, her gray hair plaited down her back. She stood beside me, silent, her gaze following mine to the mountaintop.

"This was a good day," I said softly.

She slung her arm around my shoulders and squeezed.

"There'll be more, sweetie."

. . .

In my room, I dressed for bed and turned out all the lights, save for the one on the nightstand. I sat in the rocking chair and held Bernadette's present, with its shiny silver wrapping, in my lap. It had a familiar shape and heft. For a long moment I stared at it, then began pulling at the paper.

Long before the paper was torn away, I recognized it.

It was my old tea tin. The secret one from the house outside Wheeler where I kept my Life Before. The one I hid from Jim under a loose floorboard in the storage space under the stairwell.

And it should still be there—on Insurrection Day, I'd done exactly as Bernadette had told me, and taken nothing from the house. Not even this.

I opened the tin and, one by one, pulled them out: The first-place certificate from the high school poetry contest. The clinic receipt from the baby I'd miscarried. The letter from my mother. The warning note from Terri.

They were gathered on my lap, as familiar to me as my own face. Except this wasn't my face anymore. The features might be the same, with the same curve to the cheek and jaw, the same coloring. But there was a different woman behind them now, looking back.

I stared down into the tea tin and saw something else. Something that wasn't there before. Had, in fact, never been there.

It was a small piece of white paper, folded and lying at the bottom. I picked it up and smoothed it out.

The handwriting was familiar, too. It was my Oma's, and it contained a single word: *Mut.*

Courage.

Part III

What Is Past, or Passing, or to Come

What if you slept? And what if, in
your sleep, you dreamed?
And what if, in your dream, you went
to heaven
and there plucked a strange and
beautiful flower?
And what if, when you awoke, you
had the flower in your hand?
Ah, what then?

—Samuel Taylor Coleridge

Rattlesnake

black bitter tang of copper gravity wrenching me down down down slammed against hard rock screams shards of glass twisting inside my skull screams

Laurel

eyes don't open don't open but then they open on red on red on red everywhere red my hand inches from my face red fingers twitch on red rock twitch like dying animal inches from my face

blink and blink eyes blur sting with red and salt and wet and warm running in the sockets

Laurel

pulsing roar in my ears push and push can't move rock won't let me go let me go rock *move move move* let me move twitching fingers hand jerks hard pushes out pushes away dead air rock won't let me go

let me go rock

Eyes close tight no screams now no screams. *Laurel.*

Lungs spasm, hurt, buck for air. Shuddering breath rolls into me, throws me onto my side. Temple, shoulder, hip scrape warm sandstone. Eyes open, red rocks everywhere—above and below and beside and forever.

Blink hard against the blur. Against the sun. Against skull full of nails shredding my brain.

And there's Laurel.

Dangling weightless, little cornhusk doll, from Jim's upraised fist, over the mesa's edge.

Laurel, back in her summer clothes of many colors. No parka, no snow, no trees, no valley, no farmhouse. Only mesa, sun, heat.

And Jim, his back to me. In his summer uniform, shiny oxfords, Sam Browne, just like that day in June when we last saw him.

In his other hand, the machete, slick with blood.

Something more than human strength surges in me, my limp arm twists, limp hand flops to my side, palm flat, to push off.

At last the rock lets me go.

Struggle to my feet, teeter like an old woman, head dangling, wet hair sticky on my face. Shake my head and the ends of my hair rain down splatters of blood everywhere. One step forward, then another and another toward Jim, who stands there beguiled by the power he has over life and death.

Another step, another. My foot stubs against a rock. Pale gray, not red like the others, but gray like Olin's fieldstones. I stoop, fight for balance, pick it up, feel its heft, its potential, another step, another.

I'm behind Jim now, so close I smell sour sweat, see it stain the back of his shirt along the spine, the armpits. My stomach heaves. My hand curls, clamps around the rock. The other reaches out, loops fingers through the rear strap of his Sam Browne. I yank with all my weight, pulling him with me, back from the brink. Laurel is still in his grasp, and he stumbles backward, struggling to keep his feet, legs pedaling like crazy.

As he hangs there, off-balance, he sees my face, my fist, the rock coming at him, and for a second I see it register in his eyes—the disbelief, the betrayal, the gall—before I bring the rock down hard against his head.

It sounds like an ax hitting cordwood. *Thunk.*

He hits the ground with a groan, face contorting. He loses his grip on Laurel and she falls on the ground in a heap. I lose my footing and crash down next to him. Something snaps in my wrist; pain shoots up my arm.

Jim rolls away from me, his hand flying to his forehead. "Mother*fuck*!" he mutters, sits up, dazed, swaying, blinking at the blood on his fingers as he pulls them away. He looks from his fingers to me, and his expression shifts. His dark eyes now as cold and empty as twin coffins. They move from me to the machete, dropped near the edge of the mesa, a few feet away.

Still fixed on it, he leans forward to stand back up, slow, methodical, like there's a job to do and no particular hurry to do it.

But as he leans in, bracing to stand, I swing the gray rock

again, wide and for effect, and it's as if he's moving right into the blow, in profile. I wonder that he didn't expect I'd put up more of a fight. It hits his handsome Roman nose and I can hear, can feel the cartilage crunch underneath. Blood spurts from his face, down the front of his police shirt, sprays on my forearm.

I pull back and hit him again. His face is averted now and the rock hits his cheekbone, just below his right eye. *Crack.* He falls back, his eyes roll, and in an instant, with a strength and speed from no earthly source, I straddle him, pound his face, his head, over and over and over. He catches and grips my injured wrist till I think he'll wrench it off, and white-hot pain convulses my body. My teeth sink into his fingers till I feel bones break. He screams.

"Bitch!"

And still I hit him, hit him, hit him, till his own face is blood, pulp, not Jim. Till I don't have the strength to strike even one more blow. Till he stops moving.

I roll off and kneel panting on the ground, light-headed, fighting nausea, fighting for breath. Then I straighten and let the bloodied rock go.

I crawl to Laurel and feel for a pulse at her throat. It's faint and rabbity. But it's there. Her face and arms are full of scratches, from the tumble or from Jim, but otherwise she looks whole. I close my eyes, roll on my back beside her, lungs heaving, push sticky hair from my face. The wet is still running down my scalp, seeping into sandstone. My body, too heavy to move now, wants to sleep.

A whisper, an echo, low and urgent, coming from nowhere, from everywhere, coming from the rock, calling me.

Joanna.

It doesn't want me to sleep, wants me to move move move again. I blink up at the sky, blue as a cornflower, but with a bank of gray clouds moving in fast.

I roll onto my good arm. It pushes me up till I'm sitting beside Laurel. We need to move. With my wrist, my head, I know I can't carry her, so I call to her, a croak, from tongue dry as dust, "Laurel, please wake up. Please."

She moans; her eyelids flutter but don't open.

I look around me, not sure for what. I don't know where we are, how we got here. Only that we're somewhere in the red rock mesas east of Wheeler. That somehow we went from winter to summer in a heartbeat. That Laurel and I are both dressed in the same clothes we fled Wheeler in, back in June. Miles of empty in every direction.

I push to my feet, totter to the edge of the mesa. I see the four-lane interstate below in the desert, in the distance. Now and then a car, a truck, speeds along. Getting there is our best hope.

I stagger to Laurel, kneel down to pat her cheek, my blood dripping onto her chalky skin, try to wake her, but can't. There's nothing for it. We have to get out of here. I have to stop the blood. My good hand shakes as it works the buttons of her blouse, undoing them one by one, then strips it off her, down to her yellow camisole. The sleeves are long, and I use them to tie the blouse around my head like a gypsy scarf, knotting it with my good hand and my teeth.

I pull Laurel up, nearly toppling under the deadweight of her limp body. I crouch and grasp her right arm, loop it around my neck. Then slowly I straighten, holding her slung around my shoulders in a fireman's carry.

I stand for a long time, head throbbing, to judge if I have

the physical strength for this. To climb down off the mesa carrying Laurel on my shoulders. One slip and we could fall. I could kill us both.

I turn and look at Jim, lying there motionless, arms flung out at his sides in some sort of surrender, face pulped, blood pooling beneath his head.

Then I turn away and start to walk.

I skirt the edge of the mesa till I find what looks like a steep, narrow trail going down. Maybe this is how we climbed up to begin with. It hardly resembles a real hiking trail. More of a goat track cutting between boulders.

I stare down at it and my vision blurs, fades to a sick gray. A buzzing grows in my ears; bile rises again in my throat. I close my eyes and will my vision to return, my stomach to settle.

Desperate, I appeal to the powers that be: *If I have a concussion, let it do its worst. So be it. But not yet. Not yet. Not till I make it to the highway and flag down help.*

Gradually, my head begins to clear. I shift Laurel on my shoulders and start down the track.

One small step, then another. Feet slide on loose gravel. Focus, focus, pick out a path. I miss a turn, hit a crevasse, turn, a boulder blocks the way, miss another turn, dead-end into a wall of sandstone, turn back, turn again. Focus, focus. I don't know how, but I keep to my feet. I pause for breath, steady myself against a boulder, rest, close my eyes.

A small stone pings against the boulder, inches from me, bounces off and hits the ground, tumbles ten feet down the path. I open my eyes and stare at it.

"I see you."

The voice is Jim's. It's Jim's, but it sounds off. Like he has a head cold and can't breathe right through his nose. It's coming from above, to the left.

I drag my eyes from the stone and turn to look. He's standing on an outcropping not forty feet away. A perfect vantage point to see the trail, right down to the bottom of the mesa. To see us. To see me.

He stands there, looking down, head cocked. Wipes at his face with his shirttail, then drops it.

"I'm coming."

He turns and disappears.

Adrenaline hits me, launches me from the boulder and back on the trail. No more small step, small step, but lunges down and down. Still I know I can't outrun him. Not even if I were whole and healthy. As I lunge, I glance around, frantic for a place to hide out, to foil what's coming down the trail after us. To regroup.

Finally I see it. A tangle of small boulders and rocks, seven, eight feet high. A small opening at the bottom. Panting, I move to it, kneel down too fast and Laurel slips from my shoulders. I catch her with both arms, wince from the stabbing pain that shoots from my bad wrist. As I catch her, her mouth gapes; her eyes flicker open. She looks at me, fazed, tries to register what's happening. I lay my finger against her lips. Her expression freezes. Her mouth clamps shut. No explanation needed.

I lean over and peer through the opening in the rocks. It's dark, but I can make out a space inside. Just big enough for us to crawl through.

I push Laurel through first. She digs in with her elbows and pulls herself inside. Before I do the same, I glance around again. Nothing in sight. Then I crawl in.

It's cool and dim, the hole just big enough for both of us to sit up. I hug Laurel against me with my good arm. Ready to clamp my hand over her mouth, if I have to. She's trembling, heart rabbiting faster than ever. I know she can feel mine doing the same.

For what seems like far too long, there's silence. No footsteps, no gravel shifting underfoot. I begin to wonder if Jim took a wrong turn, ended up on some other track, lost his way.

But no.

"I see you."

The voice is close. Nasal, and singsong. Like he's playing a child's game.

I squeeze Laurel against me. Whisper in her ear: *"Shhhh."*

If he can see us, he can see us. If not, the bastard's just trying to flush us out.

I won't play.

"You stupid bitch. If I can get Bernadette, you think I can't get you? She was ten *times* the woman you are. And it was easy. *Easy.* Knock-knock. Who's there? Payback, baby. Vengeance is *mine.*"

Payback? Vengeance? What's he talking about?

"You think I wouldn't find out? Put it together? I'm a cop, you idiot. It's what I *do.* I know it was her. At the house today. Must've been right after I left for work. Munoz calls me, tells me you're gassing up the car. Or *trying* to." He's chuckling. "Only there's a little problem, huh?"

The voice is moving, to the left of us, to the right, then back again. Hunting us down.

Laurel shifts, her hand groping for something in her pocket.

"Like I wouldn't find out. Like I wouldn't see the bike tracks in the yard."

I gasp. I remember that. Bernadette peeling out from the house, bike wheels hitting the grass, throwing up sod, just as they threw up snow when she came up the mountain road to Simon's cabin . . .

"Knock-knock. The maid's gonna have a helluva time cleaning up *that* mess."

I shake my head. He's lying. He has to be. I just saw Bernadette. We're meeting at the pub. She's invited to the wedding.

But I know he's not lying. Somehow I know.

My head starts to spin again. It throbs till I want to vomit. I close my eyes tight, lean back against the rock wall. But I still feel like I'm falling.

He's talking like the last six months never happened. Like it's just today that I saw him off at the front door, today that I sat in the chair under the sunburst clock, waiting with my heart in my throat for Bernadette to show up. He's talking like he went after Bernadette just like he's going after me now. Like she's not checked into the Wild Rose back in Morro at all. Like she's still at the Palomino. *A helluva mess for the maid to clean up.*

I can't draw a decent breath. Can't think.

From winter to summer in a heartbeat.

Laurel begins to whisper. So quiet I can hardly hear her. Holding something to her lips like a Catholic with a crucifix.

"Fly away, fly away," she's saying. So faint, like a release of breath. "Fly away."

She whispers it over and over, like a chant.

Fly away, fly away, fly away.

I look close and see then what she's holding to her mouth.

A tiny wooden doll carved of cottonwood root, barely three inches tall. Painted aqua and yellow, wearing a white leather skirt, green mask, moccasins. Crowned with a ruff of Douglas fir.

It's the Hummingbird. The messenger you send to ask the gods for rain. The creature that warriors who die in battle are transformed into. The only bird that ever flew high enough to see what was on the other side of the sky.

I lean close and whisper in her ear: "Where did you get that?"

She turns her head to whisper back.

"Simon."

There's shuffling nearby, and we freeze, the kachina pressed against Laurel's lips again. No whispering now.

I wait for a shadow to fall across the opening of our little cave, but none comes. Soon the shuffling moves off.

I don't trust it. Could be a trap. More games. Or Jim could've moved on, and the shuffling was only a fox, a rabbit come back to find its home invaded.

But we can't stay here and I know it. Sooner or later, moving up and down the trail, Jim's bound to see the opening. Bound to check.

I shush Laurel one more time and maneuver around her toward the opening. I wait, bated breath, then slowly peer out, glancing all around as I go. Ready to pull back at the slightest movement.

Nothing.

Jim's gone for now.

I crawl through the opening, turn to Laurel, who looks ready to follow me through. I push her toward the rear of the little cave.

"No. You can't come with me. You stay here. Quiet as a mouse."

"Like Warrior Mouse?"

I nod. "Quiet as Warrior Mouse. Just as clever, just as brave. No matter what you hear. No matter what happens. Promise me."

Her face settles into something stubborn, and for a second I think she won't promise.

Then she does.

"If I'm not back, stay here till morning," I say. "Then make your way down the trail, careful as can be. At the bottom, you'll see the highway. Go stand near it and wave your arms till somebody stops. Tell them to call the state police. Understand?"

Suddenly she pushes through the opening toward me and I think all bets are off. That she's changed her mind and she's coming with me, like it or not. Instead, she wraps her arms around my neck and for a long minute squeezes tight, like she won't let go.

Then she does. Without looking at me, she turns to dart back through the opening and out of my sight.

I stand on shaky legs, leaning against the big nest of rocks for support. A strange, cool wind buffets me. I glance up at the sky and the cornflower blue is nearly gone now, replaced by storm clouds practically stampeding in from the east. The air temperature has dropped and I shiver in my thin blouse, my slacks; my skin prickles from a snap in the air. I can smell rain moving in on the wind.

I move away from the rock nest, not sure yet which way I'm going. Just that, if and when Jim spots me, I don't want to be anywhere near it. I need to get him away from Laurel's hiding place. My best guess is he's searching farther down the trail by now, but I want a better vantage point. The outcropping he used to spot us would do.

There's a thick branch, like a staff, lying off the trail. I pick it up to use as a walking stick. I lean on it heavily, climbing up and up toward the ledge.

By the time I reach it, my head is pulsing, the pain so bad my eyes are running with tears. A light rain is falling, deepening the red sandstone to a dark brick. My foot slides on the slick surface. The temperature has dropped even more; the wind's picked up, slapping the sleeves of Laurel's blouse around my face. I move carefully to the edge of the outcropping, wary of being seen from below, in case Jim is down there, looking up toward the top of the mesa. The goal is to spot him first.

I peer over the edge. My eyes sweep the desert landscape. A flash of lightning arcs across the sky, stabs at massive black clouds tumbling over one another at a rapid boil.

"I see you."

It's coming from right behind me.

My blood freezes, but there's no panic. No hurry to turn to face him. Nowhere to go.

I straighten, leaning on the staff. Then I shuffle around, till there he is, standing just a few yards away. His face is streaked with blood, misshapen. His eye's swelling shut, nose bashed in.

I look at the damage and feel a swell of pride.

"What are you smiling at?" He's frowning. I notice he's slurring a little.

"Missing some teeth, are you?" I ask calmly.

His good eye narrows to a slit. He takes a step toward me and I see he's unsteady on his feet. A stiff gust of wind hits him and he staggers back. Thunder rolls in the distance like a growl.

And suddenly I remember. I remember the missing bits of that ride out from Wheeler, the mad dash to Albuquerque. The first place for gas was the big truck stop halfway to Grants. The same one where Trang, heading for San Francisco, hitched a ride one day. I was pumping in regular, not sure how many gallons the punctured tank would hold, but sure it would let me know. A redheaded boy with a cowlick and an earplug, who didn't look old enough to drive, wearing a Rolling Rock T-shirt, was at the pump next to me when the gasoline started running out from under my car. "Whoa, lady!" he cried. "You're leaking!"

I bought three gallon containers, filled them with gas and threw them in the trunk. Back in the car, back on the road—I never got the chance to use them. Twenty miles out, I glanced in the rearview and saw a sheriff's unit in the distance, lights flashing, sirens screaming, coming up fast. I knew I couldn't outrun him, so I careened off the road and headed straight for the red rocks, praying for a miracle.

That was where Jim caught up with us. Six months ago. Two hours ago.

I remember it. Like a bad dream somebody told me once. But not my dream. Not anymore.

Now I'm untouchable.

I tip my face to the wrathful sky, eyes shut. Cold rain streams down my cheeks as the storm overtakes us.

"Like it?" I ask. "It's for you."

He doesn't say anything, and I open my eyes. He's staring at me. Staring like he's not sure if I'm contagious.

But he's not moving toward me.

I feel a rush of adrenaline. Not sure what I'm doing. What I'm saying. Why I feel with all my might that I want to poke the rattlesnake.

I stare back, certain I look as bad to him as he does to me.

"You're fucking nuts," he says.

"I'd say you'd know, but that's giving you too much credit. To know what *nuts* is, you need a point of reference. You'd have to know what *sane* is. Do you know what sane is, Jim?" I shake my head sadly. "That would be no. A thousand times no."

The rain is coming down harder now and starts to sting. Tiny ice pellets. Sleet. Jim looks at the sky, at the boiling clouds. He looks at his bare arms, like he's seeing something unusual.

"What the fuck—?"

"Dear God, get a vocabulary," I snap. "Buy a vowel, Alex! Get some consonants! Mix them together. They're called *words.* I'd get better conversation out of a monkey."

His arms drop to his sides. He moves forward. But only a step.

He snarls deep in his throat. "Finally grow some backbone, eh? Didn't know you had it in you."

The adrenaline is pumping so hard now it feels like my head's splitting open. Like I'm levitating off the ledge. Like I'm bristling with clarity. My face is hot. I lean on the staff, eyes locked on his, drilling him down. I can feel a shift in the air between us. Can feel him waver. The dynamic is changing.

"You have no idea what I'm capable of," I say.

Thunder explodes above our heads. Rolls along the mesa like a diesel train. The air shudders with it.

The sleet is gone. Now it's hail the size of peas, the size of golf balls, rattling, thudding against the sandstone rocks, bouncing off, pelting us both.

Jim looks more uncertain than ever. Like he's not expecting this. Like he doesn't recognize me, or what's happening. He holds up his arms to protect himself, shoots a last glance at the cold-blooded sky.

Then he makes a choice. The only choice a man like him can make.

He heads toward me, an odd hitch in his step, fists clenched. "How did you think this was gonna end?" he shouts above the clatter.

He sounds desperate. Petulant. A grown man pitching a fit.

"And, Jim," I tell him. "Bernadette? Don't worry about her. She had a soft landing. You won't."

He's coming at me like a bull. Like old times. When he reaches me, I know the staff is nothing against him. The adrenaline took me this far, but it can't alter muscle mass. Can't unbreak my wrist or teach me judo in seconds flat. I hold it ready anyway. Ready to fight back, even with no chance of winning.

He's reaching for me, his ruined face like a Halloween mask, when I swivel and pivot on the staff at the last second, a clumsy move that puts me no more than a couple feet to the side, but just enough for him to overextend. He has no time left, no balance, when one spit-shined oxford hits an icy patch of red rock and slides right out from under him.

He brushes against me as he topples over the edge, so close I can see the startled look in his good eye.

Sixty feet below, the rocks break his fall.

After the Storm

The hail won't stop. It falls like a blizzard. A stiff wind keeps shoveling it into drifts. The hike back down the trail is slow. Plant the staff one step ahead, inch my way forward. Plant the staff again. Adrenaline's gone. Body's on fire. I slide on the slick path, but don't fall.

The rock nest where I left Laurel is nearly covered with a thick coat of ice and hail. For the first time I notice its shape—a rough dome, like a little hogan.

I call Laurel's name and her face appears at the opening. She scurries out, takes my hand, helps me inside. She's still dressed only in shorts and camisole and sandals. I'm soaked through, feverish. We curl up together on the floor to wait for the storm to pass.

In less than an hour, it does.

Blistered clouds roll off to the west; the sun splits through for the last hour of daylight. When Laurel peeks through the opening again, the air is already so warm the melting ice drips on her head.

She leaves me in a fitful sleep and makes her way down the hail-covered path, not once losing her way. She passes an indistinct shape a few yards off the trail, buried in a four-foot drift. She'll never know it's the body of her father.

She jogs to the highway and stands well to the side.

Minutes later, a plow driver out of Grants is clearing the interstate of the accumulation from a freak June hailstorm when he sees a little girl dressed in green shorts and a yellow camisole jumping up and down, arms flailing. He pulls over to see what on earth is going on.

Epilogue

As it is

It was Sam who told me about Bernadette. I was still in the university hospital in Albuquerque when he showed up with a bouquet of coneflowers he'd bought in the gift shop in the lobby, looking just as grizzled as the one and only time I'd seen him that night in the Javelina.

It wasn't the maid who'd found Bernadette, but Sam.

Sam had known about the escape plan, of course. In fact, he'd pitched in to help fund it. So when Bernadette was discovered, it wasn't hard to come up with a suspect.

Others came to visit while I recovered. Munoz and his wife. Sandoval and CeCe. The sheriff, who couldn't quite meet my eye.

The investigation was brief. Jim hadn't bothered to cover

his tracks. Maybe he'd figured to just disappear once he was finished with us. Start over in some other incarnation. Or maybe my flight had taken him by surprise and he hadn't thought that far ahead.

The first person I saw when I woke in my hospital bed, though, was Terri. Ten years older, beaming at me as if merely waking up was an achievement.

"Girl," she said, "you're *back*!"

When Laurel and I hadn't arrived at the airport in Boston as planned, she and her husband, Greg, had placed enough calls to Wheeler to find out why. They flew out at once. They took care of Laurel till I was released.

It's been two years since Insurrection Day, and I haven't been back to Wheeler since. I sold the house, leased a small one in Albuquerque near the university, started classes again. I'll get my English degree in June. After that, Terri and Greg have invited us to spend the summer with them in Boston—they have a daughter close to Laurel's age, and the two have become great friends. In the fall, I'll start working on an MFA in creative writing, and have accepted a job as a teaching assistant.

On weekends, we drive up to Taos. I found my Oma's little house outside town, abandoned, in disrepair. I used the money from the sale of the Wheeler house to buy it. To replace the rotting boards, repair the leaking roof. We painted it inside and out, and sowed fields of wildflowers all around.

Then we drove stakes of all sizes into the soil and tied links of pretty chain from branches. We used them to mount and hang a dozen hummingbird feeders—sequined glass, brushed metal, a crystal lantern, a dewdrop, giant strawberries and oranges, a red rose, a cobalt blue bottle, a tiny glass chandelier.

When we talk about Morro, about Jessie and Olin and Simon, it's usually there in Oma's house.

Although I've never been back to Wheeler, I did get close once.

It was a few months after I was released from the hospital, a day in late autumn when Laurel was still in school. I rented a four-wheel drive, hit the interstate and drove west. About thirty miles this side of Wheeler, I began scanning the landscape hard.

In time, I spotted the makings of an old dirt road cutting off south from the highway. Or, rather, the remains of a road—overgrown and pitted from rain and wind and disuse, sloping up toward a toothy break of hills and disappearing over the other side.

I pulled off on the shoulder and cut the engine, torn about whether to drive up this particular path or turn around and go back, even if I had just come a hundred miles to find it.

Finally I switched the engine back on and turned off the highway.

It was slow going over the rough terrain, up and up the sloping hills, then over. A mile or so farther on, I stopped again.

This time I left the Jeep and walked to the edge of the road.

The valley cuts east-west here, just as before. But now it's filled with wild grasses, brush, piñon, juniper trees. Gone are the wheat fields, the cornfields, the orchards, the trees of every kind, the wildflowers of every color. There is no Willow Creek tumbling down the Mountain.

There is no mountain.

At least, not the one I was looking for. What's here now has the bulk, the breadth, of a mountain, but it's barely a third the size of the one I knew. Just a moderate incline to a smooth summit of moderate height. Much like any other in the range. Nothing extraordinary.

And from where I stood, I should have been looking at Olin and Jessie's farmhouse. But there was no farmhouse. There'd never been one. At least, not the big house with the wraparound porch, built of gray stones dug up from the soil every spring.

Instead, next to the road were the remains of a little wood-frame, long collapsed in on itself, its fallen timber now scattered and rotted. The only portion still marginally intact was a brick fireplace rising out of the ruin, its chimney toppled.

This was where Olin and Jessie had lived.

It had taken a while to track them down, searching through the microfilm in the periodicals section of the university library. Two small obituaries in the Wheeler newspaper, both dated 1939. Jessie had passed first, in late April. By July, Olin had joined her.

I noticed far off the road a large mound of gray stones, cracking apart from erosion, sprouting so many weeds you could mistake the pile as part of the landscape—not collected over years of farming. But there weren't quite enough stones, not quite enough years, for Olin to build Jessie that farmhouse.

Finding Reuben, Bree and Jean had been easier. They were so recent, by comparison, that an Internet search was all it took. And Trang was difficult only if you didn't know what to look for. His was a brief newspaper notice: Asian male, mid- to late teens, no identification, discovered under an overpass along the interstate just outside Wheeler, hypothermia.

It was a while before I had the heart to look for Simon.

In the periodicals section, I skipped the computer and turned again to the microfilm. Wheeler newspapers, starting with 1942. Reel after reel, month by month, year by year until, in December 1944, a notice that U.S. Army Sergeant Simon Greenwood, thirty-five, 2nd Ranger Battalion, had gone missing in action in the Hürtgen Forest, on the border between Belgium and Germany.

It mentioned a fiancée, Margaret Dahl, but no other family.

I ran through more reels of microfilm, to the end of the war and beyond, but there was no other mention of him.

Margaret eventually married William Carmody in late 1946. There was a picture with the wedding announcement, the couple smiling at the camera, looking much as they had the night I met them in the pub. A computer search turned up a William Carmody who died in Denver fifteen years ago, a retired businessman, survived by his wife, Margaret, his five children, twelve grandchildren and four great-grandchildren. Margaret "Meg" Carmody passed away only two years ago, at the age of eighty-six.

I turned and headed back to the Jeep. When the engine kicked in, I gripped the steering wheel and, for the barest second, wondered if I was going to continue south toward the foothills. If I'd round the bend to see what was left of Morro, the mining town where the copper had played out half a century ago. And to see if, just on the other side of town, there was a road cutting off to the right, heading up to a cabin in a clearing halfway up the mountain.

Instead, I wheeled the Jeep around in a tight arc, kicking up dust, heading back to the highway.

I would leave Morro as it was.

As it is.

As it will be.

READING GROUP NOTES

FOR DISCUSSION

- In what ways do the sense of self and its loss/growth permeate the novel? How does the author explore this theme?

- Jim's power over Joanna goes further than physically hurting her – he isolates her, mentally and physically, and is 'the unmaking' of her. Discuss how the author portrays this and how Jim takes control of his wife.

- Often objects, people and places seem to embody either hope or dread for Joanna and can shift from meaning one thing to the other. Identify and discuss these moments within the novel.

- 'No rack can torture me,/My soul's at liberty'. Discuss the significance of poetry and music within the novel and the larger role they play in the characters' lives.

- In the Place of Truth, Joanna is slowly able to rebuild her sense of identity and self-worth. What and/or who helps her to do this?

- What do the kachinas represent in the story? And does the Hummingbird kachina have a deeper meaning for Joanna? Discuss the significance of Navajo culture and folklore within the novel.

- Does the 'Bee in a Thunderstorm' chapter have significance for you? Did it evoke any symbolism or underlying meaning? What do you learn about the women who attend?

- Discuss the author's choice to change the chapter titles from dates to a more descriptive format between the first and second part of the novel. Why do you think she did this?

- '. . . the Mountain was a massive silhouette under its snowcapped peak. I stepped off the porch, averting my gaze as I sensed *it* still watching *me*'. Why do you think Joanna feels such a pull towards the Mountain?

What does it symbolise to you, and what do you think is 'pulling' her?

- 'Courage is a kind of salvation'. How important is the theme of courage within the novel? How and where do you think this is most strongly conveyed?

IN CONVERSATION WITH TAMARA DIETRICH

Q How did the idea for the novel come about? It begins with quite a domestic setting, and then transitions into the 'supernatural' – was the idea for one backdrop born from the other? Do you often use this technique when writing?

A I used to live in the American Southwest, where countless small towns have lived and died over the past 150 years. Many of these ghost towns are typically tourist destinations today, but I was intrigued by the idea of a ghost town – a town of ghosts – rescuing someone in need. In this case, a severely abused wife and her young daughter. I'm not religious, but I'm fascinated by the spiritual. By the idea of an afterlife, and what that might look like. I'm frequently drawn to the otherworldly, and how it might intersect with the world we inhabit. A book I'm working on now has a character who mysteriously rises up out of the sea one day, a young man with no history or name, to interact with a very real, very troubled family.

Q Tell us a bit about your writing process. Does it differ greatly from the work you do as a journalist? How does writing a novel compare?

A Because I've been a journalist for so long, I thought writing a novel would be relatively easy. I was very wrong. Daily deadlines aren't difficult for me. But sustaining a story, characters and plotlines over the course of a year or so is pretty challenging, calling for completely different creative muscles. I salute anyone and everyone who manages it. Many writers I know can write in snatches – grabbing an hour or so here and there. But I write on weekends only, because I need long blocks of dedicated time to get into gear and live there for a while. I feel incredibly fortunate in having a journalism career because I can take so much of what I've experienced and use it in novel-writing (I've interviewed many abuse survivors, for instance, which gave me insights for *The*

Hummingbird's Cage), or I set ideas aside for future use. I have many, many folders full of them! Journalism also involves a great deal of research, which I love, so I find myself happily conducting tons of it for novels – even if it doesn't end up on a page, it helps flesh out a story or my understanding of a character.

Q **There were moments of real desperation and terror for Joanna and Laurel that could be hard to read at points, they were so visceral! Did you find these difficult to write, or were you able to separate yourself from them?**

A I was able to separate myself – and I credit the years of journalism experience kicking in. I felt I was chronicling terrible events, which offered a level of emotional remove, even as I was trying to get inside Joanna's skin as she experienced them. In fact, there was a scene in a draft version that my agent and editor both urged me to tone down or even take out because it was just too raw and painful. I resisted at first because I thought readers could handle it – I knew of similar incidents that had actually happened and been reported – and because I felt it was a key moment in understanding what finally broke Joanna's spirit. But eventually I understood their point and rewrote it, toning it down considerably. If you're curious which scene it was, let me pass on what I discovered is one cardinal rule of book publishing in the States: 'Don't kill the dog.' Yes, this is an actual thing. Perhaps it's true in the UK, too!

Q Prior to Joanna meeting Bernadette or finding the Place of Truth, she struggles to find support from others in 'the real world'. Alicia is quick to judge, Frank is Jim's fishing buddy. Was this a conscious decision, and was there an overarching reason for this?

A Yes, it was a conscious decision. What I've found is that women suffering abuse are often reluctant to admit to it, and, in many cases, incapable of accepting help even if it is offered. I've experienced that with at least two friends over the years. Both felt helpless and trapped. That's the goal of abusers, of course – to isolate their victims and make them feel as if they deserved, or somehow caused, their own abuse. And then there are people like Alicia and Frank who simply turn a blind or judgemental eye, for any number of reasons. I wanted to explore that feeling of Joanna's of being completely alone and desperate.

Q Joanna slowly starts to rebuild herself again with the help of Olin and Jessie, but poetry and music also play a key role in this too. Do these things hold importance for you? Do you think they are, in part, a reflection of ourselves?

A Poetry and music are, indeed, important to me! I studied poetry in college – my degree is in creative writing/poetry (as opposed to prose). I believe very much in poetry power. And some poems just lent themselves to the storyline here, like Yeats' 'The Stolen Child', about leaving a world 'full of weeping' to live happily with otherworldly creatures. And Emily Dickinson's lines 'my soul's at liberty/behind this mortal bone/there knits a bolder one' was perfect for Joanna's journey. It's also why I use a lot of bone imagery in Morro.

And music in the book holds important clues to the timelines of the characters in Morro. Jessie and Olin listen to music from the 1920s and 1930s, for instance; Simon from the 1940s. Later, Joanna – and the reader – understand why.

Q The chapter titles differ slightly between parts one and two of the novel – they begin as set dates and then become more descriptive. It felt as if this was a way of further separating 'reality' from the 'other place' – can you explain why you changed them in this way?

A For me, that was important to lay the foundation for an abrupt shift in time and place. The dates heading up the chapters of the first section were intended to show the passage of time in the real world. Much like a diary for Joanna. In Morro, though, where time really isn't an issue, I changed to descriptive chapter headings. I wanted the reader to notice, and to understand immediately, that a fundamental change had occurred.

Q The strength and courage of the human spirit in the face of adversity really shone through in the novel and it is, ultimately, a very uplifting story. Is this a key message for you?

A It is, indeed. I'm confronted every day on the job with the harsh realities of life, of people, of circumstances. Yet I consider myself an optimist at heart. And I'm drawn to real stories of people who face those harsh realities and manage to overcome them, whether through sheer grit or pluck, or with the help of others. They're an inspiration for my work – and my life, too.

SUGGESTED FURTHER READING

The Color Purple
by Alice Walker

Picture Perfect
by Jodi Picoult

I Let You Go
by Clare Mackintosh

Room
by Emma Donoghue

A Streetcar Named Desire
by Tennessee Williams

The Awakening
by Kate Chopin

Wide Sargasso Sea
by Jean Rhys